A DANGEROUS LOVE

EXCLUSIVE CHRISTIAN FAMILY BOOK CLUB EDITION

A Dangerous Love

MICHAEL
PHILLIPS

COMPLETE AND UNABRIDGED

Since 1948, The Book Club You Can Trust

Visit Tyndale's exciting Web site at www.tyndale.com

Scripture quotations are taken from the *Holy Bible*, King James Version.

Library of Congress Cataloging-in-Publication Data

Phillips, Michael R., date
  A dangerous love / by Michael Phillips.
    p. cm. — (Mercy and Eagleflight ; v. 2)
  ISBN 0-8423-3921-3
  I. Title. II. Series: Phillips, Michael R., date   Mercy and Eagleflight ; v. 2.
PS3566.H492D36 1997
813'.54—dc21   96-40459

Printed in the United States of America

02 01 00 99 98 97
 7   6   5   4   3   2   1

First Hardcover Edition for Christian Family Book Club: 1998

CONTENTS

Map – Central United States, early 1890s ix

1 Second Thoughts 1

2 Stranger in a Shoot-out 6

3 Toward Home 12

4 Doing What's Right 16

5 Deeper Levels 21

6 Fathers and God 24

7 Holdup 28

8 Surprise Homecoming 35

9 Happy Homecoming 40

10 Human Acorns 46

11 Banker's Holiday 54

12 Seven Years 60

13 Denver 64

14 Getaway 67

15 A Sisterly Talk 72

16 A Timely Friend 79

17 Unpleasant Reunion 82

18 Change of Plans 88

19 Two More Talks 92

20 Questions 96

21 Thunderclouds and Families 102

22 Rain 108

23 Tornado 112

24 Home 119

25 Recovery 124

26 Ultimatum 128

27 Break-in 132

28 Caught Red-handed 137

29 Capture 142

30 Hot Vanilla 146
31 Growth, Wisdom, and Intellect 150
32 Ominous Question 155
33 Offer of Trade 160
34 Surprise Appearance 165
35 Questions 170
36 From Out of the Past 174
37 What Next? 180
38 Following Loretta 184
39 Another Hostage 188
40 A Dangerous Love 194
41 Back in Denver 203
42 Surprising Friendship 208
43 First Faltering Prayers 215
44 Pneumonia 220
45 Tearful News 224
46 Return 228
47 Revival of a Different Kind 233
48 Out of Denver 241
49 A Familiar Sight 247
50 Back at the Ranch 251
51 Memories 257
52 Beula's Plans 261
53 Festive Season 268
54 Christmas Eve at the Bar S 272
55 Bethlehem 278
56 A Louisville Christmas 281
57 Christmas Prayer 288
58 Spring Comes Round Again 295
59 Gratefulness for a Full Life 301
60 Arrival 304
61 Procession of Happiness 310

62 *Mercy and Eagleflight* 314
63 *On Wings of Eagles* 322

SECOND THOUGHTS

An unseasonably warm late-autumn sun beat down upon the wide grassy expanse of Kansas prairie where the thoughts of a lone, dusty, and perspiring ranch hand kept drifting away from the rigors occupying his hands. Jess Forbes was stretching long strands of barbwire between the fence posts he and one of the other Bar S hands had set in the ground yesterday.

He set a metal staple in place, pounded it halfway into the post, gave the wire a final tug with the curved iron claw, and held it taut in his left hand. Then he gave the staple one last blow with his hammer. He stood back, dropped his tools on the ground for a moment, and wiped the sweat off his forehead with the sleeve of his shirt.

He surveyed the line of fencing he had finished that morning. As work went, he supposed this wasn't as bad as some. Work was hard when the sun was hot, no matter what it was. He'd done worse.

But he was beginning to wonder if he was cut out for this kind of life. He felt as though someone were stringing up fences in his life, enclosing his freedom, hog-tying him down. It was the first time he and his partner had been separated like this, and he had the feeling it wouldn't be the last.

And separated over a woman, for crying out loud!

When they had first landed in Sweetriver, two or three miles north of the ranch, earlier this year, they had only planned to stay for a few days of poker. Then his partner had taken it into his head to befriend a stray preacher woman left alone and penniless on the prairie. Then he'd taken a job here on the Simmons ranch. And now their stay in Sweetriver was beginning to look more and more permanent.

Jess would never have believed it, but Jeremiah Eagleflight had done gone and gotten himself in love!

Mercy was a nice enough girl, nicer than most they met on the trail. And pretty, too. Those green eyes of hers were really something, and that light brown hair. It wasn't anything against her, it was just the idea of settling down in one place that he couldn't get used to. Sure, she had said nothing would change. And sure, they all had it pretty good here at the Bar S. Zeke was more than a decent man and a fair boss. Jess could probably have a good future here.

But was it the kind of future he wanted?

And things *would* change. There was no denying that, no matter what anyone might say. After Jeremiah and Mercy were hitched . . . then what?

Maybe he ought to get on with his own life without waiting to find out. Maybe he ought to just wish his old partner good luck and move on, like he'd been going to do before Mercy talked him into staying.

Jess grabbed up another string of wire. He didn't like the feel of fences, that was the trouble—especially ones strung up around *him*.

How long should he stay on here at the Simmons place?

The boss and his wife, along with Jess' partner, were up at Fort Hays right now, where Mercy and Mrs. Simmons were leaving for Louisville. It would be Mercy's first visit home to see her family since coming to Sweetriver. Maybe she'd go home and stay, and that would be the end of it. Then he and Jeremiah could move on and forget this little episode in their lives.

A rider approached, interrupting his thoughts.

"Hey, Forbes!" called Dirk Heyes, the foreman of the Bar S. "Come on in for lunch."

Jess tossed his tools into the dirt. He didn't need to be told twice. Heyes had already spun his horse around and was a hundred yards on his way back to the ranch house by the time Jess was in the saddle and chasing after him.

Twenty minutes later, after washing at least some of the dirt from his hands—though he wasn't quite as careful now that Jody Simmons, the boss's wife, wasn't here to scold him—Jess Forbes walked into the dining room with a couple of the other men.

"Hard biscuits and watery stew again?" said one of them, looking over the meager supplies spread out over the table.

"Don't complain, Rice," rejoined the foreman, "or I'll add even *more* water to your bowl. Zeke'll be back tomorrow or the next day."

"What good's that do us? It's his wife whose face I'm wanting to see in the kitchen!" said Wood.

"Don't worry, Bart. Zeke's nearly as good a cook as Jody," rejoined Dirk.

"Anything's better'n your grub, Heyes!" added Clancy Phillips.

"Aw, sit down, all of you!" yelled Heyes good-naturedly. "If you don't like it, ain't nothing you can do about it 'cause it's all the vittles you're gonna get."

As Jess slowly ate the soup that Dirk Heyes was trying to pass off as stew, his eyes fell absently on the calendar on the wall of the kitchen.

November 3.

His eyes slowly rose to the top of the page, where the year was posted—1891.

Suddenly the day's date jumped off the wall and straight into his brain with the force of a slug between the eyes.

It was November 3 . . . *1891!*

In another six days—

"More stew, Jess?" asked Dirk Heyes, interrupting his thoughts.

"Uh . . . uh, no—no thanks, Heyes," mumbled Jess. "But it's mighty good."

"What're you looking at with them wide eyes, Forbes? You look like you seen a ghost."

"Oh, nothin'—just looking at the calendar, that's all. Is that right?" he added, nodding his head toward the wall. "Is it 1891?"

"'Course it's 1891."

"That bullit ol' One Eye gave you knock out yer memory or somethin', Jess?" added one of the other Bar S hands, followed by a general chuckle from the others at the table.

"No, just reckon I lost track of time," muttered Forbes.

His memory, in fact, had sharpened up considerably. He hadn't thought of that night in years. He'd almost forgotten all about it. Now suddenly many events from out of the past came tumbling back to him like they had happened yesterday.

Six days from today.

In six days it would be seven years—*seven years exactly* since November 9, 1884.

If ranching wasn't the life he was cut out for, Jess thought to himself as he finished his stew and ambled outside for a short rest in the bunkhouse, then maybe this was just the opportunity he'd been waiting for.

STRANGER IN A
SHOOT-OUT

While a preoccupied and scheming Jess Forbes
returned to his wire fence later that same afternoon, some
seventy-five miles to the northwest, his boss and partner
stood gazing eastward as a chugging locomotive of the
Union Pacific disappeared from their sight.

Sitting in the last of three cars rode the two women they
each loved.

When the train had retreated beyond earshot, and as it gradually became but a retreating speck on the horizon, the two turned and walked slowly back across the wooden landing of the Fort Hays train depot in silence, making their way toward Zeke's wagon, which stood in front of the station.

"That's some young lady you found yourself, Eagleflight," said Zeke as they climbed aboard beside each other.

"Yeah, I'm a lucky fella, all right," sighed Jeremiah. "But no sooner did I find her but she's gone!" he added with a laugh, swinging his arm back in the direction of the train. He looked after the train and realized with a start how much he was going to miss her.

"You and she won't be parted long. Next time you see her, you'll be all duded up in front of Louisville society, getting ready to say *I do.* Giddap!" Zeke called to the two horses, clicking his tongue and giving the reins a flip with his hand.

"You and Jody'll come to the city for the wedding?"

"You bet—wouldn't miss it!"

"I'd be honored if you'd stand beside me along with Jess."

"The honor would be mine. When you two figure on tying the knot?"

"Don't know," replied Jeremiah. "I reckon I'll be there before Christmas. 'Course I gotta talk to Mercy's father and see what they think."

"Parents never want to move too fast with things like this."

"Yeah, well I reckon we'll all talk about it, then decide."

"Ever gotten yourself tied up with a lady's ma and pa before?"

"Never in my life," laughed Eagleflight. "It'll be a new experience, that's for sure."

"You'll survive it," rejoined Zeke. "Ain't no better way to

start off than by getting involved with the parents right from—"

Zeke's voice was interrupted by the sound of a gunshot.

Both men glanced about quickly toward the buildings they were passing. Unconsciously Jeremiah's hand sought the place where his gun used to hang on his hip.

The next instant the swinging doors of the saloon crashed open. The figure of a man tumbled out, staggered a few steps backward across the boardwalk, and fell into the middle of the street.

Zeke's startled horses shied and reared.

"Whoa, boy!" called Zeke, reining them in to one side.

As he did so, another figure appeared in the doorway of the saloon, gun in hand. He emerged into the sunlight, paused on the boardwalk, then shouted down to the man in the street.

"Next time it won't be my fist that sends you reeling, Kramer!" he said. "And I won't give you no warning shot neither. I'll put a slug right between your eyes."

On the ground, as Zeke calmed his horses and pulled them to a stop, the man called Kramer struggled to his knees and glanced up. Unconsciously he wiped at his bleeding lip with the back of his hand.

"Any man who calls me a cheat at cards, Pherson—," he growled.

"You *are* a cheat, Kramer!" interrupted the other. "I caught you red-handed, and now I'm telling you to get on your horse and hightail it outta town before I kill you."

As he spoke, Kramer slowly rose to his feet, keeping his gaze locked on the man whose fist had sent him flying out of the saloon. The glint in his eyes was an evil one, clearly bent on revenge. As he rose, his hand moved almost imperceptibly toward the gun on his hip.

"Hold these," said Zeke softly, handing the reins to Jeremiah. The next instant, the rancher had jumped down to the street and was walking slowly toward the argument in progress.

"If you're thinking what I think you're thinking, Kramer," taunted Pherson, "then you're a bigger fool—Hey, what the—?"

"Put your gun away, mister, and go on back inside," said Zeke calmly, stepping directly in front of the man called Kramer as he spoke to Pherson at the saloon door.

"This ain't none o' yer fight, stranger," said Kramer from behind him, rising to his feet, then taking a step toward Zeke and laying a rough hand on his shoulder to force him aside. That someone was trying to save his life roused no sense of gratefulness in his heart—it only deepened his anger. "Now git outta my way or yer gonna git yerself shot along with Pherson."

In a motion so swift that none of the three onlookers could quite tell what he'd done, Zeke grabbed Kramer's hand off his own shoulder and turned to face him. Then holding Kramer's wrist in a vise grip, he spun the ruffian around and wrenched his arm up behind his back, where he held him momentarily powerless to move. As the man suddenly cried out in pain, with his free hand Zeke yanked Kramer's Colt from his holster and threw it off down the street where it thudded in the dust.

"No one's going to get shot here," he said calmly. "Now, Mr. Pherson," he said to the man on the boardwalk, "why don't you put your gun away and go back inside."

"This ain't none of your fight," rejoined Pherson angrily.

"Maybe not. But as you and everyone else can plainly see," replied Zeke, glancing about the street where a crowd had begun to gather, "neither I nor Mr. Kramer has a gun. I don't know you, Mr. Pherson, but I wouldn't take you for a coward, and no one but a coward would shoot an unarmed man who wasn't trying to do him any harm."

As Zeke spoke, Kramer struggled to free himself from Zeke's grasp but without success.

"So put your gun away, Mr. Pherson," Zeke went on. "You're not going to shoot anybody today."

Glancing about a little nervously, and somewhat cowed by Zeke's calm and commanding demeanor, Pherson slowly holstered his gun, then turned and walked back through the swinging doors into the saloon.

"All right, then, Mr. Kramer," said Zeke, loosening his hold and letting the man go, "why don't you give both your own and Mr. Pherson's temper a chance to cool down? I suggest you go on home."

"Why you dirty interfering —," began Kramer, taking a hostile step toward Zeke. He clenched his fists and raised them to strike.

Zeke lifted his hand, index finger pointed upward in warning. As he did so, he stared with a serious expression straight into the other man's eyes.

Kramer paused, uncertain. He found himself intimidated by the calm determination of Zeke's expression. He seemed to sense that it would not go well for him if he continued what had been in his mind to do. Slowly his fists relaxed. Then his hands dropped to his side.

"That's better," said Zeke.

He turned and walked up the street, stooped down, and retrieved Kramer's gun. As he returned, he turned it upside down in his right hand and emptied the bullets from their chambers into his left.

"Here you are, Mr. Kramer," he said, handing the pistol and its bullets to their owner. "I suggest you leave it empty for a while. Better yet, leave it at home altogether. You'll get into less trouble if you're not carrying a gun at all."

Kramer took it, still with a bewildered expression on his face, and slowly eased the weapon back into its leather holster. He had never seen a gunfight broken up in quite such a manner, much less one he was in the middle of.

"All right, then—you going home?"

"Uh . . . uh, yeah—sure, mister," muttered Kramer. He turned and walked from the street to the boardwalk, where he continued on slowly past the saloon. Zeke kept his eye on him for a minute, then returned to the wagon and climbed up beside Jeremiah, while the crowd of silent onlookers kept watching with faces as perplexed as Kramer's. Neither had any of them seen such a thing as an unarmed man walking straight into the middle of a gunfight.

Zeke took the reins from Jeremiah, who eyed him with something between amazement and disbelief, and a moment later the two men were again on their way out of Fort Hays.

TOWARD HOME

In the passenger coach of the Union Pacific train chugging eastward toward Kansas City, Mercy Randolph sat smiling beside Jody Simmons, unable to get Jeremiah's face out of her mind. The rancher's wife knew well enough what she was thinking.

As the train had pulled out of the station, they waved through the window to Zeke and Jeremiah until they could see them no longer. Then they settled back and talked almost nonstop for the next hour and a half, until now a thoughtful silence fell between them.

"I think you've found yourself a fine man," Jody said at length.

Mercy sighed contentedly. "It is so hard to believe," she said. "Everything was so wrong, and now everything is so right. I never dreamed that when I went back to Louisville, it would be to make plans to be married!" Mercy looked out the window across the flat prairie and let out a deep sigh. She would not see Jeremiah for many weeks.

"God's ways always have good for us at the root of them," Jody said.

"I am excited to be going back. I hadn't realized until recently how much I've missed my family."

"How did you come to be so far away from home?" asked Jody.

A pained expression came over Mercy's face.

"I'm afraid there is no other way to say it but to say I was a very naive and foolish girl," she answered. "I suppose I was anxious to do something on my own. I told myself I was serving the Lord, but I went against some good advice. I suppose I wanted my own independence."

"That's not always a bad thing," commented Jody. "Every young person eventually has to test their wings."

"Yes, but I did it against my parents' wishes." She went on to explain a little more fully than she had to Jody before what had happened and how it had led to meeting Jeremiah.

"Your parents were not against your going to the Missionary College, were they?" asked Jody.

"No, they agreed that perhaps it would be a very good

experience for me. But when I told them about Reverend Mertree, they warned me not to go with him."

"Well, God has the same lesson to teach us all," replied Jody. "He just has to do it through different circumstances and events with each of us."

"What lesson?"

"Learning that we aren't so smart as we think we are and that life will go better when we trust him and trust those around us rather than think we are completely capable of everything within ourselves."

Mercy laughed. "That's the lesson, all right. And I learned it the hard way!"

"I think most everyone who learns it, learns it the hard way," rejoined Jody. "The important thing is that we do learn it."

"When I first came out this far west," said Mercy, gazing out the window at the flat brown landscape as it passed, "especially after things started going wrong, it seemed so bleak and barren. I hated it and just wanted to go home. But now the plains are wonderful to me. It is such a spacious land. I love it now. You can see the blue of the sky forever, with white clouds all about."

"Yes, and you can see storm clouds coming from far off, and they're on top of you before you know it. I sometimes think the storm compels you to watch it," Jody went on, "until suddenly it is right over you and you're drenched in it!"

"Oh, that sounds exciting!"

"Wait until you see a tornado coming. There's nothing wonderful or exciting about that!"

"Tornadoes or not, I love the prairie now," said Mercy. "This is where I met Jeremiah, and he is such a wonderful man."

Jody smiled at Mercy.

"That is not to say I do not love Louisville too. After all, that is where I grew up. And when I think back to when I was little, there are happy memories."

"Such as?" said Jody.

"Oh," Mercy said with a smile as she reminisced, "my brother and I climbing trees and throwing acorns at each other. My sister and I going out of town to collect nuts every autumn and wild onions in the spring. Exploring my grandmother's old house where we lived for a while before my father bought the house they live in now. And then all the seasons—I loved the seasons."

"In Kansas we have only two," laughed Jody, "hot summer and cold winter."

DOING WHAT'S
RIGHT

As Zeke and Jeremiah rode silently in the wagon
southeast out of Fort Hays toward the Bar S, Jeremiah
could not get the incident that had just happened out of his
mind.

"Mind if I ask you a question, Zeke?" asked Jeremiah
after he and Zeke had ridden a short distance in silence.

"'Course not."

"How come you were so levelheaded back there?"

"How do you mean?"

"I mean, most men would've pulled a gun or started swinging with their fists or else run and hid and let the two men kill each other. But you were cool as a watermelon in a stream of water and never once got ruffled. You coulda got yourself hurt."

"I couldn't let the two of them kill each other," replied Zeke.

"But what if you had gotten shot?"

"I reckon that's a chance I had to take."

"But why did you care? They were just a couple of hot-heads, and who knows but what they'll kill each other tomorrow anyway."

"Maybe. But today I was there. I had the chance to do something, so I had to."

"But why?"

"Part of being a Christian's doing things most folks wouldn't do and don't do. Looking out for others is the *main* thing a Christian's supposed to do. I reckon I'm always on the lookout for a chance of being some use to somebody."

"Lotta folks would say you're crazy for what you did back there."

"Yeah," laughed Zeke. "That's another one of the things about being a Christian."

"What—being crazy?"

"No, doing things that *seem* a mite loco to folks that don't understand."

"Why'd you do it?"

Zeke did not answer immediately. As the wagon bounced along, he thought how best to answer his young friend.

"Well, I reckon what I'd say," he answered at length, "is

that quite a few years ago I made a decision about what kind of man I wanted to be."

"You mean when you became a Christian?"

"No, it didn't really have anything to do with that. I'd already been a believer for a while. But then one day I found myself looking around at all the folks I knew—Christians, unbelievers, men, women, all kinds of people. And I found myself wondering where they were all going."

"Where they were going?" repeated Jeremiah. "How do you mean?"

"What kind of people were they becoming? Were they growing to become *better* people than they were then?"

"Oh, I get you."

"I had to say," Zeke continued, "that most of them seemed pretty comfortable just like they were."

Zeke paused, and a slight smile came over his face.

"Then I found my eyes looking inward at myself," he said with a chuckle. "That's always a dangerous thing to do! And what did I find but that I couldn't see that I was going much of anyplace either! That's when I made the decision I mentioned."

"You mean about what kind of fella you wanted to be?"

"Yep. That's when I decided I didn't want to just stay the same as I was. I wanted to *grow*, to change, to become better. I wanted to become a man who could look himself in the mirror when he was old and say, 'Well, partner, you did OK. You're not perfect, but you became a man with some guts and character down inside. You kept *growing*.'"

"I still don't see what that's all got to do with breaking up that fight."

Zeke laughed. "Just this," he said. "When I decided I wanted to grow and change, I realized that meant I couldn't do things the easy way, couldn't do things the way other people might. I had to judge by what was right, and then just do it, come what may."

"You figured that was the way to get better?"

"Sure. How is a man to grow and become something better than he is unless he's always looking for what's the right thing to do?"

Jeremiah nodded. "I suppose I always try to do right, too, even when I don't know what'll come of it."

"I know you do," said Zeke. "That's one of the reasons you're a growing man, Eagleflight. I don't say it's easy, but ever since I made that decision, I've tried to make it a habit to look for what's right and then jump straight into doing it without stopping to think what might be the consequences."

"Sounds like a way to get yourself into a fix."

"Yeah, sometimes that happens. But as believers, we're called to take a stand, whether it be to share my faith with someone—or step between two fools bent on fighting. I have to do what is right. I remind myself that if something's truly *right*, then good has to come out of it somehow, wouldn't you say?"

"I don't know. I reckon," answered Jeremiah.

"So with things like what happened back there, I try not to stop and think about myself. Somebody was about to get killed. I don't know which of the two it would have been, but one of them was bound to be at the undertaker's before nightfall. The right thing to do was to try to prevent it. So I just jumped out of the wagon and walked into the middle of it."

"Did you know what you were going to do ahead of time?"

"'Course not. You can't usually see around the next bend

in the road until you get there. You do what's right and let what comes next take care of itself. When I hired you, I didn't know what would come of it, but I figured it was the right thing to do. Same with what happened back there."

"What if you can't do what's right just with talk? What if you got to take a gun in your hands?"

"You mean like we did with Slim Jackson?"

"Yeah, like that."

"Sometimes that is necessary, but not as often as we probably think. Usually there are other ways, and if we trust God, he'll see to things coming out right."

"But if you don't know what's the right thing to do?"

"Then I suppose all you can do is try to leave it to God and not take matters into your own hands. Though that's a mighty hard lesson for most men to learn when trouble comes their way."

"And what if you'd been shot back there, by leaving it in God's hands like you say?" asked Jeremiah.

"Like I said, I try not to think about that. If a man's doing what's right, then maybe what happens to him doesn't matter."

Jeremiah let out a whistle and a sigh.

"Well, you got guts, Zeke," he laughed. "That's all I got to say."

DEEPER LEVELS

"It sounds like you had a fun childhood," said Jody.

"Were you always a Christian?"

"My parents read the Bible as long as I can remember, if that is what you mean," answered Mercy. "We always went to church."

"From the tone of your voice I detect that there is more to the story."

"A year ago I wouldn't have known just how much more," sighed Mercy.

"Meaning?"

"That I thought I was a Christian and that my growing up active in church and my participation at the Missionary College was enough. Now I see how incomplete it actually was."

"Do you think you weren't a Christian all that time?"

Mercy thought a moment.

"No, I can't say that. I just wasn't a *complete* Christian."

"How do you mean?"

"I believed in God. I believed what the Bible taught. I believed that Jesus died for me. Yet . . . it hadn't become personal *to me*."

She paused, then looked at Jody seriously.

"Jody, do you think there are levels of being a Christian?"

"I think so—now that I think about it, yes, I do believe so."

"I've wondered if I was at a level of faith that wasn't very deep—that was more just going along with what I had heard and been taught."

"There are many Christians exactly like that."

"How do you get off that level, then?" asked Mercy. "Why did it take me so long to see that there was more to it, that I had to begin living my faith rather than just taking it for granted?"

"God speaks to everyone in their lives," replied Jody, "not always at the same time as another. He wants us all to go deeper in those waters of faith. He wants us to live knowing more about him. He wants us to think. He wants how we think about things to be pleasing to the Lord and to be under his guidance. That's what the word *Lord* means—that he is our master. It happens all through life. It never stops. He always wants to take us to a deeper level."

"How do you live at a deeper level?"

"Heeding his voice when he speaks. He cannot take someone to a deeper level if they do not pay attention now."

"But looking back at my own life, I do not think I was paying very close attention."

"I can't say," replied Jody. "But when he spoke, you tried to heed him."

Mercy smiled as she recalled her first discussions with Jeremiah about faith. "Through an unlikely messenger," she said. "I see now that the lessons were all there for me, but I didn't know how to let them inside."

"God will speak to everyone at some time," said Jody, "more often than not in a way we might not recognize as his voice. But those are his promptings to step down deeper into faith. When we do begin to listen to these lessons, we will hear him all the louder."

"What about *your* past?" asked Mercy.

"I grew up in New York," answered Jody.

"Then the contrast in coming to Kansas must have been even greater for you than it was for me."

"It was a change, all right," laughed Jody.

"Tell me what New York was like."

Jody complied and fell into an hour of reminiscences, some pleasant, some not so pleasant, accompanied by the rhythmic sounds of the train wheels speeding along the track beneath her and Mercy.

6

FATHERS AND GOD

After a long silence of several miles, Zeke was the first to speak again.

"What kind of pa'd you have, Jeremiah?"

"Normal kind, I reckon. Made me work hard, tanned my britches when I crossed him—a decent man, I suppose."

"Still alive?"

Jeremiah shook his head, then was silent a moment

before replying. "No, I left when I was nineteen—got a job that I thought was gonna make me a rich man. Regretted it ever since."

He paused again. "My pa died two years later," he went on. "Never saw him again. Always wished I hadn't been so anxious to grow up and make my own way in the world. Those years could have been good ones with my pa if I'd have been there."

"Your ma?" asked the rancher.

"She died three years later."

"Brothers . . . sisters?"

"Nope. Just me—me and Jess, that is. Jess is as good as a brother, even though he's my nephew."

"The reason I asked about your father was a roundabout way of continuing on what we were talking about a while ago—about growth."

"How so?"

"Growth is what being a Christian's all about," replied Zeke, "growing in character, becoming more like the Lord himself. Ain't nothing else there is to being a Christian. And for a man, a fella's father's just about the most important person in the world in the way of setting the direction he's going to grow."

"But my father never thought about God, at least not that he ever let on. I never heard him say a word about any of this kind of Christian stuff you and I talk about."

"It's not that a man's father has to do or say anything about it at all. He's still the most important person—for a man anyway. I'm not sure how it is for women."

"I'm afraid you lost me," laughed Eagleflight. "If a man's pa never says or does anything—"

"It's not our fathers I'm thinking of," said Zeke, "but *us.*

You see, it's like this—if a man obeys his pa, he's going to know how to obey God. If a man respects his pa, he's going to know how to respect God. If a man honors his father, he's going to know how to honor God. And the same thing's true in reverse, too. A man who doesn't show his father respect, why, that man's going to have a hard time showing God respect. You see what I mean? It doesn't have anything to do with the father at all, but everything to do with the son."

"But what if a fella's father's an ornery cuss?"

"I know there's plenty of fathers that aren't so easy to honor and respect. But that doesn't mean a fella's got to carry around anger and resentment about it all the rest of his life. A man can have a good attitude about anything or a bad attitude about anything. And the thing is—it's his *choice* which, not what kind of man his pa was. There's lots of men carrying around anger toward decent and hardworking fathers, and there's just as many who've got good attitudes toward fathers who were pretty mean to them. That's what I mean when I say it isn't the father so much as the kind of attitude a son *decides* he's going to have. And whatever kind of attitude he chooses to have toward his own pa, that's the kind of attitude he's going to have toward God, too."

Jeremiah let out a whistle and shook his head. "I got to tell you, Zeke, I never heard anything like that. The way a lot of men think of their fathers, it doesn't sound too promising that they're gonna do too well with God. Lot of men hate their pas."

"You're right, Jeremiah. And not just gunfighters either. Lot of Christians keep all sorts of hurts and pains in their heart, not doing anything to get rid of them. And then they figure they can have a good partnership with God. But it never works. In the end, a man's always going to think about God like he's thought about his father. If he resents the one, he's eventually going to resent the other. That's why I say, a man's growth has more to do with how he thinks about his father than anything else. That's why I asked you about your own father a few minutes ago."

"How about for women?" asked Jeremiah. "Is it the same?"

Zeke thought for a few minutes.

"I think so," he said at length, "but maybe not quite so much. Or maybe I'd say her mother's equally a part of it. I think for a woman, the father *or* mother can be the one that either helps or hurts how they think about God. I don't think you can say that it's always one way or the other like you can say it always has to do with a man's father. But I'm not sure—probably ought to ask Jody about that."

7

HOLDUP

The following morning, after a pleasant night in a Kansas City hotel, Mercy and Jody boarded the Missouri Pacific for the second day of their journey east toward St. Louis. The morning passed uneventfully. Mercy was just beginning to tire when the train stopped to take on passengers. The two ladies got out for a short walk on the station platform. They stopped to buy apples from a small boy to eat later with their remaining sandwiches from yesterday.

A large and jovial group was milling about on the opposite end of the platform in the midst of what appeared to be some kind of party. As soon as the conductor cried, "All aboard!" the train began to refill with passengers, Mercy and Jody among them. The noisy party made its way toward the train as well, and from its midst a young man and woman now boarded to the boisterous cheering of their friends.

"It's a wedding party!" said Mercy.

"No wonder everyone is so festive," remarked Jody.

The young man and his new wife came bursting into the carriage, passing the length of the aisle and on into the next one. The bride was dressed in a plain but lovely muslin dress with a short pink jacket. The skirt of the dress was covered with a layer of pink lace, with a pink ruffle at the bottom that matched the jacket. The groom wore a brown suit that looked perfectly ordinary—except for a bright pink tie at his neck! The faces of both of them were happy and beaming.

As she watched them pass, Mercy took special note of the bride's dress, already beginning to think about what she might wear at her *own* wedding.

"Oh, Jody, were you that happy?"

"Yes, we were."

"Will Jeremiah and I be that happy?"

"Yes, you will," laughed Jody. "Every bride beams like that."

It fell quiet for a moment as the train began to move, then pick up steam.

"You know, Mercy," said Jody, "there is more to making a marriage work than a happy wedding."

Mercy laughed.

"Of course I know that, Jody," she replied. "But Jeremiah and I won't have the same problems that others have because of all that has already happened."

"You think you know each other so well it will prevent misunderstanding?"

"Of course."

"How long has it been?"

"Six months."

"That's not very long."

"I know, but Jeremiah and I have already talked about everything, and we agree on almost everything!"

"It's not always the two people themselves who account for the troubles that come to a family. You can't imagine what life can throw at a young couple. There can be emotional tornadoes, just like ones that come in the middle of a storm."

"Oh, Jody, I don't want to hear all that right now. Tell me about your wedding. What did *you* wear?"

But Jody did not have the chance to reply. Suddenly the train jerked, and she and Jody lurched forward in their seats. At the same instant, the screech of the huge metal wheels against the iron track indicated that the engineer had thrown the brake lever. As the two women regained their balance, they felt the train beginning to slow.

"I wonder what the problem is," said Jody, glancing out the window, then back. "We're out in the middle of nowhere."

Mercy leaned to the side and also peered outside.

"There are some riders on horses out there," she said, then gasped.

"What is it?" asked Jody in alarm.

"They're wearing . . . they've got bandanas pulled up over their noses!"

Jody leaned over for a look from her seat opposite Mercy. But before either had a chance to contemplate their fate further, the coach door behind them crashed open.

In strode an outlaw with a heavy-booted step, a dirty black hat on his head, and his face hidden by a red handkerchief.

"All right, ladies and gents," he said, waving his pistol about in the air, "if you'll be so kind as to put your jewelry and cash in the bag when it comes by, we'll be off this train lickety-split and you can all be on your way!"

Behind him, a second figure, smaller and slight of build, entered, squeezed past him, and began making its way down the aisle, shoving a small open carpetbag in front of every passenger.

"Ain't no cause for alarm, folks," said the man, "and there ain't no reason for anyone to get themselves hurt, just so long as you do what we say."

All was silent as the second figure walked slowly down the center of the car collecting money and valuables. The only things that could be heard were the sound of steam escaping underneath the locomotive now that they had come to a complete stop and an occasional clink of watch or bracelet or loose coins falling into the bag. Mercy and Jody glanced at one another with white faces. Slowly Jody removed the locket from around her neck, and Mercy unclasped the brooch from her dress.

Suddenly the carpetbag appeared rudely between them. Reluctantly they each deposited their belongings inside.

Mercy glanced up. With astonishment she realized that the bag was being held by a woman. Her long blonde hair had been pulled up inside a gray cowboy hat, though a few strands had escaped around the edges, betraying its length, and the red-striped bandana could not hide a woman's eyes and complexion. The former were green and close set, the latter pale except for a small pink birthmark between the left eye and temple. For the merest moment Mercy caught the two green eyes with her own.

"Your handbags," said the woman sharply, looking away and motioning with her head to the seats, "put them in, too!"

"Please," said Jody calmly, "we're—"

"Shut up, lady!" barked the man with the pistol, taking two large menacing steps forward. "Do as my partner says!"

Mercy and Jody both complied, and the woman moved on. They sat silently, watching her proceed to the next seat as the man moved alongside them, eyes roving about to make certain everyone obeyed his instructions. His gun, which was now only a foot or so from Mercy's face, was clutched in readiness.

Fifteen or twenty seconds passed.

Suddenly the wooden floor creaked behind them. The next instant, the metallic *click* of a gun cocking echoed in the tense stillness.

"Drop the gun, Fletcher," said a quiet but commanding voice. "I've got the barrel of a .45 between your shoulder blades."

Mercy glanced sideways. There was the robber's gun right next to her! His fingers tensed imperceptibly. Her eyes widened in panic.

As if reading her mind, the new voice spoke again. "Don't even think about trying anything, Fletcher. I see that trigger finger of yours move so much as a quarter inch, I won't mind dropping you where you stand. Dead or alive don't matter to me." As he spoke, he jammed the point of his gun sharply into the outlaw's back.

"Hey, Nichols! Ain't no call for that. You got me dead to rights."

"Take that gun outta the varmint's hand, will you, miss?"

It took Mercy a moment. Then suddenly she realized that the man called Nichols was talking to *her!*

"What? . . . I, uh—," she stammered, finding her throat suddenly very dry.

"Take his gun," he repeated.

Trembling, Mercy reached out and gingerly grasped the pistol.

"Let go of it, Fletcher!"

Imperceptibly the man's fingers relaxed, and a moment later Mercy found the gun in her two hands.

"Get going, Fletcher—you too, Loretta. Just leave that carpetbag on the man's seat there. Then you two get up to the next car where the rest of your gang will be waiting for you with another of my men."

Nichols shoved the train robber forward, then came alongside Mercy and Jody's seats.

"Much obliged, ma'am," he said, taking the gun from Mercy's hand. "Marshal Brad Nichols," he added, nodding. "Been on the trail of this no-good bunch of thieves all the way from Laramie."

"How'd you know we'd be here, Nichols?" growled Fletcher as the three made their way forward.

"One of your bunch we nabbed back in Salina. Seems his loyalty was more to his own skin than to the Medicine Bow Gang. He told us you were planning to hit the K. C.-to-St. Louis run."

"How'd you know it'd be today?"

"Didn't. I grew me a beard and got me a businessman suit, and me and my boys have been sitting in the backseat of these cars every day for two weeks now."

"That blamed Butch! I never trusted him!"

"Well, you'll get a chance to tell him so yourself, 'cause you're both gonna be behind bars for a long time."

"Don't bet on it, Marshal," spat Fletcher. "We got us other friends than Butch."

"Like McLeod?"

"He's one—him and Stoner."

"Yeah, well neither of them's gonna do you any good now," laughed Nichols. "We got McLeod the same time we nabbed Butch, and one of my men's on Stoner's trail right now. Your gang's finished, Fletcher. It took seven years since we nailed Hotchkiss, but finally we got you all rounded up. Get going. Sorry about the inconvenience, folks," the marshal said over his shoulder as they reached the end of the car. "I'm sure you can all retrieve your own things while we get these no-goods off the train. You'll be on your way in no time."

Applause and a few cheers broke out from among the passengers for the marshal as he shoved the two through the door and followed them out. Sighs and exclamations of relief spread around the car. The last man to be robbed now stood, holding the carpetbag.

"I guess I'll send this back around the way it came!" he said with a relieved smile. He reached inside, pulled out his own small pocketbook and watch, then handed the bag back to the seat just behind him.

SURPRISE
HOMECOMING

Zeke Simmons, ranch owner, and Jeremiah
Eagleflight approached the Bar S shortly before noon. Each
man was lost in his own thoughts, each very different from
the other.

Zeke had built the ranch house and barn that loomed in
the middle of the prairie in front of them with his own two
hands, and over the years he had turned the Bar S into the

largest and most productive spread for miles. This was his home, and nowhere on earth did he feel the contentment he felt right here. As they crested the ridge after crossing the river north of Sweetriver and caught sight of the Bar S spreading out below them in the distance, he exhaled a long sigh of satisfaction. The fact that his wife was gone only slightly diminished the sense of homeyness he felt at the sight.

An odd feeling of inexplicable disquiet began to come over Jeremiah as they approached, however, and it could not be explained merely by Mercy's absence. He would soon discover its cause.

Even before they reached the ranch house, Dirk Heyes spotted the boss' wagon from where he sat on the top rail of the corral fence, watching a couple of his men attempt to break two wild stallions they had captured out on the range. The foreman leapt down and walked over as Zeke reined in his team.

"Howdy, Zeke . . . Eagleflight," he said, shaking both men's hands. "Glad to have the two of you back."

"Looks like everything's OK," said Zeke.

"Except that the men hate my cooking," laughed Heyes. "I told 'em you'd take as good a care of 'em as Jody."

"We'll see," rejoined Zeke as the three men entered the house.

"Women get off all right?"

"Yep, right on schedule."

"Let's see," said Jeremiah, "they were going to spend last night in Kansas City. They're likely past St. Louis by now."

"When will they arrive?" asked Heyes.

"Get to Louisville sometime this evening," answered Jeremiah.

"By the way, what's for lunch?" asked Zeke.

"Only what's left of the stew I made. I was hoping you might whip up some of Jody's fresh biscuits to go with it. They gave most of mine to the pigs after last night's supper."

"I'll see what I can do," laughed Zeke. "Eagleflight, how about putting the wagon away and unhitching the team?"

Jeremiah nodded and turned to leave the house.

Forty or fifty minutes later, the Bar S men began to wander into the house for lunch, Jeremiah among them. Gradually they settled themselves around the table. Jeremiah glanced around, looked toward the door, then strode toward the window and peered outside.

"Where's Jess?" he said. "You got him out working for the whole day, Heyes?"

"Oh, I knew there was something I forgot to tell the two of you," replied the foreman, glancing first to Zeke, then over to Jeremiah. "Forbes is gone."

"Gone" exclaimed Jeremiah.

"Yep," Heyes said with a nod, grabbing a hot biscuit from the middle of the table.

"Gone where?"

"Don't know."

"What happened?"

"He came in about the middle of the afternoon yesterday. Said he'd decided maybe the ranching life wasn't for him after all. Said he had someplace he had to go anyway."

"Where?"

"Didn't say. Just said he wasn't worried about the pay he'd lose by taking off before payday 'cause when his business was done he wouldn't need it anyway."

"Which way'd he head?" Jeremiah asked after a moment.

"Don't know—toward town's all I could tell."

"No message for me?"

"Sorry, Eagleflight."

Jeremiah sighed, more thoughtful than disappointed.

"I just can't figure it,"he said to himself. "Where could he have been heading off to?"

"Which road he took to town, I couldn't tell," said the foreman.

"He wasn't going to Fort Hays," mused Jeremiah, "else we'd have seen him. We ain't ever been to Dodge, so it ain't likely he had business there."

"You figure he's headed to Denver, then?" asked Phillips.

"More'n likely," Jeremiah said with a nod.

"You're his partner, Eagleflight," said Heyes. "I figured you'd know where he was bound."

Jeremiah shook his head. "That's one thing about Jess," he said. "He's always been a mite too impulsive for his own good."

It was silent around the table for a minute while everyone finished serving up and began eating.

"You sure he didn't say anything more?" said Jeremiah at length to no one in particular, glancing around the table.

"Nothing I can recall," said Heyes.

"He was looking at the calendar there kinda peculiar," said Wood.

"Hey, that's right!" added Clancy.

"Yeah, asked you what year it was, remember, Heyes?"

"Sure enough," replied the foreman, "you're right, Bart. Then he mumbled something about losing track of time. Yep, that's right. Didn't say much more the rest of lunch, then two or three hours later he was packed up and heading outta here."

Jeremiah looked over at the calendar.

Today was November 4. The year was 1891. What could Jess have been thinking about? There must be *something* on that calendar page that held the clue to his friend's hasty departure from the Bar S.

If only he could figure out what.

HAPPY HOMECOMING

As Mercy lay down in her own bed for the first time in three years, she pulled the familiar patchwork quilt up to her neck. Her mind drifted back to her arrival earlier in the evening. . . .

From the train window she saw her parents and brother and sister standing on the landing even before the Louisville-and

Nashville train had come to a complete stop. The conductor was scarcely able to open the door before she was through it and in her mother's arms.

"Mercy . . . dear—"

"Oh, Mother!"

"You look so much older and so beautiful!" her mother whispered into her ear.

"I am so happy to see you. You can't know how good it feels to be back."

Both women stood a moment in a tight embrace, tears streaming down their faces.

Mercy stepped back. Beside her mother, her father's arms were outspread in invitation.

"Oh, Daddy!" she cried, moving toward him slowly and letting his arms close gently around her shoulders. This was the home she had missed even before her adventures—right here in her father's loving arms.

"Welcome home, Mercy," said Mr. Randolph shakily, struggling with his own tears and with the lump in his throat.

"I'm so sorry, Daddy," said Mercy. "Will you ever forgive me for being so foolish and for thinking I could just take off by myself?"

"Of course. You need not even ask."

"I'm so sorry for not listening to your advice."

"Whatever forgiveness you feel you need has been in my heart all along," replied Mr. Randolph. "Take however much you want, and there will always be more where that came from."

"Oh, Daddy," laughed Mercy, wiping at her eyes, "you always have such a way of saying things!"

"From the sound of your letters, I half expected to see

you looking pale and haggard and thin. Why, you look positively radiant and healthy, my dear."

"I have been very well taken care of—oh, but you must
meet Jody!" exclaimed Mercy, glancing around. Jody was
just stepping down from the train and now began walking
toward them. Mercy reached out and took Jody's hand and
pulled her toward her parents.

"Jody Simmons, meet my mother and father, Ernestine and
Sinclair Randolph. Mama, Daddy, this is Jody Simmons."

They all shook hands and exchanged smiles and pleasantries.

"Hi, Tom . . . Rachel," said Mercy, turning to her brother
and sister, who were standing to one side. "Wow, you've
both grown six inches since I saw you!"

"You look different, too," said Rachel, a shy girl of eighteen years, "but not because you're taller."

"I think I've grown more *inside*," said Mercy, "than the
two of you combined on the *outside*. I'll tell you all about it.
And, Thomas, how are your experiments in the attic?"

"How did you know?" said her brother, a lanky lad of
fifteen, whose voice was teetering on the awkward balance
between fading soprano and approaching baritone.

"Mama wrote me. You'll have to show me everything."

"Let's get your bags, ladies, and get home!" said Mr. Randolph. "Your mother has a feast prepared for us, Mercy,
with all your favorite things."

"Pumpkin pie!" exclaimed Mercy.

"Of course—what else?"

"Let us be off, then," repeated Mercy's father, "because
I for one am eagerly anticipating it!"

After beginning a letter to Jeremiah, Mercy found herself
too sleepy to concentrate. She snuggled deeper into her bed

and contentedly drifted off to sleep. Meanwhile, downstairs, her mother and father and Jody Simmons entered a small parlor off the dining room. Mr. Randolph closed the door behind them.

"I hope you do not mind our asking to speak with you privately like this," he said once the three were seated. "I know it is late, and you are no doubt tired. But we did not know when an opportunity would come to see you without Mercy, and we did not want to delay what we have to say to you."

"I am fine." Jody smiled. "I think I shall be able to fend off sleep for a while yet."

"Would you care for some tea?" asked Mr. Randolph. "I know some people do not like it before retiring, and yet I happen to be one of those peculiar ones who finds that it helps me sleep."

"Zeke and I often have tea in the evening," replied Jody, "but I think tonight I shall refrain."

"You cannot know how much we appreciate all you have done for our daughter," said Mrs. Randolph sincerely as she poured a cup of tea, handed it to her husband, then resumed her seat. "That is what we wanted to say to you."

"She is a dear young lady," replied Jody. "I am privileged that the Lord allowed me to be there when she needed someone."

"We are so grateful to you and your husband," added Mr. Randolph, "for opening your home as you did. From the day Mercy left for the Missionary College in Jefferson City we could not help but be concerned."

"She was so young—at least she seemed so to us," put in his wife.

"We prayed for the Lord's protection and that he would

mature her through the time away from us. But I must say these years have been ones of trial for Ernestine and myself. We could not help but be anxious for her, even though we had committed her to the Lord's care and knew she would not stray from his sight, even if she did from ours. I hope he will forgive us our lack of trust in his providence, but parenting is sometimes no easy task for sensitive emotions."

"We are not of the mind, you see, of many parents," said Mrs. Randolph, "who are glad to see children leave home. We dearly love our son and two daughters and have always looked forward to these young maturing years prior to marriage."

"We had hoped to share this special time of emerging adulthood with our three children remaining with us," said her husband, "learning to be friends together as Christian brothers and sisters, so to speak."

"But Mercy was—well . . . she was always an independent girl," said Mercy's mother, "who had to try things for herself without stopping to ask if she was ready for them."

"And in many ways," said Mercy's father, "she was not ready for what she did."

"It was not that she was rebellious," added her mother. "Far from it. She has always been a good girl. It was just that she had an independent streak."

"We knew," said her father, "that Mercy's faith was, in a sense, a shallow one, untested, untried, without deep roots. Yet we see now that perhaps the maturing of her faith was not meant to come through us. God always seems to have others of his people ready to stand in a parent's stead when a son or daughter wanders from the fold prematurely. And we are grateful that the Lord had you there for our daughter."

Jody was silent a moment, then glanced down, struggling with deep emotion. Mr. and Mrs. Randolph waited.

At length Jody took a deep breath. "My husband and I have never had children," she said, wiping once or twice at her eye. "So you see, for *me*, knowing Mercy was like getting the opportunity to enjoy the daughter I never had of my own."

She looked up at Mercy's mother and father and smiled. "I appreciate what you say, Mr. and Mrs. Randolph," she said, "and I appreciate your words of gratefulness. But I feel as though I am the most blessed of all in this."

"The Lord does manage to work good for everyone in very complex ways," said Mercy's father.

"I am more than happy to share my daughter with you, Jody," said Mrs. Randolph. "And, please, you must call us Ernestine and Sinclair. My husband may be a banker," she added, glancing toward him, "but we do not stand on ceremony around here at home."

"Neither do we on our ranch. Of course, with the kind of men you meet out on the prairie, it would be impossible, even if we tried!"

HUMAN ACORNS

Jeremiah awoke early the morning after he and
Zeke returned. The other men were still asleep in the
bunkhouse.

He got up, dressed, and went outside into the still air of
dawn. *What should I do about Jess?* he thought to himself.
Thoughts of his nephew's leaving had kept him awake half

the night. He had a feeling Jess was going to get himself
into some kind of trouble.

It wouldn't be the first time. But always before, Jeremiah
had been there to help, to bail him out, to talk some sense
into his thick skull. Now he didn't even know where Jess
was! If only he could figure out what Jess had been thinking when he'd looked at the calendar.

Jeremiah wandered about the corral, then toward the
barn. He thought he smelled coffee. *How can that be?* he
wondered. It was too early. But somebody must be up. He
opened the creaky barn door and walked inside. He was
right—the aroma was coming from within.

"Morning, Jeremiah," Zeke's voice sounded from somewhere within the dim interior.

"That you, Zeke?"

"It's me."

"My nose was following the trail of your coffee," laughed
Jeremiah.

"I just made a fresh pot in the house—not too bad either."

The next moment, Zeke appeared, walking toward him
out of the semidarkness with a tin cup in his hand. The two
men left the barn together and walked between the corrals
to the house.

Once they were inside, Jeremiah sat down at one of the
kitchen worktables. "You're up early," said Zeke as he
poured Jeremiah a cup of the steaming black brew from the
pot on the stove, then joined him on the other side of the
table.

"Didn't sleep too well," said Eagleflight. "Thanks," he
added, sipping at the edge of his cup. "Whew, that's hot!"

"Got the young lady on your mind, eh?" said Zeke.

"Actually, I do," replied Eagleflight, "but this time it's Jess I'm more concerned about."

The rancher nodded. He was concerned, too. He didn't know Jess Forbes well, but in the time of their short acquaintance he had discerned Eagleflight's partner to be the kind of man who was likely to land in more than his fair share of hot water.

"I haven't been able to get out of my mind what you said before about what kind of man a fellow's growing into," said Jeremiah after sipping again at his coffee. "I know you aren't supposed to look at other folks and try to figure out what's wrong with them when there's plenty wrong with yourself. But I can't keep myself from worrying about Jess."

Jeremiah paused thoughtfully, then went on after a moment. "You know, the things you said about growing into something better than you are. The thing about Jess is that I don't think he's ever given a second thought to the man he's becoming. He just flies off and does whatever comes into his head to do."

"That's the way it is with most folks," remarked Zeke with a sigh. "The consequences of how their actions and thoughts affect who they are inside and who they're becoming—those kinds of things rarely occur to them. If they did, folks'd be a little more particular about what they do and the attitudes they let take root in their hearts and minds."

"You were talking about *growing* into a certain kind of person yesterday," said Jeremiah. "How do you mean that exactly? I reckon I'm asking for myself, too, not just for Jess."

Zeke smiled. "That's a mighty big question, Eagleflight."

"Yeah, well, maybe just my saying I'm a Christian isn't enough anymore. Maybe I gotta do a little more about it."

"You're right there—and you'll be working on it the rest of your life. I'll do my best to explain."

Simmons paused and thought for a minute or two, taking two or three small swallows of coffee as he did.

"You noticed the trees planted all around the house and out up the road?" he asked at length.

Jeremiah nodded. "Yeah, I noticed. You got quite a variety."

Zeke nodded. "Planted every one of them myself," he said. "Brought them all the way from Wichita as seedlings. I wanted my house surrounded with all kinds of trees. So I brought in several oaks and maples, a half-dozen pines, lots of fruit trees—apple, cherry, the like—birch, ash, syca-more. I like trees, Eagleflight, so I planted probably two, maybe three hundred all around my land."

"I'd have never known it," said Jeremiah. "They're all so big now. I just figured—well, except for the fruit trees—that they were here when you came."

"Nope. I planted the tiny things, then carried water to every one for the first three or four summers afterward. I lost a few, but most of them grew and finally were able to take care of themselves, and now they're full grown."

He paused. "More coffee?"

"Yeah, thanks."

Zeke stood, walked to the stove, took the pot from it, and filled each of their cups.

"That's what growth is like for people, too," he said after he was seated again. "We're made to become full-sized trees. Every one of us is different just like every tree is different. Every man and woman is going to have different bark, dif-ferent leaves, all kinds of different characteristics, and will bear a different kind of fruit. But the one thing that's the same with us all is that we've all got to grow to become the tree we're supposed to become."

Jeremiah nodded as Zeke spoke.

"There's a purpose we're supposed to fulfill," said Zeke, "just like an apple tree is supposed to grow apples and an oak tree is supposed to become tall and strong with wide outspreading branches that produce acorns for the squirrels to eat. We're planted for a purpose, just like I planted my trees on the Bar S for a reason. You see what I'm driving at?"

"I think so."

"What would you think of an apple or an oak tree that remained a seedling forever or else grew up middling, without anything on it but a few withered leaves and scrawny branches?"

"I reckon I'd say it wasn't much of a tree."

"And you'd be right. It wouldn't be. An apple tree with no apples, an oak tree with no acorns—those trees aren't being what they're supposed to be. There's no fruit. You might as well chop them down. You see what I mean?"

"Yeah. And you're saying that's how it is with people?"

"Yep. Exactly the same. We're made to bear fruit, to become full-grown trees. We're not just here by accident. We've been planted, Jeremiah. Why, the Bible even talks about God being a gardener. That's why I said it's what we're becoming that's so important. If we're not becoming a tree capable of producing apples or acorns or whatever it is we're supposed to produce, then we're not doing much good to him that planted us."

"What *are* we supposed to produce?" asked Jeremiah. "Are you talking about having young'uns?"

"No, I'm talking about the kind of trees we become. There's lots of different kinds of human trees with lots of different things growing on them. But we're all kept alive the same way. We've all got the same sap running up and down inside us that God made to keep us alive. When the sap flows, we're alive and healthy. When it doesn't, we gradually die inside. And it's this sap that helps us grow and produce the fruit we're supposed to produce."

"Sap? In people?"

"The sap running up through all human trees, *whatever* kind they are, is supposed to be unselfishness."

"Sounds simple enough. I was expecting you to say some highfalutin spiritual thing I might not have heard of before."

Zeke laughed. "That's one thing about the Christian life, Jeremiah—nothing highfalutin about it, just down-to-earth and simple. That's the sap that gives us life—nothing more complicated than putting others first, doing for others before you do for yourself. That's what makes growth possible. That's the sap that comes up out of the ground and eventually makes a seedling's trunk get stronger and taller and then send branches out and roots deeper yet. If that sap is flowing up the trunk like it's supposed to, then all kinds of other little fruits—like acorns and apples and pears and cherries and seedpods and cones—start to appear at the ends of the branches. But it's the sap of unselfishness that causes them to start appearing all over the human tree."

"I still don't understand—what kind of fruits? You're talking about acorns and apples, but we don't grow acorns and apples."

Zeke laughed again. "You're right there," he said. "We've been planted to grow something else. Ever heard of the fruits of the Spirit, Eagleflight?"

"Can't say I have."

"That's what they're called—fruits. If the sap's flowing

like it ought to, they start growing all over you, even in places you might not see them."

"So what are these fruits?"

"*Patience* is one, and *kindness.* Can't be patient and kind toward folks if you're thinking about yourself instead of them. But as soon as the sap of putting others first starts flowing, patience and kindness just happen without you thinking much about them. Patience and kindness are like *human* acorns."

"So you're saying if the sap's flowing inside you, then you're *growing* like a man's supposed to and you're *becoming* the tree you were planted to be, and then those acorns'll grow?"

"That's it."

"What are some of the other things that grow when you put others ahead of yourself?"

"Oh, there's lots of human acorns—cheerfulness, gratefulness, goodness. Then there's being faithful and gentle, being a person of self-control. There's all kinds of 'em."

"Doesn't sound like you're saying much more than just being *nice.*"

"That's more or less how you could sum it up—loving people as Jesus loved them. That's another of the fruits—love. It's the most important of them all."

They spoke for a few minutes more. Then silence fell.

Jeremiah set down his cup, rose, and walked outside. The sun was climbing in the sky now, and he could hear the men in the bunkhouse getting ready for the day. He walked behind the house in the direction of a large oak tree. Suddenly he beheld it with new eyes. He tried to imagine it as a small seedling when Zeke planted it and carried water to it in a bucket.

He walked underneath its vast outspreading branches,

then placed his hand upon its rough trunk, easily two feet thick. The sap in this tree had truly run vigorously, he thought, for it had made of Zeke's seedling a mighty tree. Around him on the ground were hundreds of fallen acorns.

Jeremiah stooped down and picked one up, then turned it over in his hand, beholding it with new understanding.

"Help *me* grow into the tree you want me to become, Lord," he prayed. "Help me be a man like Zeke. Help me be unselfish. Help me grow into a man . . . with character like an oak tree. And," he added after a brief pause, "help me know what to do about Jess."

BANKER'S HOLIDAY

Mercy rolled over in her bed on the morning after
her arrival and lazily opened her eyes. Rays of sunlight
streamed through the window of her old room and made it
seem warm and homey.

It had been over three years since she had gone off to the
Jefferson City Young Women's Missionary College. She
had left young and naive about life and her faith. As she had

said to her sister, she felt like she had grown up years on the inside since then. She only wished it hadn't had to come as a result of going against her parents' wishes. God had worked it out for the best, but she would always regret that she hadn't trusted her father and mother's warnings.

Oh, it was so good to be home!

So much had happened, and yet now that she was back, it seemed like no time had passed at all.

Breakfast at the Randolph home that day was the happiest anyone could remember in a long while.

"Well, Mercy, my dear," said Mr. Randolph from the large woodstove, where he was overseeing a skillet full of scrambled eggs while his wife removed a pan of fresh muffins from the oven beneath it, "what would you like to do today? This is your day, and we shall all be your servants."

"Will you not be at work, Daddy?" asked Mercy.

"Not I!" he answered. "I have declared what they call in England a 'banker's holiday'—at least for this one particular banker."

"Can you do that?" exclaimed Jody.

"When you are the vice president you can!" rejoined Ernestine.

Now they all laughed.

"Sit down, everyone," said Mrs. Randolph. "I do believe we're ready."

"And as for Thomas," Sinclair Randolph went on as they sat and the platters of eggs, muffins, butter, and bacon began their rounds, "we shall conduct school in the home for today. What do you say, Tom? We can tour Louisville and reacquaint your sister with the city and show our honored guest all its fair sights. Then we shall dine—what do you think, Ernestine?—at L'Henri's on the river."

"That will be perfect."

"My," said Jody, "this will be more culture and refinement than I've had in years. Quite a change from the dust and hay and smell of horses at the Bar S, isn't it, Mercy?"

Mercy laughed in knowing agreement.

"Are we all ready?" said Mercy's father, glancing up and down the table. "Then I shall give thanks." He bowed his head, as did the others.

"Heavenly Father," he prayed, "it is with hearts full of more gratitude than we can possibly express that we give you thanks for this moment, for bringing our dear Mercy home to us, and for her friend, and now ours as well, Jody Simmons. Thank you, Lord, for protecting and watching over Mercy while she has been away and for guiding her to your servants, Jody and her husband. We stand in awe of your sovereignty in our lives, dear Lord, and we ask you to reveal more and more of the personal aspects of that sovereignty to each of us every day. We take this opportunity to pray for Mr. Simmons and also for Mercy's new friend Jeremiah. Touch them with your love and your life this day, and we pray that for each one of us as well. Thank you now for this food. Use it to strengthen and nourish us. Let us never take your provision for granted. We give ourselves to you this day, as your men and your women. Let us be your bold and humble and grateful servants in all we do. Thank you, our Father. Amen."

A few quiet *amen*s sounded around the table.

"That reminds me," said Mercy as they began to eat, "one thing I *must* do today is finish the letter to Jeremiah I began last night."

"I am anxious to hear about this young man," said Mr. Randolph. "You must tell us the truth, Jody. Mercy's eyes are clouded over, you see, with the malady which I believe is commonly referred to as *being in love.*"

"Daddy—they are not!"

"Be honest now," added Mercy's mother to Jody with a smile.

"He is as upright and considerate a young man as I have met in all my years on the prairie," replied Jody. "You will like him very much."

"When *will* we see him, Mercy?" asked Mrs. Randolph.

"As soon as you and Daddy tell me I may ask him to visit," answered Mercy.

"Then by all means, invite him!" boomed her father.

"I thought maybe he could spend Christmas with us."

"What about his own family?"

"He has no family—except for his nephew, Jess."

"Then tell him that he and his nephew will be welcome for Christmas," said Mercy's mother.

"From what I understand," remarked her father, "we have him to thank as much as the Simmonses for watching out for you so far away from home."

"He was like my own guardian angel my first few days in Sweetriver, Daddy—though neither of us knew it at the time," she added, smiling to herself.

"How long will *you* be with us, Jody?" asked Mrs. Randolph.

"Oh, only a few days—perhaps a week. Mercy suggested I come along with her, and I did want to meet the two of you. But how long my husband and his hands can get by without me in the kitchen may be doubtful. Not that they wouldn't manage to find food to eat, but it's the condition of my kitchen that I'm worried about!"

"I understand what you mean," said Mercy's mother. "A

houseful of men with no woman to keep them in line could prove a dangerous situation!"

"You will want to visit Rev. Walton at the church, won't you?" asked Mercy's father, turning toward Mercy.

"He has been asking about you every day," added Mercy's mother, "and I know he is most anxious to see you."

An embarrassed expression came over Mercy's face. "It will be awkward."

"Why would you say that?"

"He is the one who told me about the Missionary College," replied Mercy. "I know he had high hopes for me there. He said he thought it would mature my faith as a Christian. After what I did—leaving the school early—it will be embarrassing to see him. It is almost as though I let him down."

"Believe me, dear, nothing could be further from his mind. He may want to talk to you as well, Jody. Our pastor is very interested in the building of churches in the West."

"There is no church within miles of us," said Jody. "Zeke and I do what we can in our home for just the two of us. Once in a while one or two of the hands join us. And I meet with some Pawnee children nearby. There is a small settlement not far to the south of our ranch."

"Oh, they are dears, Mother!" added Mercy. "You should see them."

"You have gone to an Indian reservation?" asked Mrs. Randolph, not exactly knowing what to think.

"It is not on reservation land," replied Jody.

"Yes, I've gone two or three times with Jody," added Mercy.

"But to get back to the idea of a church," Jody went on, "Zeke and I have occasionally thought about the possibility of building one in Sweetriver."

"Why haven't you?" asked Mercy's father.

"Somehow neither the prompting from the Lord nor the right circumstances have seemed to exist," answered Jody.

"Without those, you are wise to wait," he replied.

"Is your husband a minister, Jody?" asked Mrs. Randolph.

"Oh no—just a rancher who loves God. Maybe your minister would like to come out and help us begin a church in Kansas."

"You never know," laughed Mr. Randolph. "Harold Walton is a pretty adventurous fellow for a minister. I wouldn't put anything past him."

SEVEN YEARS

Halfway through the following afternoon, Jeremiah suddenly realized why Jess had been looking at the calendar. He'd glanced over toward the wall himself at lunch and again found himself puzzling over the date — November 5.

Why had Jess been so interested? Why had he asked Heyes what year it was? What was so significant about the year 1891?

Just a couple of minutes ago the thought had occurred
to him that possibly it wasn't *this* year Jess had been thinking of at all.

Then it struck him—they'd been in Denver seven years
ago at exactly this same time of the year. They'd been there
right at the time of the famous Donahue robbery.

When had it been? he thought to himself.

The ninth. November 9 . . . 1884.

The next instant the truth crashed into Jeremiah's brain
like a hammer. The sapphires had never been found—some
said two hundred thousand dollars' worth. And just four
days from now—seven years after the famous night—the
statute of limitations would run out on the robbery.

There had been reports, of course, all through the years,
about where Kid Hotchkiss had stashed them and stories
about his gang waiting till the seven years were up to
retrieve them. Jeremiah'd never believed any of the rumors
himself, though, now that he remembered it, Jess had
always taken an unusual interest in the case.

That was it!

Jess had taken off after the sapphires! If he got his hands on
them after the ninth, he would figure they were his to keep.

But he could well get himself killed in the process. If they
didn't have them already, the Medicine Bow Gang was sure
to be snooping around. Hotchkiss had ridden with the gang
before getting himself killed that night, and if his former com-
rades had any inkling what he'd done with the sapphires,
they'd be converging on Denver, too. If Jess got himself in
the middle of it, there was no telling what might happen.

Already Jeremiah had dropped his hammer and was heading back to the ranch house. He had to go after Jess before
Jess got himself into trouble!

The minute Zeke Simmons glanced up from the horse's hoof he was shoeing and saw Jeremiah walking into the blacksmithing shed, he knew something was up.

"Zeke, I gotta talk to you," said Eagleflight.

"From the worried expression on your face, I'd say it looks serious."

"I think I figured out why Jess took off."

"Denver?"

"Yep, and I think he could be in danger."

"And you want to go after him?"

"I got to."

Zeke nodded. He knew what kind of man Jeremiah Eagleflight was and that whether it was a fruit of the Spirit or not, *loyalty* grew on Eagleflight's tree. Zeke understood. He'd ridden into a few hornets' nests himself in his time for the sake of a friend.

"I know you're my boss," Jeremiah went on, "and I know you'd have every right to fire me for leaving on you without warning. But I'm hoping you'll understand."

"I do, Eagleflight. Go on—get your saddlebags packed, and hit the trail. You got a job with me anytime and for however long you want it."

"Thanks, Zeke. You're a real friend."

"What about Mercy? You going to telegraph her?"

Jeremiah shrugged and sighed.

"I been debating with myself what to do," he said. "I kinda hate to spoil her first day home, especially knowing she'd worry about me."

"She'll be expecting to get a letter from you."

"I was hoping maybe you could write to Jody and mention that I had to go to Denver for a few days. That way Mercy won't think it's anything serious."

"*Is* it serious, Jeremiah?" asked Zeke.

"It could be, Zeke. . . . It just could be. But don't worry, I'll be back in a week, inside two weeks at the most. I'll be at the Grey Falcon Inn. The owner's an old friend of mine, and we always stay with him when we're in Denver."

Jeremiah looked at Zeke's face, seeing the concern written there. Zeke reached for his wallet as if he was about to offer a loan, knowing that Jeremiah was not flush with money.

"I'll be fine, Zeke," Jeremiah said, putting his hand on Zeke's arm. "I sold my extra saddle last week."

Zeke looked surprised.

"The one with the silver studs and the fancy carving?"

Jeremiah nodded.

"I hated to part with it, but the cash does me more good than a saddle I don't use."

Zeke nodded. Something about marriage makes a man look at priorities different.

"Just don't take all the cash with you to Denver," he warned. "You can leave the rest here in the safe."

DENVER

Riding into Denver alone just doesn't seem right,

thought Jess Forbes as he looked down the familiar street.

He loved Denver, but it just wouldn't be as much fun

without Jeremiah.

But he would be rich before he left the city this time, and

then *everything* would be fun!

He had been riding so hard he hadn't allowed himself the

luxury of pausing to think about what he had done by leaving his partner of so many years without so much as a note of good-bye. Well, Jeremiah would understand once Jess had a chance to tell him his errand, Jess thought. Maybe he'd even be able to talk him out of getting married, and the two of them could go out to San Francisco for a while.

He rode up and dismounted in front of the Rocky Mountain Hotel, glancing up as he looped the end of his reins around the hitching rail. The place looked different than he remembered it, though it had been several years since he'd seen it, and it looked like it had been painted recently.

He walked to the counter.

"I'd like a room," he said.

"How long?"

"Two, three days . . . maybe four."

"Just yourself?"

"Just me," answered Jess. "Listen, mister," he added, "I'm kinda sentimental. Be possible for me to have the corner room that looks up the street at the mountains, the one on the top floor?"

The clerk eyed him quizzically. "What for?" he asked.

"Like I said, I'm sentimental. Me and my wife stayed in that very room for our honeymoon—before she passed on, that is," he added, with just a bit too much sorrow in his tone.

"Well, let me see," mumbled the man, turning and glancing over his keyboard. "Yes, it is available at that. I suppose you can have that one if you like."

"Much obliged."

"That'll be a dollar a day—in advance, Mr. . . . ?"

"Uh . . . uh, Eagleflight—Jess Eagleflight."

Jess dug into his pocket, then plunked a coin down onto the counter.

"Just sign here in the register, Mr. Eagleflight, and I'll get you the key."

Five minutes later, Jess turned the lock, swung the door open, and walked inside room 4-G. He glanced around. Nothing fancy, just a hotel room.

He threw his saddlebags down on the bed, looked around again, opened a couple of the drawers of the dresser, then pulled open the door to the small wardrobe, the only two pieces of furniture in the room besides the bed and a chair. Both were stark empty.

He had no idea where to even start looking. But he had a couple days to try to figure it out. In the meantime, he was thirsty.

He turned and headed downstairs to the saloon.

GETAWAY

"Now it's my turn, Nichols — drop it."

"What are you talking about, Fletcher?" laughed Marshal Brad Nichols. "I got you dead to rights, and you ain't got nothing that could pass for a weapon."

The marshal gave his reins a flick and shouted at their horses to keep moving, his own following close behind those of his prisoners. After taking them into custody, Nichols and

his deputies had returned with the robbers by train to Gree-
ley, north of Denver. Now he and one of his men were trans-
porting them overland to Fort Collins, where the original
warrants had been issued and where they would stand trial.

"Yeah, maybe I ain't," said Fletcher over his shoulder,
"but I just wanted to hear how the words sounded. And
even if I got no gun, my friend over there behind that rock,
he's got a carbine taking a bead right at your forehead."

Nichols laughed. "You expect me to believe —"

A shot echoed through the canyon. The marshal tumbled
off his mount with a groan. He hadn't taken the slug in the
forehead, but rather in the thick of his thigh. As the echo from
the shot died away, a man rose, carrying a small-caliber
varmint rifle, and walked forward. Nichols' deputy already
had both his hands in the air.

"Come on, hurry it up, Stoner!" cried Ross Fletcher,
leader of the Medicine Bow Gang. "Get me and Loretta and
Red outta these ropes."

"No word of thanks, Ross?" asked the other, with more
than a little sarcasm.

"Yeah, yeah, *thanks*, Stoner — now get us loose!"

The man called Stoner walked slowly forward and gave
a kick at the marshal where he lay.

"Off yer horse," Stoner ordered the deputy, who warily
complied.

Stoner took the deputy's gun, shoved him to the ground
near where Nichols lay, yanked the marshal up to a sitting
position, then proceeded to tie both men to each other back-
to-back. His job would have been easier with help, but he
seemed to relish leaving his cohorts in their own bonds yet
a few more minutes.

"How'd you get loose, Stoner?" said the marshal, grimacing and holding his bleeding leg until his arms were bound behind him. "Last word . . . last word I had was that Silverstein . . . had you holed up in an old mine shaft with no way out."

"Yeah, well I ain't the fool Butch is, Nichols," replied Stoner, "or the fool your deputy took me for neither. I got out of there all right, but not where he was watching for me."

"What about McLeod?"

"You got him and Butch . . . for now. I'll get 'em out."

"Well, if you're going to kill us, go on and get it over with."

"Don't worry, Nichols, I ain't gonna shoot you again. I don't figure on getting a murder charge stuck to my name."

"Doesn't matter. You're gonna hang all the same."

"I ain't gonna do any such thing, Nichols. You seem to forget, I got the gun."

The marshal seemed to think better of further discussion and was silent. Meanwhile, the prisoners let forth another volley of shouts and curses at their slow-moving savior. Stoner turned and glanced at them, as if trying to decide whether to let them loose or not.

"Stoner, I tell you — "

"Shut up, Red. You ain't gonna do nothing," said Stoner, at last withdrawing a long knife from his waist and giving Loretta's cords a quick slice.

"Whew — thanks, Stoner," she said. "I don't mind thanking you."

"What do you think, Loretta?" he said. "The way these other two are jawing at me, I've half a mind to leave them here with Nichols and the other fella, and you and I go see if we can find the jewels ourselves."

"You do and I'll kill you, Stoner!" shouted Fletcher.

"Yeah, you probably would at that," said Stoner, who now

walked slowly over to their horses and released the two men. They immediately quit their grumbling.

"What're we gonna do with them?" asked the man called Red, nodding toward where the marshal and the deputy sat back-to-back.

"I say we kill 'em," said Fletcher.

"Not with me around," said Loretta. "I'm with Stoner — nobody gets killed."

"We'll take the horses and leave 'em here," said Stoner. "Nichols ain't hurt too bad. Somebody'll find 'em, and by then we'll be long gone."

He took the varmint rifle, turned, and aimed carefully. A shot rang out, followed by a suppressed cry of pain as the deputy took a bullet in his leg. Like the previous shot, the wound it made was small and would not prove lethal. But it would make walking any distance nearly impossible.

"They won't get far now," said Stoner, "but they ain't gonna die. By the time we get our business done, we'll be back up in Wyoming where nobody'll find us."

He walked over, grabbed the reins of the two mounts, and led them to where his own horse was tied.

"You three ride OK?" he asked the others as he mounted.

"We can ride," answered Fletcher.

"Then let's go," said Stoner. "We ain't got no time to lose."

The three followed, leaving the two where they sat. When they were out of earshot, Stoner spoke again.

"I got my kid brother down in Denver keeping an eye on the place," he said. "Some fella showed up day before yester-day poking around. Don't know if it means nothing, but he asked for the room on the top floor, overlooking the moun-tains. I think he thought it was the Kid's room."

"He better not be setting out to find them jewels before we do," growled Fletcher.

"What are we gonna do?" asked Red.

"We're gonna find out what he's up to, then we're finally gonna cash in on the Kid's job like we been waiting to."

A SISTERLY TALK

Rachel Randolph was not only the middle child of Ernestine and Sinclair Randolph's three children but she had also always been the most agreeable. Neither parent could ever remember seeing Rachel, who was of even temperament, truly angry. Not only was her customary attitude one of obedience but she fell in so naturally with the desires of her parents as she grew that she scarcely even had to be told what to do. It was easy to overlook her because of her passive and gentle demeanor. Her parents occasionally wondered if this compliant demeanor was the result of her weaker and sometimes sickly constitution.

Like her older sister, Mercy, and her younger brother, Thomas, Rachel had grown up familiar with the ideas of the Christian faith. Sinclair Randolph's reputation for integrity and uprightness in the business community of Louisville was unequalled. If the devout man of God possessed a fault as a Christian father, it lay in the assumption that his children would grow to inherit his belief system. He and his wife had carried out a nominal share of spiritual instruction through the years. But the last three years had jolted them into a deeper realization of the truth that the day would come when each of their three offspring would have to step out from under the parental wings of belief and develop a personal faith. Both were now fully aware that that process had occurred in their eldest. They were, however, unprepared for the direction it would take in their second.

Mercy had known something was bothering Rachel from the very first day she had arrived home. Her younger sister was normally more quiet than she, and Mercy realized that she had matured a great deal in the three years Mercy had been gone. Yet she recognized Rachel's withdrawn expression as indicating more than Rachel was telling. Now it had been three days, and Mercy decided to have a talk with her.

Rachel was sitting quietly in her room reading when a knock came at her door. She spoke and Mercy entered. Rachel glanced up, uncharacteristically unsmiling. Mercy looked about the room as she sat down. It was so orderly, like Rachel herself. The two girls had always been so different. While Rachel's room was always tidy and in order, more often than not Mercy's looked as though a storm had recently blown through. While Rachel dressed in pastel feminine colors, Mercy had been in the habit of choosing dark solid colors until Jody Simmons had taken her in hand. And Mercy's flashing green eyes and light brown hair contrasted noticeably with the gentle blue eyes and deep black hair of her sister, who now sat silently before her in a rocking chair.

"What are you reading?" Mercy asked.

"Oh, nothing—just some book by Mrs. Alcott."

"Which one?"

"*Little Men.*"

"Is it good?"

"I suppose."

"Didn't she write one called *Little Women,* too?"

Rachel nodded.

This was even more difficult than Mercy had anticipated. Rachel obviously did not want to talk. She sat unmoving, staring into her lap.

"Rachel—," Mercy said, then paused with a sigh. Still Rachel did not look up.

"Rachel," she repeated, "we used to be friends. . . . We used to talk. Now . . . now you're as silent as a statue. . . . You never even smile at me—"

Silence.

"Oh, Rachel—please," implored Mercy. "What's wrong? What have I done to make you so angry you won't say a word to me?"

"I am not angry with you," said Rachel softly, speaking at last but still not glancing up.

"Then what is it? Why are you so quiet? I've never seen you like this."

Rachel said nothing in reply.

"Something *is* bothering you, Rachel."

"I just have some things on my mind, that's all."

"What kind of things? Is it about me?"

Rachel did not answer. It *was* about Mercy, but how could she tell her sister when she hardly knew herself what emotions were swirling about inside her heart?

"It does have to do with me, doesn't it? Please, Rachel — I wish you would tell me. I will not be hurt, whatever you say."

"It's just that —," Rachel began, then sighed.

"What? . . . Please tell me."

"It's just that all these years I've hardly done anything wrong!" Rachel blurted out at length. "I've never so much as raised my voice at Mama and Daddy. Yet it's always Thomas this and Thomas that, and Daddy's always telling everyone what a young genius he is. And now that you're home, Daddy takes a day off from work and goes all over the city with you and Mrs. Simmons and takes you out to an expensive restaurant. He's never taken *me* out to dinner like that. He never brags about me. He doesn't even *notice* me. As far as Mama and Daddy are concerned, you and Thomas are all they need. I might as well not even be here for all they care."

Already Mercy's eyes were filling with tears of compassion as she listened.

"And I'm not sure you and I were all that close anyway," added Rachel. "I just tagged along with whatever you wanted."

"Oh, Rachel!" said Mercy, rising and walking several steps to where Rachel sat. She sat down and put her arm around her sister's shoulder. "Rachel, I'm so sorry!" she said tenderly. "I never meant for my coming home to be this way for you—oh, I *am* sorry!"

"I know you didn't," said Rachel. "It's not your fault. I almost envy you in a way for what you did."

"But I did wrong, Rachel."

"At least they notice you. That's better than being taken for granted every day."

"They don't take you for granted, Rachel—you must know that. They love you dearly. The fact that you're more obedient than I have been doesn't mean they take you for granted."

"Maybe you're right, but you don't know how many times I've wished I could trade places with you and be out West somewhere."

"But it was dangerous!" said Mercy.

"And exciting," added Rachel.

"Perhaps, but not altogether in a good way. If God hadn't protected me, I can't imagine what might have become of me."

"Do you really believe that?"

"You mean that God protected me?"

Rachel nodded.

"Of course. Why do you ask?"

"I don't know. I've never seen God do anything to protect *me.*"

"What about keeping you here, keeping you safe, giving you an obedient heart—don't you think those things are gifts from God?"

"If they are, they're not very nice gifts. I'm beginning to wish I *hadn't* been so obedient. My life might have been a little more interesting."

"Rachel . . . please—"

"It's true. Evangelists come to our church and talk in loud voices about how God works miracles and changes lives and how we're all sinners. Well, I don't feel like I'm any more a sinner than I am a saint. There've never been any miracles in *my* life. I'm just boring Rachel doing what I'm supposed to do, day in and day out. I'm of no use to anybody."

"Oh, Rachel, don't say such things!"

"Why not? That's how I feel. I've never felt that God paid any more attention to me than Mama or Daddy do."

"Do you talk to him about it?"

"Talk to who?"

"God."

"You mean . . . *pray?*"

Mercy nodded.

"You mean . . . talk to God about all these kinds of things you and I are talking about?"

"Of course."

"No, I don't suppose I ever did."

"Do you think he would understand if you did?"

"I don't know. I never thought much about God as being someone who would understand me. When I think about him, he always seems like one of Daddy's banker friends — you know, old, with white hair, and not very interesting."

It fell silent for a few moments.

"Do you mind if I ask you another question?" said Mercy at length.

"No, that's all right."

"Have you ever talked to Mama and Daddy about this — have you ever told them how you feel, you know, about me and Thomas and that you don't feel they care much about you?"

"Of course not. I couldn't say that to *them*."

"Why not?"

"They wouldn't understand."

"Do you think they'd be angry with you?"

Rachel thought a moment. "No, I don't suppose they would be," she answered.

"Do you think they love you?"

"I suppose," Rachel said with a shrug.

"What do you think they would do if you told them?"

"I don't know."

"Think, Rachel—what do you think they would do? Inside your heart you know, don't you? Mama would cry at first. Then they would wrap their arms around you and tell you how much they have always loved you. You know that's what they would do."

Again Rachel looked down into her lap and was silent.

"You must talk to them," said Mercy gently. "They do love you, Rachel, and they need to know how you feel."

Mercy remained where she was for another moment or two.

"I love you, too, Rachel," she added, then slowly rose and left her sister's room.

16

A TIMELY FRIEND

The two days he had thought would make him a wealthy man had passed.

He still wasn't rich. And he was getting further and further from it every minute.

Jess Forbes had now been at the blackjack table for three hours and hadn't had any more luck than he'd had upstairs. He was down to his last four dollars and was just about to give it up, when suddenly it seemed that fortune might smile on him and his luck might change after all.

"Hello. . . . Mind if I sit down to watch?" sounded an attractive voice next to him.

Jess turned. The face that went with it was just as pretty as the voice. The girl who had spoken wasn't decked out like a saloon girl—he could tell that immediately. She had on a pretty green calico shirt tucked into a brown riding skirt. He didn't stop to think what she was doing in the saloon, though she seemed comfortable enough.

"Sure . . . sure," he replied, smiling. "Have a seat."

"Looks like you could use some help," she said.

"How'd you guess?" he laughed.

"I've been watching you for a while. I'd say the cards are running against you."

"You're right there. Maybe you'll bring me some luck! What're you drinking?"

"Nothing for me, thanks—but you go ahead."

"Hey, bartender," called Jess, "how 'bout bringing a bottle of whiskey over?"

A minute later the bartender appeared with the bottle and two glasses. "Four bits apiece," he said.

Jess reached into his vest pocket. "I'm about out," he sighed. "My luck had *better* change, and soon!"

"Let me get it," said the young lady, handing the bartender a dollar.

"Hey, thanks," said Jess. "I'll pay you back as soon—"

"Never mind that," she said. "Get back in the game, and let's see how that luck of yours is running now."

The pretty young lady seemed to know some of the others at the table as well and called them by name. But whenever Jess glanced in her direction, she was looking at him.

It turned out Jess' luck *had* changed.

Within an hour he was ten dollars ahead of where he'd started the day, had drunk more whiskey than was good for any man, and had been a little too free with his thickening tongue than he ought to have been.

UNPLEASANT
REUNION

Jeremiah Eagleflight wasn't exactly sure how he was

going to find his partner once he got to Denver. He hoped

Jess would be registered at the Grey Falcon.

He wasn't.

"You haven't seen a thing of him, Boone?" he asked

their friend.

"Nope. But you know," he added thoughtfully, "come to

think of it, there was some ruckus down the street at the
Rocky Mountain night before last. Didn't give it much
thought before now, but seeing you suddenly makes me
curious."

"About what?" asked Eagleflight.

"Well, seems to me I heard that there'd been a fellow that
might have been called Jess somebody arrested," replied
Boone.

"What was it about?"

"Don't know. Something about damage to the hotel, I
think."

Eagleflight was already turning on his heel, heading for
the door. He paused halfway across the floor and turned
back. "Save me a room for tonight, Boone," he said. "I'll be
back."

A few minutes later Jeremiah walked into the sheriff's
office. Suddenly he was conscious again of the holster and
gun at his side. He'd put it on before leaving the ranch. This
was the first time he'd worn it since the summer, and he still
hadn't gotten used to it again. He glanced around a few
times, but the cells were not visible from the outer office.

"You by any chance got a fella by the name of Forbes
here?" he asked the man behind the desk. The deputy
glanced up and looked Jeremiah up and down.

"Can't say as I have," he replied.

"Man I'm looking for's just under six feet, twenty-five,
though he sometimes looks about nineteen, with bushy
brown hair."

"Well," said the deputy, rubbing his chin, "reckon it could
be . . . but I tell you, mister, we ain't got no Forbes. Got a
drunk in cell one, and some fellow that broke up a hotel
room and calls himself Eagleflight in cell six."

Hiding his reaction, Jeremiah glanced away momentarily. "Any chance I can see the man in cell six?" he said to the deputy.

"Just unstrap your gun belt, mister, and leave it on the desk there," said the deputy, getting up out of his chair. "But I thought you said the name you wanted was Forbes."

"Maybe I was mistaken," mumbled Jeremiah. He followed the deputy across the office, then down a long hall with cells on either side.

"There he is," said the deputy, indicating the last cell on the right.

Asleep and turned the other way on the bunk, was Eagleflight's partner. Hearing voices, he groggily turned over and tried to bring himself to one elbow.

"Jeremiah!" he exclaimed as the deputy left them and returned to his office. "What in tarnation are you doing here?"

He rose and came toward the door.

"The question is," rejoined Jeremiah softly through the bars as soon as the deputy was out of earshot, "what in tarnation are *you* doing using *my* name?"

A sheepish look came over Jess' face.

"Sorry, Jeremiah," replied Jess, looking down at the floor and shuffling his feet a time or two. "I didn't plan to. It just kinda came out when the hotel clerk asked me my name."

"Well, what in blazes for?" asked his uncle with obvious annoyance in his tone. "If you were up to something illegal, then what were you thinking of—trying to get the law on *my* trail instead of yours?"

"Heck, I don't know, Jeremiah. I said I was sorry—what more do you want?"

"I want some kind of explanation. And what in thunder

are you doing in jail? Man, can't you even get by a week alone without getting yourself into trouble?"

"It wasn't nothin' illegal. Just wait till I tell you—"

"What am I to think anyway? You go running off from the ranch without a word. Then the next time I see you, you're in jail . . . using *my* name!"

"If you'll shut up a minute, I'll tell you."

"All right, all right . . . I'm listening."

"You remember the Donahue robbery?"

"I figured it had something to do with that. Come on, Jess, you ain't going to get your hands on those sapphires."

"And why not? I got me the same room in the hotel Kid Hotchkiss had when he pulled the job, and the sapphires have never been found. Rumor has it he stashed 'em somewhere before Nichols got to him. I figure they're in that room someplace."

"Yeah, you and everyone else—including Marshal Nichols and the whole Medicine Bow Gang."

"But, Jeremiah, tomorrow night at midnight—"

"I know," interrupted Eagleflight. "The statute runs out."

"If we can find them, we'll be rich, Jeremiah."

"And you think *you're* gonna find them when no one else can? Come on, Jess—they went over every inch of that room seven years ago."

"Maybe they missed something."

"You're dreaming, Jess. Ain't nothing can possibly come of it but trouble. Which reminds me—what are you in here for anyway?"

"Aw, they caught me tearing up the floor."

"Of the hotel room?"

Jess nodded.

"Tarnation, Jess!"

"Well I had to find 'em," whined Jess.

"You ain't gonna find no sapphires in the floor. Kid Hotchkiss wasn't a fool."

"He'd have had to act quick. He knew Nichols was onto him. Why not in the floor?"

"'Cause they'd have found them by now, that's why. I tell you, Jess, they've been over every inch of that hotel with a fine-tooth comb."

They fell quiet a minute.

"Well, what's the charge?" asked Jeremiah at length.

Jess sighed but didn't answer immediately.

"Don't tell me it's worse than you told me?"

"Drunk and disorderly," said Jess finally.

"Drunk and disorderly!" exclaimed Eagleflight. "Shoot, Jess, what were you thinking?"

"Well, there was this girl, and—"

"A girl! So she told you to get drunk and tear up your room?"

"It wasn't like that, Jeremiah. She's different. She's the only friend—except for you, now that you've come—I got in the whole town. She was trying to help."

"Oh, and you told her about the jewels, too?"

"Sure, she's got a share coming. I tell you, Jeremiah, she's a friend. You'll like her."

"Aw, Jess, I don't know what to do with you sometimes."

Eagleflight turned and took a couple steps away from where his partner stood holding onto the bars of the cell, looking more forlorn than ever.

"Hey, Jeremiah, you're not gonna just leave me here?"

Jeremiah stopped and looked back. "Maybe I oughta at that," he said, shaking his head.

"You gotta get me outta this hole!" whined Jess, suddenly worried that maybe his partner meant it.

"I'll talk to the sheriff," Jeremiah sighed. "I'll see what I can do." He turned again and walked back out into the sheriff's office.

"What'll it take to spring my friend?" he said to the deputy.

"I thought you were looking for Forbes," said the deputy.

"That's Forbes," replied Jeremiah. "*I'm* Eagleflight. But we're kin."

"Well, you'll have to talk to the sheriff, Eagleflight," said the deputy. "The hotel owner wants twenty-five dollars or he's pressing charges. As for the drunk and disorderly, sheriff'd probably let him go with twenty-four hours, as long as there's no warrants on him and you keep him out of trouble."

"When'll he be back?"

"Couple hours."

"Thanks. I'll come up with the twenty-five bucks," replied Eagleflight, "then I'll be back and see the sheriff."

18

CHANGE OF PLANS

Even as Mercy Randolph saw the letter from Zeke
Simmons to his wife, Jody, something in her heart gave a
brief skip.

She had been watching the mail eagerly every day since
her arrival home in Louisville, hoping to see an envelope
with her name on it addressed in Jeremiah's hand. And now
when this letter came, just two days before Jody's scheduled

return to the Bar S, still without anything from Jeremiah, she immediately sensed that something was wrong. Jody's silence as she set the letter down after reading it only made matters worse.

"What is it, Jody?" she asked. "Is something wrong at the ranch?"

"No . . . nothing wrong," replied Jody. "Here . . . you read it—the P.S. down at the bottom."

She handed Mercy the last page of Zeke's letter.

P.S., Mercy read, *Tell Mercy Jeremiah had to go to Denver for a few days. I don't expect him to be gone more than a week or ten days. He said he'd write her and explain first chance he got.*

Mercy handed the sheet back to Jody.

"There *is* something wrong," she said softly.

"I don't think you ought to jump to conclusions, Mercy. I'm sure everything is fine, otherwise Zeke would have said something."

"No, I can feel it," rejoined Mercy. "I don't know what it is, but some kind of trouble's come up. Jeremiah wouldn't leave like that otherwise."

Agitated, Mercy rose and left the house. She was gone about an hour. When she returned, the determined expression on her face was one both her father and mother recognized. They could tell immediately that some kind of decision had been reached.

But when Mercy asked them to join her in the kitchen that evening, they were nevertheless surprised.

Mercy knew what she wanted—what she felt she *needed*—to do. But she had begun walking down a new road upon which are learned the necessary lessons many are too proud to learn voluntarily. She was determined not to squander this first opportunity.

"Mother . . . Father . . . ," she began.

Mr. and Mrs. Randolph looked at one another with expressions of cautious anxiety, unable to prevent memories from the past from rising into their hearts.

Mercy hesitated. Unconsciously she glanced about the familiar kitchen. Suddenly she realized how much she really did love her home here in Louisville and the two people before her who were responsible for making it such a warm, pleasant, secure, and loving place.

"I am feeling very concerned about Jeremiah," she went on after a moment. "I feel strongly . . . I am *sure* something is wrong."

Again she paused, taking in a deep breath.

"My first thought is to return to Kansas," she continued. "Something inside tells me I should be there. But . . . but I don't want to run off impulsively again like I did last time. I . . . I want to know what you think."

Again she paused, her voice trembling slightly.

"No," she added, "it is more than just that. I want your *advice.* I want to practice listening to those the Lord has put around me and over me. I . . . well, as funny as it sounds after all I've done in the last year . . . I want to give the decision to you. I will do what you think is best."

Again Mr. and Mrs. Randolph looked at one another. This time, however, how very different were the expressions they exchanged. Neither knew quite how to respond. None of their three children had ever said such a thing to them before.

"You will be twenty-three in two months, Mercy," said her father at length, "and you have been more or less on your own for a year, making larger decisions than this one for yourself."

"I know," Mercy said with a nod. "Even if that is true, perhaps that is all the more reason for me now to go back and learn what I was too independent to learn earlier. I didn't really learn about life at the Missionary College. I think it is time that I do."

All three fell silent.

The next to speak was Mercy's father. In that wonderful, mysterious process whereby trust imbues and calls forth latent wisdom from the reservoirs of character, the answer was now given to him to pass on to his daughter.

"Let us wait upon this decision for two days," he said solemnly. "Let us each pray that God would make his will known. If, at the end of that time, Mercy, you still feel as strongly as you do at this moment that you are to go, we shall take that as indication of his answer. If, however, there comes a lessening of that impulse, however slight, then we shall take that as an answer to the contrary."

Mercy nodded as she listened to her father.

"Only you must be careful," he added, "to pray that the Spirit of God will press upon your heart *his* will and purpose rather than your own. Of all things, we must not listen to our *own* desires and confuse them with answers to prayer."

"Yes, Daddy," Mercy replied with simple childlike obedience. "I think I can do as you say."

19

Two More
Talks

The following afternoon, now that the possibility of
leaving Louisville again loomed in her considerations,

Mercy realized she must delay no longer the matter of her

sister. If she was herself involved in the problem, then per-

haps she ought to do what she could toward a resolution.

She sought Rachel again.

"Rachel," she said, "I may return to Kansas soon. I do not

want to leave until you have spoken with Mama and
Daddy."

"I will talk to them," sighed Rachel. "But what is the
rush? Can it not wait until you are gone?"

"These kinds of things cannot wait, Rachel. Once you're
aware something needs tending to between yourself and
someone else, immediately is usually best. I'll talk to them
with you if you'd like."

They were silent a moment.

"I'll think about it," Rachel said at length. "Although if I
do tell them what is bothering me, it seems like I ought to do
it alone."

It was later that day, as soon as Mr. Randolph arrived
home from his office, when Rachel asked if she could speak
with both her parents.

They were together an hour. As they emerged from the
parlor, the eyes and cheeks of both mother and daughter
were red, though the smiles on their faces indicated that the
tears had been well spent and had accomplished their purpose. Rachel's father was subdued and did not speak much
throughout the evening. From that day forward, however,
he lost no opportunity to speak from out of the love of his
heart toward both his daughters and his son.

The next morning before leaving for the bank, he took
Rachel aside.

"I want to thank you, Rachel," he said, "for saying what
you did to your mother and me last evening. I know it was
not easy for you."

"You're welcome, Daddy," Rachel said with a smile.

"Parents sometimes do not know what their sons and
daughters are thinking and feeling. Sometimes we need
help. I never meant to take you for granted—"

"I know that now."

"Believe me, I will never do so again. I love you more than you can know."

"Thank you, Daddy. I love you, too."

He kissed her, then turned and left the house, glad for the half-mile walk to the bank ahead of him. For now it was *his* eyes that were red, and when he reached the bank he hoped the exercise would be able to account for his flushed countenance.

Later that morning the two sisters, this time at Rachel's initiation, left the house for a walk.

"You were right," said Rachel after they had walked five or ten minutes in silence, enjoying the fresh morning air.

"About what?" said Mercy.

"What you said Mama and Daddy would say when I talked to them."

"They apologized and said they loved you no less than me?"

"Yes. Mama cried, just like you said, and they both said they were sorry it seemed to me as though they didn't notice but that they appreciated my obedience more than maybe they'd said."

Mercy smiled. "Do you feel better after talking to them?"

"I suppose," answered Rachel. "I mean—yes, I do. It always helps just to *tell* someone. But it doesn't make everything I was feeling disappear all at once."

"But it is a beginning."

They walked on a while longer without saying anything.

"I told them something else," Rachel went on at length, "something you and I *didn't* talk about."

"What?" asked Mercy.

"I said—" Rachel paused and gave a little laugh—"you are probably going to think I'm crazy."

"I won't—I promise!" said Mercy.

"I told them . . . if you went back to Kansas like you said you might last night . . . that I would like to go with you."

Mercy looked at her sister in shock, then smiled, then finally began to laugh.

"My sister, the adventure seeker!" she said. "What did they say?"

"Mama said she wouldn't hear of it. Daddy said maybe the change would be good for me and that it might be a way they could show me that they trusted me and believed in me."

"How did you leave it?"

"In the end they said if you agreed, and if you did in fact go, that Daddy would pay my train fare—as long as it was for a *round-trip* ticket!"

QUESTIONS

Jeremiah, Jess, and Jess' new friend were sitting together in the dining room of the Grey Falcon Inn.

Jess had been right. This girl was different, in a subtle sort of way. Jeremiah could not help taking to her immediately.

To Jess, of course, she was just a pretty and friendly young lady. But to Jeremiah, whose heart was already spoken for and whose wings therefore did not flutter so readily as his nephew's, a hint of vulnerability, almost lostness, invaded the edges of the girl's happy smile and shining eyes and drew him toward her. There was something down there, he thought to himself, deeper inside than she was willing to let show, and the natural compassion of his nature could not help but be curious.

"That was extremely generous of you, Miss Morgan," Jeremiah was saying, "to help us out with the other half of Jess' bail. I didn't quite know what I was going to do."

"I'll pay you back, Doretta," said Jess, "as soon as we get our hands on those sapphires."

"Keep your voice down," said Jeremiah. "We don't need any more eyes looking at us than already are. And I'm telling you again, if there ever were any sapphires, which I'm beginning to doubt, they're long gone by now."

"What makes you say that, Mr. Eagleflight?" asked Doretta.

"You ever heard of the Medicine Bow Gang?"

"Uh . . . I'm not . . . uh, yes, maybe I have," she answered hesitantly.

"Well, they're not the kind who would just sit and wait for someone else to take what they figure is theirs."

"Maybe they don't know where the sapphires are either," she suggested.

"I suppose that's a possibility."

"If we could only get back into that room!" exclaimed Jess. "I'm sure if we had enough time —"

"Forget it, Jess," interrupted Jeremiah. "You're not going to get *any* room in that hotel ever again. Besides which, you tore up Kid Hotchkiss' room, and it'll be a week before they let anybody inside it."

"Are you *sure* you didn't find any clues?" asked Doretta.

"'Course I'm sure," answered Jess. "You think I'd be sitting around here if I'd found anything?"

They were silent a minute or two.

At length Jeremiah rose.

"I'm going over to the hotel to ask around. Not that I think there's any sapphires, mind you, but just to keep *you* away from there."

He turned and left.

As Jeremiah stepped into the street to cross to the Rocky Mountain Hotel, he saw a figure walking toward him down the boardwalk on the other side. He paused and squinted momentarily. Then recognition dawned on him.

Stoner! he exclaimed to himself.

He turned aside for a moment, watching out of the corner of his eye as Stoner walked into the lobby of the hotel.

If Stoner was here, Fletcher and McLeod couldn't be far behind!

What could they possibly be doing in Denver . . . unless they were after the Donahue stash, too!

Jeremiah waited another minute or two, then moved cautiously across the street and followed the other man inside. He glanced around. Stoner was nowhere to be seen. Jeremiah walked to the desk.

"Fella just came in," he said to the clerk, "friend of mine named Stoner. What room's he in?"

"Three-G," replied the clerk.

Jeremiah took a few steps toward the stairs as if to follow, then, when the clerk glanced away, turned instead into the saloon and paused.

That's curious, he thought. *Why would Stoner be in the room directly underneath the one Jess had? Or is it only coincidence?*

Maybe he would snoop around and ask a few questions, Jeremiah thought to himself.

He glanced about. It was early in the day for most of the saloon's business. One or two men stood at the bar, and a poker game was in progress at a table in the opposite corner. An old man was pushing a broom over toward the entrance of the dining room. Jeremiah moseyed toward him.

"Hey, old-timer," he said, "I understand there was a pretty famous robbery around here a few years ago."

"That's right, mister," the man replied, looking up, glad for the chance to rest his broom. "Seven years ago last night it was."

"Were you here then?" asked Jeremiah.

"You bet I was. That's a night I'll never forget. Why, the marshal—"

"That'd be Marshal Nichols?"

"Brad Nichols, all right—why, he shot it out right there in the Kid's room at point-blank range, and it was Hotchkiss that went to meet his maker that night."

"Right up there in that top-floor corner room, the way I hear it?" said Jeremiah, motioning up in the general direction with his head.

"Yep, top floor all right."

"Four-G, eh?"

"No, no, young fella—weren't no fourth floor back then. They remodeled this place four or five years ago. Top floor then was the third."

"So the Hotchkiss room was 3-G?"

"That's it, young fella."

"But they didn't find the jewels?"

"Ol' Nichols likely tore that room apart from top to bottom—floors, ceiling, walls. But there weren't no jewels nohow. And nobody's seen nothin' of 'em since."

"You figure the sapphires are still in Denver?"

"Oh, they're around all right. I figure they're still right here in this blamed hotel—it's just that nobody can figure out where in thunder the Kid hid 'em."

"You figure Hotchkiss' partners'll be back looking for them?"

The old man did not reply immediately. He put his hand on Jeremiah's lapel and pulled him gently toward him until their faces were only two or three inches apart.

"I'll let you in on a little secret, young fella," he said confidentially, adding a wink. "Ain't no figuring to it—they're here now! I seen two of 'em already, and I'll bet money that Fletcher and McLeod'll show up any day, too."

Jeremiah nodded. "Well, that's mighty interesting, old-timer. I reckon I'd better keep away from here, then."

He left the hotel, his mind suddenly turning over many new thoughts.

He found Jess and Doretta in the saloon next to the Grey Falcon. He walked toward their table. As Jess saw him approach he opened his mouth to speak. Jeremiah brought his finger to his lips. He sat down, then motioned Jess closer.

"There may be something to all this after all," he said in a low voice, and then proceeded to tell about the conversation he had just had.

"You mean I tore up the wrong room?!" exclaimed Jess.

"Keep your voice down—and yes, that's what I'm telling you. Kid Hotchkiss was in the room right underneath yours—where Stoner is right now."

"Dad blamed!" muttered Jess.

"The only one missing is Brad Nichols. I'd have figured if anything was up with the Medicine Bow bunch, he'd be right in the thick of it. I wonder where the marshal is."

THUNDERCLOUDS
AND FAMILIES

The ride on the westbound train from Louisville

was more subdued than when Jody and Mercy had first

traveled to Mercy's house a little more than a week earlier.

For Rachel, however, the trip was full of excitement. This

was the beginning of a great adventure. Her older sister did

her best to keep pace with Rachel's enthusiasm and sustain

her end of the conversation. But having heard nothing from

Jeremiah gradually weighed more and more on Mercy's spirit, and by and by her mood became more contemplative.

After two or three hours, silence fell between the three women, each of them becoming absorbed in her own thoughts. Mercy was thinking not only about Jeremiah but also about the conversation she had had with her father and mother the evening before.

"What do you think, Mercy?" Mr. Randolph had asked her.

"I still feel as though I ought to go," Mercy had replied.

"As strongly?"

"If anything, even more so. But I want you and Mama to make whatever decision *you* think is best for me. I think at last I am learning to trust you more than I have in the past."

"I know that, Mercy," he had replied. "Your trust means more to me than I can say. The very fact that you are asking my advice demonstrates a new maturity. You are becoming wise not only from experience but also by decision. And this enables me to return that trust to you. Sometimes that is the way—trust must flow mutually, or else it does not flow at all."

"So what should I do, Daddy?"

"In this case, I believe that God has impressed this matter upon your heart. There are answers of *no* as well as answers of *yes* between parents and their sons and daughters, as well as from God. I cannot say that when you place a decision in my hands my response will always be in accordance with your wishes. But it would seem to be so in this case."

As Mercy relived the conversation, the poignant realization stole upon her that in trusting her parents she had in the end relinquished nothing of her freedom at all but had actually gained a higher freedom altogether—a freedom based on trust rather than independence. If only she had been able to see it sooner, she thought. She wondered if it was the same with God—that freedom came with *trust* rather than trying to do things for oneself. She wondered, too, if God might sometimes reply to her prayers in a manner similar to how her parents had answered her request for help concerning the decision about returning to Kansas. Might God entrust her with more and more of her *own* decisions the more she was able to place her life into his hands? It was a new idea. Was such a process an element of growing into spiritual maturity, trusting God so thoroughly that God *returned* the trust as had her father? Was that perhaps the basis for Jesus' bold confidence in so much of what he did and said—his *total* trust in his Father?

Slowly the hours passed, and the train continued to clatter westward across Missouri.

As Mercy gazed absently out the window, thick clouds could be seen gathering on the horizon toward the west. The train appeared to be heading straight toward them. Other things than rain and storms swirled about in her brain. Neither Jody nor Rachel paid the clouds much attention either.

By evening, however, as they arrived in Kansas City, the storm into which they had traveled was not one they could ignore. They walked into the hotel where Jody and Mercy had spent the night a week and a half earlier, just as the rain started to pour down. Driving drops of heavy rain pelted so loudly against the windows of their room after they had checked in that the panes seemed likely to break from the force.

"I hope it's not pouring like this between Sweetriver and Fort Hays," exclaimed Jody, "or Zeke will get so bogged down in mud he will never get through to meet us!"

"What will we do?" asked Rachel.

"Oh, he'll manage to get through," laughed Jody. "I didn't mean to alarm you. Zeke is not the sort of man to let a little weather intimidate him."

"I had hoped to show you some of the city," said Mercy to her sister, "but with this rain, I'm afraid we would be drenched before we were a block from the hotel."

"Let's freshen up and go downstairs for dinner," suggested Jody. "That much we can do safely."

They sat down together some minutes later in the hotel restaurant. Even as they descended the stairs, Mercy noticed Jody becoming pensive and thought at first that she might not be feeling well.

"Do the two of you realize how fortunate you are?" asked Jody quietly after they had placed their orders.

Mercy and Rachel looked at one another, both puzzled.

"In what way?" asked Mercy.

"For the parents you have," replied Jody. As she spoke, her voice grew soft, then she glanced down and sought her handkerchief. Mercy saw that there was more to her statement than met the eye.

Jody dabbed at her nose and eyes for a moment or two. "It's been so long since I was in the midst of a family," she said, "like I have been with yours this past week. I . . . I didn't realize how much I missed it."

"I suppose for too long I took it for granted," said Mercy. "But I think this visit did make me realize more than ever before the truth of what you just said."

"I guess I have been taking it for granted, too," added Rachel. "It has only been in the last day or two that I have been trying not to. I still have a lot to learn."

They fell silent for a few moments.

"Not having children," Jody went on after a minute, "well, I've accepted it. But there is still something missing for a woman like me to know that I will never have a daughter of my own. You cannot imagine how wonderful it is to see a family where love flows like it does in yours. That is why I asked what I did."

"It is easy to forget," sighed Mercy, "or to think your parents expect too much of you, or to think they want to prevent you from growing up. I thought those things, even though I now see I was wrong—wrong in two ways."

"What two ways?" asked Rachel.

"I was wrong to think it," replied Mercy. "And what I thought was wrong, too—Mama and Daddy *weren't* expecting too much, nor did they want to keep me from growing up."

"Oh, but even if they had—what a joyous burden for a young person," said Jody.

Both girls looked at her questioningly.

"How do you mean?" asked Rachel.

"Even if one's parents *do* expect too much—to be part of a family in itself is such a privilege, even if there are hardships along with it. And I wouldn't call it a hardship to have people who love you enough that they want to protect you from your own youthfulness."

"I never thought of it like that—as a privilege. Everybody has a family, don't they?"

"Not everyone has that privilege," answered Jody. "You can't think how deep is the emptiness and loneliness of so many of the men we meet on the prairie. Half or more of those who come to work for us have no family at all. They're drifters—tough, hard men who would never admit it but who would give everything they had to be able to remember a mother's arms around them or to have had a father to laugh with or ride with or romp with."

Mercy and Rachel listened reflectively, each thinking of pleasant memories from childhood, which now began to come back to them for the first time in years.

"They have had such hard lives," Jody went on. "They would even treasure the arms of a mother who might have been harsh or a father who whipped them when they did something he thought was wrong—not to mention what they would give to have had parents that cared deeply for them. Oh, you mustn't take for granted what you have in your precious mother and that dear, humble, sensitive father of yours! It is so clear that they love you," Jody said, glancing deeply into Mercy's eyes, then into Rachel's, and speaking with an earnestness Mercy had not heard in her tone before.

Rachel and Mercy were both silent. They knew Jody was right, for both had recently been coming to see that very truth. Fortunately, they were realizing it at a young enough age to appreciate the privilege, as Jody called it, of their family before it was too late.

22

RAIN

It had not rained in western Kansas anything like in Kansas City, though it had rained steadily enough for an experienced westerner like Zeke Simmons to know that the rivers would rise quickly if it continued.

The storm calmed for a day or two, and after receiving Jody's telegram Zeke had made it to Fort Hays without being caught in a downpour. By the time he was halfway back from Fort Hays to the Bar S with the three women, however, Zeke knew serious trouble was brewing in the sky above them.

As they made camp for the night at their usual stopover site, Zeke glanced about with a concerned expression. He felt the wind whipping up dangerously.

"We'd better tie everything down tight tonight!" he called out to Jody as they unhitched the horses and began pulling the canvas cover up over the wagon.

She nodded, hair flying about her face. She felt it, too, and knew what was on her husband's mind.

Through the night and all the following morning, the rain still held off. About an hour from Sweetriver, the wind suddenly picked up even more fiercely. Ten minutes later the heavens opened. All four travelers were drenched within minutes.

Zeke shouted to his horses through the din, though their going was getting rougher by the minute. Eventually he managed to guide the weary team into Sweetriver. The winds had by now reached gale force, and it looked doubtful that they would be able to continue to the ranch.

"I'll get a fresh team at the livery!" Zeke shouted to Jody through the uproar.

"As much as I want to get home," replied Jody, also nearly shouting to be heard, "I don't think we can make it. Why don't we wait out the storm at the hotel?"

"We can make it," insisted Zeke. "It's only two miles."

"I'm worried about the girls. They're soaked to the skin."

"So are we. None of us can get any wetter than we already are."

Zeke let the three women off at the hotel.

"Go inside and warm up by the fire!" he called as they stepped down. "I'll be back in twenty or thirty minutes."

Shivering and wet, Jody, Mercy, and Rachel went inside. All around Sweetriver people scurried about for cover, most toward their homes to secure shutters and doors and barns and animals and whatever else might be damaged by the winds howling about every building and seeking whatever was not tied or bolted to the ground. The temperature had dropped noticeably in the last fifteen or twenty minutes. It felt as though worse than rain might be on the way.

The winds continued to increase. Half an hour later, soaked to the skin but with a fresh team of horses, Zeke ran into the hotel, a blast of wind following him through the door.

"Let's go!" he cried across the small lobby, where the three women stood huddled in front of a large and cheery blaze in the great stone fireplace.

"I was just beginning to warm up," said Mercy as she shivered and attempted to smile through clattering teeth.

"If you want a hot bath and dry clothes and your own bed, then we got to get home now," enjoined Zeke.

Reluctantly the three left the fire and followed him out through the hotel door back into the street.

"Zeke," Jody began to protest, "do you think—?"

"We'll be fine, Jody," said Zeke, trying to calm her. "The winds can't stay this strong for long. It'll blow over by the time we get to the bridge."

As if to punctuate the foolishness of daring to show their faces, a fierce blast of wind sent the women's dresses and petticoats flying halfway up over their faces. They all stumbled, losing their balance, and only Zeke's quick, supporting hand kept them from winding up on their faces in the mud of the street.

Zeke steadied each, helped the three up into the waiting wagon, then climbed aboard himself, flicked the reins, and called to the horses, who lethargically picked up their hooves and began plodding as best they could through the mud and rain. Not another creature, except for two dogs roaming about barking at the tumult, was to be seen in the whole town. Sensible people had long since secured themselves behind closed doors.

Five minutes later, Zeke and Jody and the two young Randolphs were on their way along the southern road out of Sweetriver.

23

TORNADO

They had not even reached the bridge over the Sweet River before Zeke realized he had made a grave mistake.

The wind was coming at them from a southwesterly direction, blowing into their faces from the right in severe gusts laced with stinging pellets of rain. By now the road was itself a flowing stream, the wheels of the carriage halfway up to the axles in water. The horses were laboring, not only from wind and rain and water and mud, but also from increasing terror, for the sky was black and by now lightning and thunder flashed and sounded all around them. Whether an early blizzard would follow it was too soon to tell.

All at once the rain ceased.

For several seconds the wind died to almost a whisper. An eerie quiet descended upon them but lasted only ten or twelve seconds.

"Zeke!" cried Jody. "Do you think—?"

Her last words were drowned out by a sudden new gust directly in her face.

"It's just a storm," he replied, "nothing to worry about . . . wrong season for—"

Suddenly a flash of lightning lit the sky in the west. Almost instantly a deafening crack of thunder echoed. One of the horses reared. Rachel screamed as the wagon lurched to one side.

"Whoa . . . easy!" called Zeke to the other three, trying his best to calm them.

"Less than a mile—," said Zeke, turning in the direction from which the lightning had come. But no more words left his lips. Zeke's mouth hung open, and his eyes shot wide in disbelief. Right season or not, the light of a second jagged electrical line in the sky revealed an ominous silhouette.

Less than a mile away, the black swirling funnel cloud of a giant tornado was bearing down upon them.

It took Zeke but a second more to recover his wits. He yanked back on the reins and brought the team to a stop.

"Out of the wagon!" he cried.

Even as he shouted the command, the outer fringes of the twister reached them, whipping the air up into a frenzy. The women had followed Zeke's gaze and now realized their peril. They needed to be told only once and scrambled recklessly onto the ground, heedless of shoes and mud and dresses.

"Run! Make for the bridge!" cried Zeke.

The river lay some hundred yards away. Any remaining sense of propriety giving way to fear for their lives, Mercy and Rachel scooped up the bottom hems of their wet dresses in their hands and splashed their muddy way up the slight incline as fast as their legs were capable of carrying them. What safety they would find at the bridge they had not stopped to consider. Zeke had said to run, and they obeyed!

"Zeke, the horses!" called Jody.

"I can't do anything for them now!" cried Zeke, whose long knife was already slashing away at the reins to free the team from the wagon. "I can't take time to separate them—they'll either live or die together. Jody, run!"

"But, Zeke—"

"Go!" cried Zeke in a voice of command. "I'll be right behind you!"

Jody turned, picked up the bottom of her dress, and followed after the girls.

With two or three final whacks from Zeke's blade, the struggling horses were freed from their burden.

"He-yah!" shouted Zeke, slapping the one nearest him on the rump.

Off they dashed as one across the prairie, in justifiable terror. Zeke did not pause to watch them to assess their chances of survival, for his own now became his paramount concern. He bolted through the mud after his wife with as much haste as water-soaked and mud-caked boots would allow.

He drew up beside Jody fifty yards from the bridge,

grabbed her hand, and pulled her along even faster. The sound as of fifty locomotives began to roar behind them, and they knew the tornado was almost upon them.

They caught Mercy and a terrified Rachel, stumbling now from exhaustion, ten yards from the bridge.

"Over the side, everyone!" cried Zeke. "Hurry—there's only seconds!"

Zeke led the way off the road, still clutching Jody by the hand, and jumped over the embankment and down the slope toward the river. The women stumbled after him.

"Underneath!"

Letting go of his wife, he grabbed the others one by one, careless of anything but getting them out of the tornado's path, pulled them down to the ground, and then pushed and shoved and exhorted all three back up under the thick timbers of the bridge.

Even as the women crept upon hands and knees into the tiny cave of safety and huddled together against the slope of the riverbank, the awesome terror roared over them, shaking the ground and rattling the boards as if the bridge were made of mere toothpicks.

"Zeke!" screamed Jody, seeing her husband thrown from his feet.

He tumbled down the slope, fortunately in a direction that sent him under the bridge. Nearly toppling into the swirling river, swollen now from the rain of the past several days, he righted himself, crawled halfway to his feet, and scrambled up the slope, where he joined the others. Jody reached out and pulled him the last few inches, where he collapsed at her feet.

"Mercy . . . Mercy, I'm so afraid!" whimpered Rachel.

Mercy barely heard the words, but she knew well enough

her sister's terror. She extended her arm around Rachel and pulled her close.

As if outraged that Zeke had outwitted it, the tornado now seemed to redouble its fury. The deafening noise was louder than anything they had ever heard. A great wrenching sounded, and suddenly three or four heavy crossbeams in the middle of the span creaked and twisted, then tore free, flying briefly into the air before crashing into the river. Several more followed. For a moment it seemed the entire bridge would give way.

Then suddenly the deafening echo lessened. The rumbling of the bridge and shaking of the earth subsided. Though the wind continued to howl, they knew the tornado had passed.

Already on his feet, Zeke scrambled out from their cover up to the top of the bridge. Only one thing was on his mind—in which direction was the twister bound?

He gazed after the ominous black swirl connecting prairie to sky. It was moving in a southwest-to-northeast direction. Unless the tornado jumped suddenly, as tornadoes could do without warning, both the town and the Bar S should be safe. But immediately Zeke thought of the Carter place. From where he stood at this moment, Zeke judged Bob's ranch to be exactly in the middle of the funnel's path.

Zeke turned and scanned through the still-howling and swirling storm for signs of the wagon and team of horses. The wagon was not far from where they had left it, overturned and with two wheels missing. It looked as though it had been lifted up and dropped only twenty or thirty feet away. He saw no sign of the horses.

"Zeke . . . Zeke!" a voice shouted through the tumult behind him.

He turned to see Jody struggling up the embankment to the edge of the road. "Zeke, we've got to get these girls home. I'm worried about Rachel."

"Look at the bridge, Jody," he replied, turning and extending his hand over the angry Sweet. "A fourth of the crosspieces are blown clean off. If the river keeps rising, the whole bridge may go!"

"We've got to get home! There's enough of it left. . . . We can get across."

"In this wind? I can hardly keep my balance right here!" As if to emphasize the point, a great blast hit them both in the face. Jody stumbled, and only Zeke's quick hand kept her on her feet.

"I can't risk taking the girls across—a gust like that'd land them in the river, and the water is high."

"I'm afraid of pneumonia, Zeke—we've *got* to get them out of this cold and wind."

As if in response to Jody's remark, a few large hailstones began to fall, clattering on the boards of the bridge.

"It always hails after one of those," said Zeke, looking up. The sky was even blacker now than before. He knew they were in for a deluge by nightfall. He only hoped it would hold off another hour.

"I've got to get across before that hail makes it too treacherous," he said. "I'll run to the ranch, get a wagon, lots of rope, and some of the boys. We'll be back as soon as we can to get you all across and home and dry."

"But, Zeke, what if—"

"You watch it close, Jody," answered Zeke, knowing what his wife was thinking. "If that bridge starts to go, you get those girls out from under it pronto, you hear?"

Jody nodded.

"If it collapses," Zeke continued, "you'll have no choice but to get back to town and wait for me at the hotel. I'll have to take the long way around. Don't worry, I'll get back before the river's much higher."

Before the words were out of his mouth, Zeke had already started across the bridge.

"Zeke . . . be careful!" Jody called after him, but her voice was lost in the wind.

She watched anxiously as he came to the first opening, where two crossbeams were missing. Scarcely slowing, Zeke leapt across the cavity and continued on, keeping his balance despite the increasing pelting of hail. The bridge seemed solid at the two ends, and in less than a minute Zeke was safely across.

Immediately, as his soggy boots hit the mud of the bank, what hail remained in the cloud directly above him suddenly fell as if a door in the heavens had been opened.

Zeke increased his speed to the extent that his soaked britches, heavy boots, and tired legs would allow. The last Jody saw of him was his running form disappearing across the prairie in the direction of the Bar S.

Quickly she turned to get out of the hailstorm and rejoined the others under the bridge.

HOME

Within three or four minutes the hail stopped.

Jody and Mercy did their best to make conversation in the little cave of protection under the projection of the bridge that had saved their lives. Before Zeke had been gone many minutes, Rachel began shivering, and Jody's fears for her health deepened. She had seen pneumonia claim more than one life out here, usually in circumstances exactly like this—an early winter storm catching its victims unaware and unprepared.

It was genuinely cold now.

Snow could well follow the hail. Jody herself was shivering by now. The wind on their soaked bodies made the situation more dangerous by the minute.

Jody did not hear Zeke shouting from the other side of the river as he approached forty-five minutes later, nor even his booted feet making their way carefully across the bridge. Mercy had begun to sing out the words "What a friend we have in Jesus," and Jody did her best to join in, although their voices were mere whispers. Her body wrapped around her sister's, Mercy soothed and reassured Rachel as best she could. Suddenly Zeke's head appeared in the opening between bridge and sloping ground.

"Everybody up!" he cried. "Let's go home!"

Mercy and Jody crept out and inched their way down the slope until they could stand, then stepped out from under the bridge. The tiny covered space had become almost cozy, a safe haven to Rachel in comparison to the wild open prairie, and she was terrified to leave it. It was all Jody and Mercy could do to get Rachel to move. They lifted, pulled, and nearly dragged her across, whispering encouragements all the way.

Meanwhile, Zeke and Clancy Phillips stood above them on the western bank, pulling tight the rope that Jack Rice had secured on the other bank. Zeke tied the rope snugly to the end post, then turned.

The women struggled with their wet dresses up the muddy slope.

"All right," he said when the women had managed to climb up to the top of the foundation embankment, "we'll walk you across one at a time, between us."

"Where's Heyes?" asked Jody, surprised that the foreman was not among them.

"I told him to stay home, start some broth on the stove, and stoke the fire. Now you hang onto the rope with your hands," he said to the women, "and we'll hang onto you."

"Take Rachel, Zeke," said Jody.

Zeke nodded. "Take hold of the rope, Rachel," he said.

She did not move a muscle.

Zeke grasped Rachel's nearly limp arm, threw it around his shoulder, and placed his left hand securely around her waist.

"Take hold of her, Clancy," he said. "We'll carry her."

Phillips reached around and put his right hand under the poor girl's right shoulder, while Jody took her left arm and pulled it up and drooped it around his neck.

"Rachel . . . Rachel," exhorted Mercy, looking into her sister's face. "We're going to be home soon. You have to try to help these men. Stand up and walk, Rachel. . . . You have to help them!"

"I'll try," whimpered Rachel, standing up a little straighter and flexing what strength remained in her two arms to hang on tightly to the two men at her side.

"Let's go, Clancy!" said Zeke.

Carefully the two men started across. When they came to the first opening, they paused. Rachel gasped in terror as she looked down to see the frothy river straight under her feet.

"It's all right, Rachel," Zeke reassured. "We won't let you fall. Let go of her, Clancy," he said. "You jump on across."

Phillips did so, then reached back across the chasm, grasping the upper portion of Rachel's left arm just below her shoulder.

"Take hold of the rope, Rachel," said Zeke.

This time, energized by the horror of what she saw below them, Rachel obeyed. With Zeke now clutching her right arm in his own grip, the two men half lifted her across the opening as Rachel held onto the rope for dear life, pulling herself toward Clancy.

Within a second she was across, nearly collapsing in Phillips' arms. Zeke leapt after her, and the three continued on their way over the bridge. Briefly stirred into alertness, from both the activity and the beneficial stimulation of fear, Rachel now became an active participant in the attempt, and the next few openings were crossed with scarcely more than a pause.

When they were halfway across, Mercy and Jody glanced at one another, both thinking the same thought.

"Are you ready for some dry clothes?" asked Jody.

"And a hot fire!" rejoined Mercy.

"Do *you* want to wait for the men to come back for us?"

"I can make it if you can!"

The next instant both women were walking briskly across the bridge, careful of the wind and holding securely onto the rope. Mercy reached the first opening, paused briefly, then leapt across, clutching the safety rope, without incident. Jody followed. They continued on.

By the time Zeke had lifted Rachel into the wagon, draped one of the dry blankets he had brought around her shoulders, and jumped down to head across for the others, his wife and Mercy were running the last few paces across the boards and onto land.

"We couldn't wait!" said Jody. She and Mercy scrambled up beside Rachel, grabbing at two more blankets.

"I'll run over and untie the rope!" called Phillips, heading off again toward the other side.

"Leave it!" cried Zeke. "We'll need it to cross again. I'll have to come back for the things in the wagon."

The next moment Zeke had the reins in his hands. Rice and Phillips scrambled aboard.

"He-yah . . . giddap!" cried Zeke, and the wagon lurched forward.

Ten minutes later they crested the ridge and clattered down the final muddy two hundred yards to the ranch house of the Bar S.

Rachel had swooned into near unconsciousness. Dirk Heyes ran out to meet them as Zeke pulled the team to a stop.

Rice and Phillips were already on the ground. Zeke and Jody lifted and cajoled Rachel into wakefulness and handed her down to the waiting arms of the men, while Mercy climbed out the other side.

"Zeke," said Jody, "just take her inside the door. Then you and all the men go out to the bunkhouse for a minute or two. I want to get every stitch of clothing off her immediately here in front of the fire and dry her off. That goes for Mercy and me as well. As soon as we're in dry clothes and decent and I've got Rachel between warm dry sheets, I'll ring the bell and you can come in and change."

"Right—we'll get the team put away, then come in for some of Dirk's hot soup."

RECOVERY

By late afternoon the fury of the storm had spent itself.

The wind died as the temperature outside continued to

plummet. As if to soothe and comfort after the devastation

they had wrought, the clouds now opened and sent a gentle

snow drifting peacefully down to the earth.

Storms and hail and rain and wind were no strangers to

Jody Simmons. This was not the first time she had been

caught out in the elements and drenched to the skin and chilled to the bone. Nor would it be the last. How could a little rain bother a robust constitution like hers? If anything, she felt invigorated by the tussle with the elements, and now she bustled about the ranch house, happy and warm again, her kitchen full of the aromas of various soups and healthful concoctions, breads, and a roast of beef—welcome smells indeed.

Jody's chief concern, however, was not for the men's appetites but for the future of Mercy's sister, who now lay quietly sleeping in Mercy's own bed under a heavy pile of blankets and quilts. Were it not for the storm, the approach of night, and the certainty that the tornado had caused more damage and possible injury elsewhere, one of the men would have ridden in search of Doc Haggerty. As it was, however, they would nurse Rachel as best they could themselves.

They had managed to get about half a cup of strong broth down Rachel after Jody and Mercy had struggled to get dry bedclothes over her limp arms and legs, then laid her down for what they prayed would be the restorative influence of healthful sleep. As soon as Mercy herself was clean and dry, she crept into the bed beside her sister and wrapped her arms tightly around her. Mercy's own body heat, now recovering quickly, would hasten the end of Rachel's chill more rapidly than the blankets alone.

Mercy lay still, gently stroking her sister's arms and shoulders, singing quietly and praying silently, until she judged Rachel's body beginning to recover its power. Within an hour, Rachel was sleeping peacefully and the goose bumps over her body had mostly disappeared. Carefully Mercy crept out of bed, tiptoed across the floor, and half closed the door, leaving it wide enough, however, for the heat from the fire in the living room to continue to flow inside. She joined Jody in the kitchen.

"How is she?" Jody asked.

"Sleeping, and mostly warmed up," answered Mercy.

"How are *you* feeling?"

"Pretty well. I was cold, but I don't think I got seriously chilled. After a warm supper and a good night's sleep, I'll feel fine."

"We've nearly succeeded in making a tough western pioneer out of you!" As she spoke, Jody gazed toward the window. Dusk had fallen, and the snow was coming down in earnest.

"Where is Zeke?" Mercy asked, as if reading Jody's unspoken anxious thoughts.

"He and Bart rode back out to the river," sighed Jody. "He wanted to retrieve as many of our things as he could before the snow buried them. But," she added anxiously, casting yet another glance outside, "they ought to have been back by now."

Jody turned again to the stove, where she continued to busy herself with preparations for supper while Mercy set plates and bowls for them and the winter crew of Heyes, Phillips, Rice, and a couple others.

It was with visible relief that she heard the approach of a small wagon outside in the darkness about fifteen minutes later. Moments later Zeke walked in the door carrying two carpetbags.

"You found them!" exclaimed Mercy.

"Soaked clean through, but otherwise in one piece. Bart and I had to comb every inch within fifty yards," he laughed. "When I found these two, both on opposite sides of the wagon, I couldn't believe they could have been thrown so far without flying open and scattering your unmentionables halfway to Kansas City!"

Jody laughed. "You're not supposed to mention them, Zeke!"

"I wouldn't, except that some of *yours* weren't so lucky."

"What do you mean?"

"Your bag's in the wagon. Unfortunately, when I found it, it had torn apart, and most of the contents *were* scattered all over the place. I gathered up what I could."

"I'll go out after the storm and try to find the rest. What about the wagon?"

"I doubt it can be fixed. But the bridge seems to be holding. I don't think the river's coming up any higher."

"The horses?"

"No sign of them. If they're alive, they'll wander back to the livery. If the tornado got them, somebody'll run across their carcasses eventually, or else the buzzards'll lead us to them."

"Everything's ready," said Jody. "You want to call the men?"

"I'll bring in what things of yours I found. Then I'll go fetch the men. I'm sure they won't waste any time getting here!"

ULTIMATUM

Lightning flashed across the distant plains to the east

of Denver, pocking the sky with flashes of light and low

rumbling thunder. It was the kind of storm that might drift a

hundred miles east, even as far as Sweetriver.

Jeremiah was glad Mercy was safe in Louisville. He

hoped the storm had caused no damage at the Bar S, though

if it had he would be able to help Zeke set it right. His plan

was to head back that way tomorrow morning—with or
without his partner.

"I tell you, Jess," said Eagleflight, turning from the window back to their hotel room, "it's a fool's errand. Forget the
doggone sapphires. They aren't yours in the first place, and
statute of limitations or no statute of limitations, even if you
do find them without getting yourself killed, you're not
going to get to keep them."

Like a boy being scolded, Jess Forbes sat backward in a
stiff-backed chair, leaning his arms and head against its back.

"But, Jeremiah," he said, "don't you want to be rich? Just
think what—"

"We're not going to be rich!" interrupted Jeremiah.
"They're not your jewels—how can I get that fact through
that thick skull of yours? Besides, there's other things than
money in this world."

"Yeah . . . like what?"

"Like staying alive, for one thing!"

It fell quiet a minute. A low rumble of distant thunder
sounded.

"Heck, Jess," said Jeremiah at length, the frustration
clearly evident in his tone, "I've tried to do my best by you.
I've tried to be a friend and maybe a little bit more besides.
I came here after you to keep you from getting into trouble. I
bailed you out of jail—with Doretta's help, that is. Now
I'm trying to give you some good advice. But when your
mind's set on something, you just don't listen to anybody.
Maybe I ought to just quit nursemaiding you and let you
be. I don't suppose there's much a fella can do for a man
who's too big a dang fool to listen to the good counsel of a
friend. Do whatever you gotta do, doggone it! If you wind
up in jail again, don't expect me to come running. I'm head-

ing back to Kansas in the morning, with you or without you."

Jeremiah turned and left the room.

Jess sat for several minutes in silence. It wasn't very often that he managed to make Jeremiah get really upset. Whenever he did, he knew he'd crossed a line and gone too far.

But this time was different, he thought to himself.

If he could just make Jeremiah understand!

It didn't matter *who* the jewels had belonged to before. Seven years had passed! They were *anybody's* now—they belonged to whoever found them!

Why shouldn't it be him?

If he could just lay his hands on them, thought Jess, *then* Jeremiah would understand. Why, shoot—he'd give half the loot to his partner. He wasn't greedy.

He had to find the sapphires, he thought. . . . Then Jeremiah would understand, and everything would be fine between them again.

Jess rose, pulled his gun out of his holster, and checked to make sure it was loaded. He walked slowly to the window and glanced outside, already revolving in his mind the plan he was sure would make him and his partner wealthy men.

He stood only a moment more. Then he, too, left the room and walked outside into the night.

Downstairs in the saloon, Jeremiah was struggling with his conflicting emotions. Had he been too hard on Jess? He hated to lose his temper and upbraid his nephew like that. But sometimes Jess frustrated him to such lengths he just couldn't help it. Was it right to just walk away and leave Jess on his own, especially in the middle of a situation like this that could prove really dangerous?

But what choice did he have? He couldn't hang around

and let Jess drag him into trouble. Now that Mercy was in the picture, that was one thing he *wasn't* willing to allow to happen. He loved Jess, but now there was someone he loved in a different way. If it came to a choice, Jeremiah Eagleflight knew which side he would land on.

Jeremiah glanced around. *Where's Doretta?* he wondered. She'd been so friendly, but once Jeremiah began talking about returning to Kansas, she had disappeared. She had asked a lot of questions about the sapphires. Maybe it was just a coincidence. Jess had said they met even before he'd told her a thing about them.

Jeremiah sighed and rose from the table where he'd been sitting alone. He still felt bad about the tongue-lashing he'd given Jess. He'd go back up to the room and try to talk some sense into his partner again, this time without getting upset.

BREAK-IN

Jess Forbes made his way stealthily up the outside stairs of the Rocky Mountain Hotel. He paused at the landing of the third floor and glanced around.

It was mostly quiet on the upper floors of the hotel. The hour was late. He had waited in the alley between the hotel and the adjacent bank since leaving his room, keeping his eye on the window of the corner room of the third floor. The shouts and laughter from the saloon on the ground floor of the hotel showed no sign of letting up.

Jess knew both Stoner's and Fletcher's faces well enough. One thing he hadn't told Jeremiah was that Fletcher also knew *him*. The two men had had a run-in several years back, and neither was likely to forget the other.

Jess walked into the saloon, hat pulled down low over his eyes. He walked to the bar and glanced about. Stoner and Fletcher both still sat occupied in a game of poker at one end of the room. Neither saw him enter.

Why, then, was the lamp in their room still burning? Jess wondered. It looked like somebody was inside. Jess ordered a quick drink, then left the saloon as nonchalantly as he had entered. Returning to his vantage point, he looked up. The room was still lit.

Jess leaned against the brick wall of the bank and waited. After a long moment, the light went out. The occupant either was going to bed or had left.

Jess crept to the street, then along the boardwalk to the window of the hotel lobby. Making sure he wasn't seen from the inside, he peered inside. A minute or two later the figure of a man descended the stairs and headed for the saloon.

This was the chance he had been waiting for. The room must be empty!

He was tempted just to walk through the lobby and up the stairs, but someone might recognize him from the trouble he had stirred up earlier in the week. He thought better of it, quickly returned to the alley, and made his way up the back fire stairs of the hotel. *Who would have thought about a fourth floor being added?* he chuckled to himself, growing almost giddy at the thought of how close he was to having his hands on the stones.

After a brief pause at the landing, he tried the door. It was open. Jess crept into the deserted corridor.

The door to 3-G stood just a few paces to his left. He tiptoed along the worn strip of carpet down the middle of the hallway, then paused.

He reached out to the knob and gingerly tried the door. It was locked.

"Drat!" Jess whispered to himself. He could not bust down the door without making more noise than he wanted to. He needed time inside to search the place.

He turned, walked back outside to the landing, closed the door, then paused to take stock of his surroundings. The window of the room was only five or six feet away from where he now stood. The lip of its sill ran just about exactly the same height as the railing around this landing. If he could just . . .

The next second Jess was hurrying back down the stairs to the alley. Somewhere down one of these streets he had seen a small lumberyard. He ran out of the alley, then down the street, past the bank, past a dry-goods store—there it was, just down the next side street! He slowed to a walk, not wanting to call attention to his late-night business.

Six or seven minutes later Jess Forbes returned to the alley beside the Rocky Mountain carrying a board of pine some eight feet long by a foot or so wide. It should just do the trick!

A minute later he again stood on the third-floor landing, holding one end of the piece of pine and stretching it across the opening, easing it down onto the lip of the sill of room 3-G, then resting the other on the landing rail. *There!* he thought. *A perfect bridge!*

Well, not *exactly* perfect, for it wobbled dangerously as he tested it with his fingers. He climbed up and eased himself precariously onto it. The makeshift bridge was tipsier than he liked, for only about six inches of the opposite end of the board were able to rest on the lip of the sill. But if it would just hold long enough for him to crawl across without the board toppling down and alerting everyone in the saloon, it would have done its job.

Inch by inch Jess crept across, teetering back and forth, until he could stretch out his hand and take hold of the frame of the window to steady himself. He knelt down and tried the window. It, too, was locked from the inside.

Jess drew his gun. A little damage now couldn't be helped. He had come too far to turn back.

Holding it by the barrel, Jess waited. After a minute or two, a loud outburst sounded from the saloon. At the same instant, with the butt end of his gun Jess knocked through one of the six panes, sending glass shattering into the room. Reholstering his gun, he stretched his hand inside the hole, unlocked the latch, then pulled the window up. It was tight, but he managed to open it to a width of ten or eleven inches. Lying flat on his bridge of pine, Jess now put his feet through the opening, then wriggled his way the rest of the distance inside.

Standing up in the darkened room, Jess glanced hurriedly around.

At least it was empty. Thank heaven for that. He was tempted to light the kerosene lantern. He saw the outlines of three beds in the darkness and knew that none of the three occupants of the room would see the lit window from the saloon. But he thought better of it. He would make do with the little bit of light coming in by the window through which he had entered.

Where to start looking for the jewels he hadn't a notion. Jess glanced up at the ceiling. They could not be hidden there. Hadn't he already torn up the floor directly above this? They must be under his feet.

He knelt down. All the boards seemed sturdy and intact. Why hadn't the outlaws looked there already themselves? Was it possible that they were in this room sheerly by accident, not knowing this had been Kid Hotchkiss' last home before his death? Could it be that the Medicine Bow Gang had no intention of searching it?

Well, none of that mattered, thought Jess. *He* intended to search it, because he did not intend to leave Denver until *he* was in possession of the Donahue sapphires.

Across the floor he crept, feeling for any loose edge that might give him a beginning point from which he could pry up a first floorboard. After that, the rest would come easily.

CAUGHT
RED-HANDED

In the saloon, things were not going well for Ross

Fletcher.

He had lost more money in the last hour than he had won

in the last two days, and his mood was surly. He would

probably already have caused trouble around the table if he

hadn't been conscious of the need to keep from being

noticed by the sheriff or either of his deputies. He knew

neither of them personally, but word was bound to spread about the train job eventually since the Medicine Bow Gang was the most notorious bunch in these parts. He only hoped they found what they were looking for before Nichols and the other man Stoner shot dragged their way into Fort Collins.

He glanced down at his hand—two lousy fours. Was his luck never going to change?

"Three," he said, tossing three cards facedown on the table. One by one he picked up the three new ones tossed his way. A six and an ace, followed by a jack.

He swore, threw his hand down on the table, and rose to his feet.

"That's it—no more for me tonight!" he said angrily.

"Aw, sit down, Ross," said McLeod, who had only just joined the game twenty minutes earlier. "You can't expect every hand to be a winner."

"If I stick around any longer, I'm likely to shoot somebody," rejoined Fletcher, "and I don't think any of you want that to happen. I learned a long time ago that when the cards turn against you, the sooner you pack it in, the further ahead you'll be."

He turned and strode toward the lobby while his two partners stared after him.

"I'll be back down in a few minutes," he called out over his shoulder. "I just need to calm myself down so I don't do nothing stupid."

He continued on and started up the stairs while the game resumed.

Still irritable, Ross Fletcher climbed to the third floor and turned down the corridor toward the corner room, thinking no more of Kid Hotchkiss and stolen sapphires than of the man in the moon. He silently cursed his recent fate around the poker table and began to think that maybe they should have finished off Brad Nichols where he lay rather than leave him alive to track them down again.

>—◆>—○—<◆—�◄

In room 3-G of the Rocky Mountain Hotel, Jess Forbes had succeeded in prying several floorboards loose, having learned a few tricks from his previous experience directly above where he now knelt, not the least of which was keeping his search quiet enough so as not to arouse complaint and bring the hotel manager investigating. With trembling hand he lit a match down by the floor and peered into the darkened cavity he had just uncovered beneath one of the beds.

The metallic sound of a key being inserted into the lock of the door suddenly echoed in the stillness of the room with as much force as if a gunshot had gone off in the vicinity of Jess' ear.

Instantly he blew out the match and jumped to his feet.

>—◆>—○—<◆—◄

Ross Fletcher expected to see no one in his room, though if the thought of a visitor had crossed his mind, she would have presented a far different appearance than that which met his eyes the moment he swung the door open.

The light from the lantern in the corridor flashed in, illuminating the face of the intruder.

The two men stood eye to eye, their gazes locked together in shock, neither moving a muscle.

"Forbes!" breathed Fletcher in mingled disbelief and

wrath. The sound of the name suddenly woke both men to action. In the time it took Fletcher's hand to touch the barrel of his gun, Jess spun about and dove for the window. When the outlaw's finger found his revolver's trigger, the glass had already shattered and was tinkling onto the floor of the alley below. Unable to believe that Forbes would leap recklessly through a third-story window, Fletcher sent a bullet after him, shattering yet more glass. The explosion of gunfire sounded in the saloon below, interrupting the game in progress and sending men running for the door, even as Fletcher darted across his room to the window to see if Forbes had survived the fall.

What he saw instead were Jess's heels scrambling the final distance across his tipsy makeshift bridge to the landing. Fletcher's next shot found lumber rather than flesh as the board at last gave way from its perch on the sill, its landing end tipping momentarily upward as a bullet shield before the whole thing crashed like the glass into the alley. A third report of gunfire sent a slug into one of the stairs down which Jess now bounded four or five at a time, and the next instant darkness consumed him. Fletcher spun from the window and sprinted for the stairs.

He found the saloon vacant as everyone stood outside, glancing up and down the street.

"Where is he?" he shouted as he ran outside to join them.

"Saw a fella come charging out of the alley—that who you mean?" said the bartender.

"That's him—which way?" shouted Fletcher in a rage. "You see him, Stoner?"

"Like the man said," replied his partner, "he went up the street. Who is he?"

"The guy who broke into our room, that's who he is.

Come on," answered Fletcher, taking off through the night in the direction indicated. "You, too, McLeod—we'll split up. We gotta find him!"

The three outlaws ran off. Gradually the onlookers wandered back into the saloon.

>-+->-o-<-+-<

Half an hour later the three gathered together about a block away from where their search had begun. The Denver night was quiet again, except for an occasional sound from one of the saloons.

Stoner and McLeod both shook their heads as they approached.

"No sign of him, Ross," said Stoner. "You see anything?"

Fletcher shook his head. "And after all that commotion, the sheriff'll be poking around. He's probably at the hotel now, asking what happened."

"We gonna stick around?" said McLeod.

"I don't know. I get nervous when lawmen start nosing around. Who knows but what this guy's already heard of what happened to Nichols and might know who we are. No, I don't relish going back there. But we gotta get our hands on Forbes."

"What we gonna do?"

"I ain't sure yet," replied Fletcher, "but I may have me a plan. If we can't find Forbes, maybe we can make him come to us."

141

29

CAPTURE

The first thing Jeremiah heard after falling asleep

was a light rapping at the door of his hotel room.

Returning late from the saloon, he had found the room

empty. Rather than going in search of his nephew, he had

gone to bed. They would sort it out in the morning, and

then, one way or another, he would be off for Kansas. His

sleep had been sound, and he had not been disturbed by the sounds of gunshots up the street.

He glanced about. From the quiet of the night he judged it to be three or four in the morning. He sat up and felt toward Jess' bed. It was empty.

Again came two or three knocks.

"Who is it?" asked Jeremiah sleepily.

"Jess Forbes," said a muffled voice in the hall, barely above a whisper. "Come on . . . let me in."

Jeremiah sighed sleepily, rose, and walked to the door. Unlocking it, he suddenly found the door swinging roughly toward him. The next instant he felt the barrel of a pistol bury itself in his stomach.

"Don't breathe a sound, Eagleflight!" rasped a menacing voice.

Jeremiah found himself shoved rudely back inside. The door closed behind them. By the thin light from the corridor outside, Jeremiah recognized his uninvited guest.

"Ross Fletcher," he said, "what do you want with me?"

"So you know the face, do you, Eagleflight?"

"I've seen it on a wanted poster or two. Don't worry, I'm no bounty hunter."

"I ain't worried, Eagleflight," laughed Fletcher. "I got the gun."

"How do you know me?"

"That ain't no concern of yours. I know you, that's all you need to know, and I know that no-good partner of yours, too. Where is he?"

"I don't know."

"Don't lie to me, Eagleflight," growled Fletcher.

"I came back to the room a few hours ago looking for him myself, but he was gone."

Fletcher did not reply immediately. The fellow just might be telling the truth. After all, why *would* Forbes come back here?

"Well, whether you do or don't know where he is don't much matter anyhow. Get dressed."

"Why?"

"What is it with you, Eagleflight? You want to get yourself shot with all these questions? Now get dressed!"

Jeremiah thought better of further argument and did as he had been told.

"All right, let's go," said Fletcher. "If you know what's good for you, you'll keep your voice down."

Having a bad feeling about the prospects of seeing this room again anytime soon, Jeremiah grabbed his overcoat and saddlebags and complied with the command without protest. They left the room. He made his way along the corridor, down the stairs, through the empty lobby, and outside into the deserted Denver street with Fletcher's gun jabbed into his back.

"Where we going?" he asked once they were outside and he was reasonably sure another question or two would not result in Fletcher's unloading his gun into his back.

"We ain't going nowhere *you* need to be concerned about," replied Fletcher in a low voice. "You just better hope that fool partner of yours has enough brains to turn over them sapphires."

"Jess hasn't got the sapphires."

"That's what you say. Keep going!" he added, shoving Jeremiah so hard he nearly stumbled in the darkness.

They reached the other side of the street, then entered a narrow alley.

"You got him?" said a voice out of the darkness.

"I got him," replied Fletcher. "You got the horse?"

"I got it."

"Then tie him up while I keep the gun on him."

Jeremiah felt himself grabbed rudely, and a minute later his hands were lashed tightly together in front of him with strong cord. He was spun around, and a thick bandana was placed over his eyes from behind, then tied in place. He was shoved forward, then felt himself bump up against the side of a horse.

"All right, Eagleflight," said Fletcher, "get up in the saddle."

"You expect me to ride like this?"

"Don't worry," laughed Fletcher, "I'll be holding onto your reins."

Rough hands now took hold of him and hoisted him up. With his bound hands, Jeremiah fumbled about for the saddle horn to steady himself. After a moment, he rode out of the city blindfolded, in what direction he hadn't a clue.

HOT VANILLA

Even though the tornado had mercifully missed the Bar S, its outer swirls had nevertheless left the ranch a mess, and much cleaning needed to be tended to. Mercy and Jody cleaned up debris scattered all over the yard while the men checked buildings, fences, and stock.

Rachel slept on and off continuously, ate little, drank a

little more, and remained in bed. Her strength did not
return, and Jody remained concerned.

It had now been two days since the tornado. Though her
vigor was restored, Mercy's thoughts had begun to return to
the reason for her coming back to the Bar S so suddenly—
the uneasiness she had felt about Jeremiah.

Still no word had come.

She had given her parents instructions to telegraph her
immediately if either letter or telegram arrived for her. But
as yet neither had come, either to Louisville or to Sweetriver.

The clouds and cold had remained, though the anticipated
blizzard had never materialized. It continued to snow fitfully
on and off, but only an inch or two remained on the ground.

Mercy had just returned from Rachel's room, where she
had fed her sister some soup and bread for supper. She
entered the kitchen.

"How is she?" asked Jody.

"She ate everything I took her," replied Mercy.

"That is a good sign."

"But she is still weak. I've never seen her look so pale."

"The food will do its work in time. Do you suppose we
might encourage her to get up and come into the living
room this evening?"

"If I help her, I think so," replied Mercy.

"Good. We'll sit around the fire and let Zeke read something to us. He'll be in for the night in about half an hour."

"Oh, that sounds perfect!" exclaimed Mercy.

An hour later a great fire blazed away in the wide stone
fireplace and darkness fell outside. Rachel wrapped herself
into a cozy bundle on the couch, and Mercy sat on the
carpet at her feet. They both stared into the bright red and
orange and yellow flames. Jody walked in from the kitchen

bearing a tray of four large steaming mugs. She set the tray down on a short table beside the couch, then handed one mug to Mercy and one to Rachel.

"What is this, Jody?" said Mercy, lifting the mug to her nostrils. "It smells heavenly!"

"A little concoction I like to make for sitting in front of the fire on cold winter nights. I know it is a little early, but the snow put me in the mood. It's called hot vanilla."

"It's delicious!" exclaimed Mercy, sipping around the frothy rim of her cup. "What's in it?"

"Thick, creamy milk, vanilla, a bit of honey, and a dash of cinnamon and nutmeg. Nothing fancy."

"Isn't it wonderful, Rachel?" said Mercy, looking up toward the couch.

Rachel put the mug to her lips and tentatively probed its edges. "It is delicious, Jody," she said softly.

Just then the door opened, and Zeke walked in bearing an armload of wood. A sharp gust of cold followed him before he could shove the door closed with his foot.

"Brrr, it's cold out there!" he said. "We may be in for a hard winter—the snow's started up again."

He set down his burden in the woodbox, brushed himself off, then turned into the room.

"Unless my nose deceives me . . . ," he said, glancing about.

Jody handed him a mug.

"Ah, my dear . . . ," said Zeke, taking it and drawing in a deep breath of the pleasing aroma. "I thought so—hot vanilla!"

"Would you read something to us, Zeke?" asked Jody, settling down on the floor against the front of the couch, facing the fire, her own mug in her hand.

"What did you have in mind?" asked Zeke, settling himself into his favorite chair.

"Would you start the book I brought back from Louisville? It is brand-new, only published last year. The bookseller I bought it from said he met the author personally in Cincinnati when he was lecturing in America eighteen years ago." As she spoke, Jody got up, walked to one of the bookcases in the room, and returned a moment later with the volume just mentioned. She handed it to her husband.

Zeke opened it and began. "'It was a day when everything around seemed almost perfect,'" he read. "'Everything does, now and then, come nearly right for a moment or two, preparatory to coming all right for good at the last. It was the third week of June. The great furnace was glowing and shining in full force, driving the ship of our life at her best speed through the ocean of space. For on deck, and between decks, and aloft, there is so much more going on at one time than at another, that I may well say she was then going at her best speed, for there is quality as well as rate in motion. The trees were all well clothed, most of them in their very best. Their garments were soaking up the light and the heat, and the wind was going about among them, telling now one and now another, that all was well, and getting through an immense amount of comfort-work in a single minute. It said a word or two to myself as often as it passed me, and made me happier than any boy I know just at present, for I was an old man, and ought to be more easily made happy than any mere beginner.

"'I was walking through the thin edge of a little wood of big trees, with a slope of green on my left stretching away into the sunny distance, and the shadows of the trees on my right lying below my feet. The earth and the grass and the trees and the air were together weaving a harmony, and the birds were leading the big orchestra—which was indeed . . .'"

GROWTH, WISDOM, AND INTELLECT

Zeke continued to read from Jody's new book for

thirty or forty minutes, pausing every so often for a pleasur-

able swallow of the soothing brew his wife had prepared.

As the story of the young lad in Italy progressed, a sense of

calm contentedness settled over his three women listeners.

At length Zeke closed the book and set it down.

The only sound to be heard in the house was the thin

crackling of the dying fire, made all the more comforting by the knowledge that outside millions of tiny flakes of white were silently piling one on top of the other.

"His talking about the horse growing into a better and better creature in the first chapter," reflected Zeke at length, "reminds me of what I was reading about earlier today."

"About what?" asked Jody

"*Human* growth," replied Zeke. "That is what I was thinking about, anyway, though not exactly the subject of what I was reading. Where's my Bible?" he asked, glancing about.

"Here," answered Jody, leaning forward and handing him the thick, worn, black leather book. "I had it ready just in case the mood came over you to share something."

Zeke took it from her, set down the mug, whose contents he had just drained the last of, and began flipping through the familiar pages. "I was reading something this morning that struck me," he said. "Let me see, where was I — in Mark, I think . . . no, or was it in James?"

He paused, glancing back and forth between the two books.

"Ah, now I remember — I was in both places. I had been going through the book of James." He paused to find the exact passage, then began. "'What doth it profit, my brethren,'" he read, "'though a man say he hath faith, and have not works? can faith save him? . . . shew me thy faith without thy works, and I will shew thee my faith by my works. . . . Who is a wise man and endued with knowledge among you? let him shew out of a good conversation his works with meekness of wisdom. . . . But the wisdom that is from above is first pure, then peaceable, gentle, and easy to be intreated, full of mercy and good fruits, without partiality, and without hypocrisy. And the fruit of righteousness is sown in peace of them that make peace.'"

Zeke paused again. "I thought of Jeremiah when I read that."

"Jeremiah?" said Mercy in surprise, glancing up. She had been thinking of him a great deal today, too.

"He and I had a long conversation on the way back from Fort Hays about growth as a Christian. I've been thinking about it ever since—what makes a person *grow?* What is it that makes a man or woman *wise?* James gives us the answer right here—a wise person is one who is pure and considerate of others, who loves peace, who does good, who is sincere and merciful . . . someone whose life shows the fruit of Christlikeness. He says it as simply as can be—who is wise? Let him show it by his good life, his deeds, and his conversation."

"Then what were you reading in the book of Mark?" asked Jody.

"I found myself thinking about all the *other* ways people try to grow wise. I thought about how so many people think that wisdom can be attained by the intellect—like the Pharisees thought. Whenever the Pharisees come into the gospel story, they try to trick Jesus with all their intellectual puzzles, trying to trap him with this argument or that inconsistency. Mark says that they 'reasoned among themselves.' In other words, they were always trying to explain away by reasoning the validity of the fruit of Jesus' wisdom. *Did* they grow wise? No. They remained angry, bitter, proud, and spiritually blind. Just like Paul says, seeking to become wise, they became fools. Well, anyhow, that's what I was thinking about."

"But, Zeke," said Jody, "I've always heard you say that Christians *ought* to think hard about what they believe and shouldn't believe things without trying to reason them through."

"Of course. God gave us brains—we ought to use them. I'm only saying that reasoning and thinking *alone* won't get you growing as a Christian and won't make you wise. Growth only comes by *doing* what you're thinking about. It wasn't asking Jesus questions that was wrong of the Pharisees. It was getting angry when he didn't give them the answers they wanted. Some of their questions were good, and if they'd have done what he told them, even the Pharisees would have grown wise. But they weren't setting themselves to be pure and gentle and considerate and peaceable and all the rest that James speaks of. All they wanted to do was argue and dispute and debate. The intellect's a good and powerful thing, but not all by itself. If you want to be wise, there's more to it. You've gotta do what the Lord says."

The room fell silent again. Zeke rose. "Looks like this fire needs a new log or two." He picked up two large chunks from those he had recently brought in and set them onto the coals. Within seconds they began popping as new flames brightened and leapt up around them.

"Do you think Jeremiah is a wise man, Zeke?" asked Mercy seriously.

"Probably not yet," replied Zeke. "There's not many men you can say such a thing of. Wisdom isn't like that. It's a process of growth. The question you have to ask is, is he *becoming* wise?"

"Then do you think Jeremiah is *becoming* wise?" Mercy asked again.

"Yes . . . yes, I think so," answered Zeke. "He's a thinking young man, a man who wants to know *why* things are, a man who values truth and asks good questions—but at the same time a man who doesn't value the intellect *too* much. There are those who are in love with their intellects. But there's none of that in Jeremiah. He's a thinker, but he sees that the intellect is only given to us as a tool to help us toward faith, not as a thing of value in itself. Most of all, I'd say Jeremiah is a man who does what he knows. And that's why he is a man who will *become* wise."

"Does what he knows?" repeated Mercy, not quite certain what Zeke meant.

"Yep. The way I see it, that's pretty much the recipe for wisdom — *doing the truth you know.* There's a lot of people doing lots of things that don't have anything to do with truth. There's others that spend a lot of mental energy on what they call seeking truth with their brains, but it doesn't have much to do with their hands. Then there's the kind of man that I think Jeremiah is — with a wide-awake brain from *thinking* and rough hands from *doing.* You gotta have both. Can't get to faith with just your reasoning, any more than you can get to truth with just good actions. There's gotta be both. Faith doesn't come from thinking alone *or* doing alone. Thinking and doing *together* make up what's called belief, and when you add to that trusting God, then you've got the whole thing called faith. There's a balance between all the parts. That's the kind of balance that grows wisdom in a man, and I figure your Jeremiah's on the right road toward it."

Mercy was quiet, but she felt warm inside. And the warmth came from something other than hot vanilla.

OMINOUS
QUESTION

Four more days went by. The clouds passed, the sun came out warm again, and within a short time the early snowfall was only a memory.

Reminders of the tornado, however, were not so quick to disappear.

Zeke and his men spent two days repairing and strengthening the bridge, the next riding the full perimeter of the property checking for downed or damaged fences, and the next at the Carter ranch helping clear away the debris from Bob's barn, which the tornado had utterly destroyed. Most of the men of the community would gather over the next two weeks to assemble a new one.

Much to Zeke's surprise, the livery's team of horses was found only a few miles downriver from the ranch. They were plenty scared and bedraggled, but alive, and for that Zeke was most grateful. Even the rigging and harness remained intact. Lars was as grateful to see them when Zeke took them back to town as the horses were to be home.

All the ranches in the area had suffered some damage, though the Carter barn was the only structure that had lain directly in the twister's path. It would be months before everything on all the ranches and farms, and in Sweetriver itself, would be completely repaired and back to normal.

Still there was no word from or about Jeremiah.

Finally Mercy could stand it no longer. She rode into Sweetriver and sent a telegram home to Louisville, asking whether they had heard from Jeremiah—the question she was afraid she already knew the answer to.

A return telegram arrived at the Western Union office in Sweetriver three hours later:

NO WORD FROM JEREMIAH. SORRY. WE LOVE YOU. GREET RACHEL AND JODY.

▸─◂▸─◦─◂▸─◂

What was she to do? By now Mercy was beginning to be genuinely worried. What if Jeremiah was in some kind of trouble?

Discouraged and full of many thoughts and possibilities, Mercy walked into her room and sat down beside the bed, where Rachel was just waking from a nap.

"From your face I assume Mama and Daddy have heard nothing from Jeremiah," said Rachel as she coughed lightly.

Mercy shook her head. "I'm sorry, Rachel," she said. "Here I am supposed to be helping you to get better, and I am moping around worrying about my own problems."

"That's all right, Mercy. You have been waiting on me hand and foot—maybe it is my turn."

"No, I want you to stay right where you are until you are completely well," said Mercy. "I'm still worried about that congestion in your chest."

"I feel so much better," said Rachel, forcing a smile, though the weakness in her voice was all too evident.

Mercy returned her younger sister's smile. "Well, you certainly got your adventure, didn't you?" she said, taking one of Rachel's hands in her own. "How many young girls in Louisville have been through a tornado?"

"Oh, it was so scary," said Rachel. "But, Mercy," she added, her eyes on their two hands, "I think I realize now why I wanted to come west."

Mercy waited, gazing into the pale face.

"I wanted to be like you," Rachel added.

"Oh, Rachel, you don't need—," Mercy began to protest. But Rachel interrupted her.

"You were so brave and strong during the tornado," she said. "You knew just what to do. You weren't the least bit afraid."

"Oh, but I was, Rachel!"

"You didn't show it."

"I have never been through anything like that. I was terrified."

"But you and Jody are such strong women. I wish I was like you. But I'm just a weak, scared little kitten."

"No, Rachel—you're not anything like that."

"I am, Mercy. But *you're* like those frontier women I've read about in the books Father brings home. I suppose I thought if I came out to Kansas I would be like that, too. But I'm not."

Mercy could not prevent a deep sadness from filling her heart, and she looked away. Mercy's sister possessed such a natural spirit of obedience and purity, yet at present she was unable to see its value alongside what she perceived as Mercy's spunk and bravery. If only Rachel had seen her during her first days in Sweetriver, thought Mercy. But she realized that nothing she could say right then would help.

It was silent in the room for several long minutes. The mood grew heavy.

Mercy glanced back at Rachel's face and saw tears rising in her sister's eyes. Rachel wrinkled her forehead in unspoken question.

"Mercy . . . ," said Rachel in a soft, trembly voice, "Mercy . . . am . . . am I going to die?"

"Oh, Rachel, dear—of course not!" replied Mercy, clasping her sister's hand between both of her own. Even as she spoke the confident-sounding reply, however, Mercy could not prevent an invisible lump from rising in her throat at the somber words her sister had uttered.

"But . . . but I'm afraid," said Rachel. She began to weep softly.

Mercy leaned down and placed her arms around Rachel's shoulders, then kissed her on the cheek. "Try not to think of such things, Rachel," she whispered. "God will take good care of you. He loves you even more than I do."

"But sometimes I can't tell if he's near me," whimpered her sister.

"That doesn't matter. He *is* near you all the same. He will take just as good care of you whether you know he is there or not."

"But how do you know?"

"Because I believe it," replied Mercy. "He kept us safe from the tornado, didn't he?"

"I suppose," consented Rachel.

"There, you see. No harm came to us. He was protecting us, even though it may have seemed we were in great danger."

"But I still cannot help being afraid."

"Being afraid is no sin," said Mercy. "It's to help us grow able to trust him."

"I will try, then," said Rachel.

33

OFFER OF TRADE

Jess Forbes didn't know what to do.

He and his partner had been in tough spots before.

They'd been in some *real* tough spots. But something told

him this was the worst and that this time Jeremiah's life was

really in danger.

And he knew it all depended on him . . . but he didn't

know what to do.

After hiding out for three or four hours in somebody's stable after his escape from Ross Fletcher, he'd crept back to the Grey Falcon. He'd made it upstairs to their room without being seen, but there was no sign of Jeremiah. He'd fallen asleep. Morning had come, but still his partner was gone. A few of Jeremiah's things were still around, and there was no sign of a struggle. Jeremiah'd said he was heading back to Kansas, but something about the way he found the room didn't feel right to Jess.

He stayed in the room most of that first day, going downstairs only long enough to get something to eat. He wasn't sure if he ought to show his face around the Rocky Mountain after the condition he'd left Fletcher's room in. Fletcher had seen him clear enough, and after the trouble he'd already been in with the hotel owner, for all he knew there might be another warrant out for his arrest. When he did get up his courage to wander out later that afternoon, however, encountering one of the sheriff's deputies in the middle of the street without incident, he realized that they were not looking for him.

After two days, he was beginning to be seriously worried. He wandered into the lobby of the Rocky Mountain in the direction of the saloon.

"Hey—," called out the desk clerk.

Jess glanced nervously toward him.

"You know that bunch that was staying in the room just below yours?"

"Uh . . . no—don't know who you mean," lied Jess. "Why?"

"Well, I figured maybe you and them was in cahoots— why, they wrecked their room just like you did! Came down yesterday morning, told me they'd had a little accident, handed me thirty dollars, and said they hoped that'd cover it, then paid their bill on top of it and said they was leaving town."

Jess took in the information with interest.

"Say where they were going?" he asked.

"Nope. But when I went up to look at the room, why, they'd torn up the floor just like you did. What is it with you fellas and tearing up hotel rooms anyhow?"

"I dunno," Jess said with a shrug.

"What do you care where they were going? You said you didn't know them."

"Just curious," replied Jess, continuing on into the saloon.

He ordered a drink and sat down. He didn't like it — Fletcher and his bunch leaving town just when Jeremiah disappeared. The thing had a bad smell to it.

"Hi, Jess," said a voice behind him. "Buy a lady a drink?"

"Doretta!" exclaimed Jess as he turned around. "Where've you been? I haven't seen you in three days."

"How about that drink?"

"Sure . . . sure—sit down! Bartender!" he called over his shoulder.

"I had to leave town for a few days."

"Where have you been?" asked Jess.

"I . . . uh, had to take the train down to Colorado Springs."

"Boy, am I glad to see you. Jeremiah's disappeared."

"I thought you said he was going back to Kansas."

"I did, but I don't think that's where he's gone. I think he's in trouble."

"Did you find the jewels?" she asked.

"Never mind the sapphires—it's Jeremiah I'm worried about."

"But did you find them?"

"Heck no, I didn't find them," replied Jess.

Doretta eyed him for a moment, doing her best to conceal her suspicions, at which attempt she was entirely successful. Jess hadn't any idea that more was on her mind than his friend's well-being or that their meeting like this was not as accidental as it seemed.

"Well, what are we going to do?" she asked after a moment.

"You mean about Jeremiah?"

"Him and the sapphires."

"I don't reckon there's much I can do about the jewels," replied Jess, "and I don't even know where to start looking for Jeremiah."

"Are you sure you didn't find any clues when you searched the other room?" asked Doretta.

"No, I didn't find a thing," replied Jess distractedly.

They finished their drinks in silence, occupied with their own thoughts. Jess rose.

"Reckon I'll wander back to my room," he said. "I figure I oughta be there, just in case. Where'll you be?"

"I'll be here, in the hotel."

"What room?"

"Uh . . . 3-F," replied Doretta.

Jess turned and left the saloon. When he arrived back at the Grey Falcon, the note was waiting for him.

Forbes,
We got yer partner. We'll keep him alive as long as you cooperate. We'll trade the saffires fer Eagleflight. You wait where you are. We'll let you know when.

R. Fletcher

Jess sat down on the edge of his bed and let out a long sigh. He'd been afraid of this.

He spent the rest of the day in his room but heard nothing.

The next morning, shortly after breakfast, another letter came. Its contents came as no surprise, however, compared with the shock that was awaiting Jess Forbes two hours later as he sat drinking a cup of coffee.

SURPRISE APPEARANCE

"They said I might find you here," came a voice

behind him.

The tone had a familiar sound, yet seemed foreign and

out of place.

Jess turned.

"Sister Mercy!" he exclaimed, nearly emptying the hot

coffee into his lap. "What in tarnation—?"

He could not get the words out.

"What am I doing here?" she said, completing the question for him.

"Yeah—what are you doing here? How in the heck did you ever find me?"

"Jeremiah told Zeke where he'd be staying. I asked at the desk. They said you were in here."

"But . . . but how'd . . . how'd you know what'd happened to Jeremiah?"

An expression of shock filled Mercy's eyes. Her face went pale.

"I *don't* know what's happened to him," she said, sagging into a chair opposite Jess. "Is he . . . ?"

"You don't know about the sapphires?"

"Jess, I don't know anything. I was in Louisville when Jeremiah came after you, and I haven't heard a word from him in two weeks. Finally I didn't know what else to do but come to Denver myself and see what the two of you were doing. I got in on the train just a few minutes ago."

Jess let out a long sigh, realizing all over again just how much trouble he had caused. From his pocket he took the first note he'd received from Fletcher. Mercy read it. Then he handed her the one that had come just that morning.

Forbes,

We'll let yer partner go when you bring us the saffires.
You try a double cross and he's dead, and so are you.
Bring them in a leather pouch inside a saddlebag. Take the
road to Boulder six miles out of Denver. A trail breaks off
in the middle of a stand of pine to the right. Take it a mile.
There's an old mine with a water tank on the ridge above it.

*Throw the saddlebag into the tank and git back to Denver.
When we've got the saffires and got word that yer back,
we'll let him go.*

R. Fletcher

A minute or two of silence followed. At last Mercy spoke.
"What's it all about, Jess?" she asked.

"Well, you see, me and Jeremiah were here in Denver
staying at the Grey Falcon seven years ago when just about
the most famous robbery ever to hit Colorado happened
right up the street."

He went on to tell her of the Donahue sapphires, the
shoot-out and death of Kid Hotchkiss in room 3-G, which
was on the top floor of the hotel at the time, and the recently
expired statute of limitations.

Mercy listened patiently to the whole story.

"Well, Jess, if I wasn't so worried about Jeremiah, I
could be pretty angry with you."

Jess looked down and said nothing.

"I thought you and I had an understanding," she went on.
"I thought we were going to be a three-way partnership,
you and Jeremiah and me. I thought you said you loved
Jeremiah enough to share him. And now you go and do
something like this. I don't understand it, Jess."

"I know . . . shoot, I'm sorry—I didn't mean for so much
trouble to come of it."

"Jeremiah's life's in danger over a few sapphires—"

"Not just a few," interrupted Jess.

"What difference does that make? How can you compare
your partner's life to a ridiculous dream of getting rich?
They aren't yours anyway. Even if you do find them, you'd

have to give them back to Mr. Donahue. I don't know what to say, Jess. It wasn't a very smart thing to do."

Jess was beginning to realize that fact well enough for himself.

"Well, Jess?" said Mercy after a moment.

"Well what?"

"When are you going to ride out there and do what it says?"

"What do you mean?"

"You do have them, don't you? Surely you're not thinking of—"

But before Mercy could finish her question, yet another interruption came to Jess Forbes.

"Why, Jess, if you aren't seeing another woman behind my back!"

Jess glanced up to see Doretta approaching the table.

"It ain't nothing like that, Doretta," said Jess, "this here's Jeremiah's gal."

Doretta sat down.

"Sister Mercy, this here's Doretta Morgan—Doretta, meet . . . uh, Mercy, who's one day gonna be Mercy Eagleflight."

The eyes of the two young women met. A fleeting question of recognition passed over Doretta's countenance, but she quickly dismissed it. She turned quickly toward Jess.

"Any word?"

Jess handed her the new letter that had come.

Mercy, meanwhile, was doing her utmost to keep her composure. She recognized the young lady instantly. If the long blonde hair and close-set green eyes weren't enough, the pinkish blemish near her left eye was unmistakable. Mercy had never seen a birthmark quite like it and would never forget it. It was her. The woman on the train. The one with the gun!

"Jess," she said softly, holding her surprise inside and concealed, "could I talk to you . . . alone?"

"Heck, Sister Mercy, anything you have to say to me, you can say to Doretta. Why, she's been helping me all this time trying to figure out what to do. She's on our side, ain't that right, Doretta?"

"You bet! But, Jess, you never told me your partner was going to marry your sister."

Jess laughed. "Mercy ain't my sister—she's a preacher, leastways she used to be."

"I really wish you wouldn't call me *Sister* Mercy anymore, Jess," said Mercy, "and I really must talk to you alone."

"Come now, Mercy, dear," said Doretta, "you can trust me. If Jess and Jeremiah do, surely you can, too."

But neither of them knows what I know about you! thought Mercy to herself. But the words that came out of her mouth instead were, "I think I'll go see about getting myself a room." She rose from the table.

"When you want to talk, Jess," she added, "come find me."

She left the room, saying nothing more to Jess' new companion.

QUESTIONS

As soon as Mercy had put the one bag she had brought with her in her room, she went back downstairs, asked directions at the desk, and walked straight down the street to the sheriff's office.

She introduced herself to the sheriff, then asked, "Do you know Brad Nichols?"

The sheriff glanced her over with the sort of interrogative

look that accompanied his job. He was used to seeing just
about anything in Denver. But this pretty young lady in her
dusty traveling suit nevertheless struck him as just a mite
out of the ordinary. She seemed to be a nice city girl and a
frontier woman all in one pretty package.

"Yes, ma'am," the man replied. "He's U.S. Marshal for
this region."

"Have you seen him recently? Is he in Denver?"

"No, ma'am, on both counts. Nobody's seen hide nor hair
o' him for a while. He rounded up several of the Medicine
Bow Gang in the East—don't reckon you've heard of 'em,
ma'am," the man added, "but they been wanted in these
parts for years. Nichols was bringing 'em in to stand trial.
Ain't been no word from Nichols since. Why you asking,
ma'am?"

"Oh . . . oh, I've just got some unfinished business with
Mr. Nichols, that's all."

"Don't know what to tell you, ma'am."

"Well, thank you very much, you've been most helpful,"
replied Mercy. "Would you happen to have a handbill on the
gang you mentioned?"

"Sure do, ma'am," replied the sheriff, pulling out one of
the drawers of his desk. "No pictures been taken of them,
but here's descriptions of 'em all."

Mercy took the leaflet and folded it, thanked the man
again, and left the office. She walked back to the Grey Falcon. Jess was just crossing the lobby toward the stairs.
Thankfully, now he was alone. Mercy hurried to catch up
with him.

"What's all this about, Mercy?" he said, a hint of irritation
in his voice. "Having to talk to me alone, and saying it right
in front of Doretta like that . . ."

Mercy said nothing, and they started up the stairs together.

"Where's your room?" she asked when they reached the landing.

"Right down there." Jess pointed.

Mercy followed him and walked in right behind him through the unlocked door. She closed it behind her.

"What's this all about, Mercy?" Jess repeated.

"How well do you know your new friend?" she asked.

"Doretta?"

She nodded.

"She's been about the only friend I've had these last few days. I tell you, Mercy, she's trying to help me."

"Help you what—find the sapphires?"

"Yeah, well . . . I reckon . . . that *and* help Jeremiah. Why—what do you have against her, Mercy? I can tell by that look in your eye that you don't take too kindly toward her."

"Her name's not Doretta, Jess," Mercy finally blurted out.

"What are you talking about? 'Course it is."

"Her name is Loretta, Jess . . . Loretta Monroe—ring any bells?"

"No . . . ," said Jess, "and there ain't no reason it should. I tell you, Mercy, her name's—"

"Look at this, Jess," said Mercy, finally growing angry with Jess' thickheadedness. "There's a description of her right down to her height and green eyes and small pink birthmark next to the left eye."

Jess scanned the paper briefly.

"Don't mean anything. Shoot, that's plumb ridiculous!"

"Jess, I've seen her before," insisted Mercy. "I *know* who she is."

"Seen her? Where could *you* possibly have seen her before?"

"On the train between Kansas City and St. Louis," rejoined Mercy. "The train was being robbed, and she was one of the robbers! Jess, what does it take to get through to you? She's working with Ross Fletcher. They've got Jeremiah . . . and your friend Doretta—who is really Loretta Monroe—is in on it!"

Jess sat down on the side of the bed, shaking his head in disbelief.

Mercy stood in the middle of the room in angry silence, like a schoolteacher who had just scolded one of her pupils.

"Shoot, I hear what you're saying, Mercy," he said in almost a whimper, "but I just can't believe it."

"Believe it, Jess. Everything I'm telling you is the truth. She's been playing you for a fool, and you fell right into it. Now Jeremiah's life is at stake because of it!"

Mercy threw the Wanted poster at his feet, then spun around and left the room.

FROM OUT
OF THE PAST

Fighting tears of anger and fear and not knowing

what she should do now, Mercy ran out of the Grey Falcon

Inn and down the street away from the center of town.

She continued at a brisk pace for twenty or thirty

minutes. She turned and changed directions several times in

the streets. She gradually slowed to a more leisurely walk for

a while longer, heedless of her direction, until she found

herself in a quiet and pleasant section of the city. The neighborhood was comprised mostly of homes, a few shops, and here and there a church building.

Though the day was not yet half over, Mercy had begun to tire from her long journey. But her anger at Jess' foolishness and her concern for Jeremiah made her forget her weariness. She needed to think.

It was approximately eleven-thirty, late Saturday morning.

She saw the white steeple of a church building in the distance. The structure drew her as an external reminder of where her internal source of strength lay. As she walked closer, she noticed that in the empty field behind it and on the grassy lawn on each side stood a number of carriages and buggies, their horses all waiting patiently for their owners to conclude their business inside.

Some kind of special meeting must be going on, thought Mercy. Yet this was a peculiar hour for a service. She slowed her walk and drew closer. As she did, a voice reached her ears from inside.

". . . opportunity for harvest of souls . . ."

What was it about that phrase that sounded so familiar? Where had she heard it before?

". . . special gathering before this evening's service for those whose hearts . ... leading of the Lord to serve him . . ."

Now it was not merely the phrases that were familiar but something in the intonation of the voice speaking. Suddenly she remembered where she had heard the exact same words. At the Young Women's Missionary College in Jefferson City, Indiana! At a special gathering held specifically for those desirous of serving the Lord on the so-called mission field of the American West!

Reverend Joseph Mertree!

". . . my dear brothers and sisters," Brother Joseph was now saying, ". . . pray concerning this wonderful opportunity to be part of this harvest I speak of . . . opening just now for a young woman . . . lead singing and play the organ, in addition to . . ."

She walked closer, gradually hearing more and more clearly through the open window the words of the man she now knew as a shyster, though he had been her onetime spiritual mentor. Many emotions raged through Mercy Randolph, from heartache to fury, from anger to spite.

Again her heart beat rapidly. Her face flushed. She wanted to run straight through the door and yell out to all those listening, "Don't listen to a word he says—the man is a fraud! Don't make the same mistake I did!"

She also wished she had the courage to run straight to the front of the church and punch him right in the nose in front of everyone. But she knew she could not. Not only did she *not* possess the courage, she knew it wouldn't be right. She didn't know who she was more angry with—Jess or Reverend Mertree.

Suddenly Mercy's thoughts turned to the sad plight of Brother Joseph's maid and companion, the former slave of his parents.

She glanced all about the church. The wagon from which the Tent of Meeting and Healing originated was nowhere to be seen. That was to be expected, she thought. He would not want to run the risk of a black woman's being seen with him. But it had to be nearby somewhere!

Unconsciously Mercy began walking hurriedly again, looking this way and that down the side streets. She hurried on past the church, glancing down one street, then another, but there was no sign of the Mertree wagon.

She paused to catch her breath and think.

He would have located it out of the way, on the road leading out of town, and near a river or stream for water. He would himself, of course, be staying in a nice hotel someplace.

Mercy glanced about. A large wide street intersected with that of the church several blocks farther on. She broke into a run. Reaching it, she looked to the right and then to the left. It looked to be one of Denver's main streets, and toward the left was the center of the city. Mercy turned toward the right. As she walked, she could see that this street did lead out of town.

A bridge stood about a quarter mile farther on. Mercy ran toward it, houses and buildings thinning now. Pastureland and prairie gradually surrounded her on both sides.

She reached the bridge out of breath and glanced all about, up and down the river that ran beneath it.

There was the wagon! It was just as she had expected, in a small field under two or three large oaks, sitting some distance up from the bank of the river. Mercy left the road and headed toward it across the field of high brown grass.

She saw no one as she approached. Suddenly the setting was so familiar. Was it really possible this had once been *her* life? She could hardly believe it, so much had happened since!

She reached the large wagon and climbed tentatively up the back to peek inside.

A large black woman sat inside. Startled at the sound of an intruder, she turned.

"What you doin' here?" she exclaimed.

"Beula!" said Mercy with a smile.

"How you know my name, missy?"

"Beula, it's me. . . . It's Mercy."

The large brown face stared straight ahead in silence, eyes wide in question, unable to connect the word she had just heard with the person before her.

"Sister . . . *Mercy?*" she said questioningly, squinting slightly, as if that might serve to bring back the black dress and old-fashioned bonnet and expression of a naive evangelist's assistant.

"Yes, Beula," laughed Mercy, "it's Sister Mercy."

"Lan' sakes, chil'—what in tarnation you be doin' here?" exclaimed Beula, half rising now and opening her arms in welcome.

"I heard Brother Joseph in a church not far from here. I came looking to see if I could find you." As she spoke, Mercy came all the way inside. The two women embraced for the first time ever.

"Why, we gabe you up fo' lost fo' good!" said Beula. "What happened t' you, chil'?"

"I'm afraid I found out that Brother Joseph was faking the conversions, Beula," replied Mercy sadly. Seeing the poor woman now moderated her own anger toward Mertree.

"I always knew somebody was boun' to fin' him out sooner or later. I done tol' him so, too. Can't go cheatin' the Lord foreber. I done tol' him, but he don' listen none t' me."

"Why don't you leave, Beula? Why do you stay with him?"

"Where's a black woman like me gonna go, Sister Mercy? Me dat ain't got a cent to my name."

Mercy was silent a moment. The next words were out of her mouth before she had a chance to even consider all the implications.

"I know a place you can go, Beula!" she said.

"What you talkin' 'bout?"

"Come away. . . . Come with me."

"Come where, chil'? I tell you, I ain't got no place t' go."

"But you do. I've got a home now, Beula. You'll be welcome — I know it. They took me in. . . . They'll take you in, too."

"Who you be talkin' 'bout?"

"Friends of mine, Beula. On a ranch back in Sweetriver. Come — I'll take you home with me."

Tears filled the eyes of the large black woman. No one had shown her the slightest attention since Joseph's mother had died. She had scarcely seen another human soul up close besides him in ten years. And now a young lady she hardly knew was offering to take her in. The sincerity of Mercy's tone went straight to the dear lady's starving heart, and she needed not another five seconds to make up her mind. Whatever affection she may once have held in her bosom for the boy Joseph for the sake of his mother had long since disappeared. In less than a minute she and Mercy were packing all her worldly possessions in two medium-size carpetbags.

"Lan' sakes, if I didn't nearly forget!" Beula exclaimed at length. "I sabed all yo things too, Sister Mercy. Joseph, he was plenty riled when you lef'. He would hab thrown dem all out on the prairie, but I hid dem all dis time."

She now pulled Mercy's old carpetbag from under her own makeshift bed. Mercy's eyes filled with tears at the sight of those few possessions she had left behind.

Ten minutes later the two women were hurrying across the field toward the bridge and the road. Mercy hoped the owner of the Grey Falcon Inn had no objection to her sharing her room with a former slave.

37

WHAT NEXT?

Once situated safely in her room with Beula, Mercy turned her thoughts back to Jeremiah—he was in serious danger! And it appeared that she was the only one capable of helping him.

She told Beula she was in Denver to help a special friend. Beula set right to work cleaning Mercy's travel suit while Mercy changed into something more serviceable.

"You just relax, Beula," she said with a smile. "I'm going to see what I can find out."

She left the room, went down one flight of stairs and along the corridor, then knocked on Jess' door. No answer came.

She couldn't depend on him, she thought. Especially if he continued to be mixed up with Loretta and refused to listen to the truth. She had seen the letters from Fletcher. Whether or not Jess had the sapphires, she didn't know. But since she knew Fletcher's instructions, perhaps *she* ought to take some action. If Jess did have them, how dependable would he be to turn them over in exchange for Jeremiah? And if Loretta got her hands on them first, would anything be able to save Jeremiah?

She'd better talk to the sheriff again, Mercy thought. He might not know what she knew. And he was likely to be more help than Jess.

She returned to the jail.

"Sheriff," she said, "I don't know what's happened to Marshal Nichols, but I *do* know that the bank robbers he arrested near Kansas City are on the loose again."

"How do you know that?" the man asked.

Mercy explained.

"You were there when Marshal Nichols arrested them varmints?"

Mercy nodded. "But they're loose now. I've seen one of them myself, and Jess has seen three of the others, right here in Denver."

"Dad blame!" the man exclaimed. "If I'd only known it was them! You say the woman's still around?"

Again Mercy nodded.

The sheriff thought a moment. "I'd better telegraph Fort

Collins and see if they've heard from Nichols." He rose from his desk and walked toward the door. "Meet me back here in twenty minutes," he added. "I'll let you know what I find out."

Mercy returned to her room to make sure Beula was doing all right. She found the old woman sitting in a chair pulled up to the window. She was doing nothing more than looking out the window, smiling from ear to ear. The idea that someone cared about her was in itself enough to make her happier than she had been in years.

"Seems you're right, ma'am," said the sheriff, leaning back in his chair with a sigh after Mercy returned. "Brad and another fella just came in this morning, shot up pretty bad. Some ol' miner found them out on the trail, took care of 'em a couple of days, then took 'em into Fort Collins. Sure enough, that Medicine Bow bunch is on the loose again."

"What are you going to do?" asked Mercy.

"Technically it's Brad's jurisdiction since they were his prisoners. Figure I'll talk to him first. Reckon I'll take the train up there this afternoon, then tomorrow, depending on what he says, I'll likely round up a posse and head up where you said they are and shoot 'em outta there. I just gotta find out whether Brad wants 'em dead or alive."

"What about Mr. Eagleflight?" asked Mercy, not liking the sound of it.

"'Course we'll do our best to keep from hitting him, ma'am, but in these kinds of situations you can't ever tell for sure which way the lead's gonna fly."

Mercy left the sheriff's office less reassured than ever. If she was going to help Jeremiah, she had to do it before the sheriff's posse left town!

As she walked toward the hotel, she saw a familiar figure walk out of the Rocky Mountain Hotel, glance about, then mount a tan horse and ride along the street leading out of town to the northwest. Her first thought was to run back in and tell the sheriff to arrest her. But on second thought she waited, watching until the rider was out of sight.

Without thinking about it further, Mercy suddenly ran in the opposite direction. A minute later she reached a livery stable.

"I need to rent a horse and saddle," she said breathlessly to the man in charge.

"Can you ride, ma'am?" he asked.

"Yes, I can ride. Please, I'm in a hurry."

The man eyed her a moment more, then turned to grab a saddle.

"I want the fastest horse you have," added Mercy.

Again he turned, glancing at her skeptically, then threw the saddle on a spirited roan mare.

Mercy opened her bag even as he was cinching the straps.

"How much for twenty-four hours?" she asked.

The man told her. She did not argue, though the price was twice what he would have quoted a man. The money was in his hand the moment he yanked the final loop tight, and Mercy was in the saddle the next, galloping up the wide Denver street in the direction of Boulder.

FOLLOWING
LORETTA

Mercy hoped she remembered the instructions from the letter Jess had shown her, but it wouldn't have mattered. Mercy rode hard, and within three miles she was in sight of a rider in the distance in front of her. She eased the mare to a canter, gradually slowing the rate at which she was closing the gap.

Over the next mile she drew within two hundred yards

and was at last satisfied that it was indeed Loretta. She eased back so as to attract no attention, and continued to follow from a safe distance.

The wide trail began to wind through a region of lightly forested hills. As the road turned this way and that, most of the time Mercy could not see her prey. As she rounded a bend, suddenly in front of her stretched a straight view of the road, uninterrupted for at least a quarter of a mile.

Loretta was nowhere to be seen.

Mercy stopped. She gazed down at the dirt below her. She couldn't tell exactly, but there didn't *appear* to be any fresh tracks ahead of her. She turned in her saddle and glanced behind. Could Loretta have turned off somewhere?

Slowly Mercy pulled on the reins and eased her horse back around. She would retrace her tracks half a mile or so. Easing her mount into a gentle trot, she again rounded the bend over the stretch of road she had just passed. On her left grew a thick grove of pine trees.

That was it—she remembered now!

She hastened toward them, then slowed. Sure enough, a narrow trail led off the road through the trees.

Mercy took it. Soon she was climbing along the face of a steep ridge.

When she had ridden for perhaps five minutes, the trail began to widen. Mercy could tell she was about to crest the summit. She stopped, took the horse some distance into the shrubbery, tied her to a tree, then continued on foot.

Just short of the peak, the trail intersected a wider road, obviously used for wagons and supplies. Mercy crept farther until she could see down the other side. A small valley appeared, cleared of trees, between where she stood and another steep ridge perhaps two or three hundred yards farther on. An abandoned mine shaft bored into the opposite hill. Above it, exactly as described, stood a circular wooden water tank.

Jeremiah was somewhere nearby!

Yet alone like this, Mercy could hope to do little for him. In the distance she heard faint voices. A thin wisp of smoke could be seen coming through a small stand of trees below and to the left of the mine shaft. That must be the cabin where they were holding Jeremiah.

Mercy glanced about. She knew she was in danger. Besides Loretta and Fletcher, there were probably two more men around. To get Jeremiah away from here, she would need help. Reluctantly, she turned, creeping back out of sight and down the hill to her horse. Untying it, she eased back down the slope until she came to the main road, then increased her pace and hurried back into the city.

On the way her brain hatched a plan that was either foolhardy and could get her killed along with Jeremiah . . . or, if it worked, that just *might* rescue him.

She rode straight to the Grey Falcon. Jess was neither in his room nor in the dining room. She found him in the Rocky Mountain saloon.

She walked straight toward him with renewed fire in her eyes. He saw the flash of intensity instantly. Not wanting a scene, he rose and went to meet her.

"How can you play poker at a time like this?" she whispered angrily.

"What else am I gonna do?"

"You're going to listen to me, that's what," she shot back. "I followed Loretta. She rode out to meet the others at that abandoned mine, exactly as that letter you got said. She's *with* them, Jess! What does it take to convince you?"

Jess looked down and squirmed.

"You be over at my room at the hotel in five minutes. You got Jeremiah into this, and you're going to help me get him out of it."

She turned and strode out of the saloon, still angry. Jess watched her go, then returned to the table, looking for the first opportunity to cash in and excuse himself.

39

ANOTHER
HOSTAGE

Jess Forbes sat silently. He didn't like being browbeaten by two women, but he'd never run into two quite as determined as these.

"Now you listen to Sister Mercy," Beula was saying. "She be talkin' some mighty good sense, but you's not payin' her no heed."

"I don't know, Mercy," whined Jess. "I still think—"

"Jess, for heaven's sake," interrupted Mercy, "if you still think Loretta's trying to help you, then you're either too blind or too stupid for your own good. Now you're either with me or else I tell the sheriff who she is, in which case she'll be arrested. Now you go down there to the saloon, and you wait, because I have no doubt she'll be back. They think you have the sapphires, and her job is to keep an eye on you so you don't skip town. When you see her, I want you to bring her over here to the Grey Falcon."

"Where?"

"When you and she come toward the hotel, you say something funny, then laugh loud. I'll hear you and know you are coming. You bring her upstairs to your room, which you will have left unlocked. Beula and I will be waiting inside. All right, go on down there—you know what to do?"

"I reckon," replied Jess, turning toward the door. "I don't want you to think I don't care about Jeremiah. It's just that—"

"I know, I know, Jess," said Mercy, without waiting for him to finish. "Just do what I've said, and all will be forgiven."

Jess left the room. He knew he had to go along, but it didn't feel right having a former preacher lady and a black woman telling him what to do.

"Dat dere's 'bout the most stubbornest an' dim-witted man I eber laid eyes on!" exclaimed Beula.

"Deep down I think Jess is good enough," sighed Mercy, "but he just hasn't yet come to the point of deciding what kind of man he wants to be. By the way, Beula, do you know what hotel Brother Joseph is staying at?"

"He don' tell me dat."

"I would certainly rather he didn't see either of us in the middle of all we have to do."

"What we gonna do 'bout him?" asked Beula.

"You mean, are we going to let him continue pretending to be a preacher and taking people's money?"

"Dat be what I mean. I don' like da idea ob some other girl goin' off wif him."

"Neither do I," said Mercy. "I have been wondering about that, and I think before we leave Denver I shall go have a little private talk with the pastor of the church where I saw him. I will leave it in his hands whether or not to notify the sheriff. He will certainly be able to keep his own congregation from being duped. In fact," she added with a thoughtful smile, "is Brother Joseph holding services tonight?"

"He sho is. He's got hissel' two or three fake testificashuns all lined up. I heerd him talkin' 'bout it near da wagon wif one ob dem."

"If we are through with all the rest of this," Mercy said to herself with a nod, "it just might be interesting to be in attendance." She smiled at the thought.

Forty minutes later, in the midst of their conversation, Mercy and Beula heard through their open window a loud laugh sound from down on the street. Mercy leapt up from her chair and went to the window, glancing down carefully from its edge.

"There they are," she said. "Headed this way! Come, Beula."

With more enthusiasm for life than she had felt in years, even if it was danger that caused the excitement, Beula followed Mercy hurriedly from the room, her wide eyes aglow in the middle of her round, black face, ready to take on the world for her new savior and benefactor. Within moments they were situated behind the closed door of Jess' room, waiting.

After another minute or two they heard footsteps and voices approaching. The door opened. Jess and Loretta walked in. The door closed behind them, and Mercy stepped out from the shadows. A momentary smile of recognition came over Loretta's face, but it quickly faded as she noticed Beula standing behind Mercy with a huge, threatening scowl looming on her brow. She realized from the expression in Mercy's eyes as well that the interview planned was far from friendly in its purpose.

"Jess . . . ," said Mercy with command in her tone.

Loretta glanced up at Jess with questioning eyes.

"She knows who you are, Doretta," he said.

"I don't know what—"

"He's right, *Loretta*," interrupted Mercy. "I know."

Hearing her real name momentarily stunned her. She glanced from one to the other, then over toward Beula, then back to Mercy. Slowly recognition began to dawn.

"I knew there was something. . . . It was on the train . . . ," she began.

"That's right," rejoined Mercy. "And now you are going to help us free Jeremiah from your friends."

"Not on your life," said Loretta, finally coming to herself and backing slowly toward the door. "Ross would kill me if—"

"Jess!" said Mercy again.

Jess continued to hesitate.

Suddenly Mercy stepped forward and grabbed the gun out of his holster, then stepped quickly back, pointing it toward Loretta.

"Stay where you are, Loretta," she said. "I don't know

how to use a gun, and I've never shot a pistol like this in my life. But to save Jeremiah, I'll pull the trigger if I have to. Even if I only shoot a hole in the wall, it'll bring people running."

Loretta froze. She well knew that the most dangerous person with a gun was the one who knew nothing about guns.

"Grab her, Beula."

"Don't you touch me!" cried Loretta, recoiling at the very idea. But the large black woman paid her words no heed. The next instant Beula had Loretta's wrists in the grip of her two large, strong hands, holding them behind Loretta's back.

"I'm going to need your hat and your bandana," said Mercy, handing the gun back to Jess, then stepping forward and taking Loretta's hat from her head. She then reached up and began untying the bandana from around Loretta's neck.

"What are you doing?" complained Loretta.

"Shut up, you," said Beula, giving Loretta's wrists a yank behind her. "If you knows what's good for you, you won' make no mo sounds."

"Take her to our room, Beula," said Mercy. "Tie her up if you need to, or just sit with your back to the door. I don't care. Just be sure she doesn't go anyplace."

"She be safe wif me, Sister Mercy," replied Beula. "You can count on dat! Come on, you," she said to Loretta, opening the door with one hand, then tugging her prisoner through it.

"All right, Jess," said Mercy, "you and I had better be going." She glanced around the room. "And bring your rifle," she added, nodding to where it stood leaning in the corner.

"Where?" asked Jess, following Mercy like a compliant schoolboy.

"We're going to get Jeremiah, what do you think?"
replied Mercy testily. "You haven't shown much backbone
so far, Jess," she added. "I hope you figure out who your
real friend is before we get there. I'm going to have to
depend on you."

Jess followed her downstairs and outside.

"Where's Loretta's horse?" asked Mercy.

"At the livery."

"Go get him and your horse. Mine's saddled and ready.
I'll meet you here in front of the hotel in ten minutes."

Jess turned and began walking toward the livery stable
while Mercy went in the other direction toward a gunsmith's
shop. She had one other errand to attend to before she would
be completely ready. She stopped at the window and peered
in at the collection of guns on display, gulped once, then
walked into the store, hoping that her precautions were not
going to be needed.

A DANGEROUS
LOVE

Mercy and Jess rode along the Denver-to-Boulder

road at a brisk trot. They did not want to risk tiring their

horses too much in case they needed to make a fast getaway.

Beside them, reins in Jess' hands as he rode, trotted

Loretta's tan filly.

The ride out of the city, thoughts about what might lay

ahead, as well as the very real danger facing his partner at this very moment, had succeeded in restoring some sense into Jess Forbes' head. Mercy's courageous levelheadedness and her willingness to risk her life for Jeremiah had not gone unnoticed. Now he found himself wondering how he could have been so stupid as to let a woman like Doretta— or Loretta, if that was her name—blind him so.

Well, he thought, he would show both Mercy and Jeremiah that they *could* trust him. He would not let his uncle down again.

"There are the pines," said Mercy, slowing and pointing ahead of them off to the right.

She urged her horse into the lead, leading off the main road into the woods and up the ridge. About two-thirds of the way up the slope, she led a little ways off into the woods, stopped, and dismounted, motioning for Jess to do the same.

"It's less than half a mile from here," she said softly. "I'll give you ten or fifteen minutes. Go the rest of the way up the path there. From the ridge you'll see the mine shaft with the water tower up on the hill behind it. Work your way around to the right, through the woods, and up the slope to where the mine is. If you can get to the tank, I think you'll be above the cabin and will have a clear view down to it. But be careful in case someone's standing guard up there."

Jess nodded. "What about you?" he asked.

"I'm going to ride up to the cabin and get Jeremiah," answered Mercy. "That's why you're going to cover us from up on the hill. As soon as you see that we're safe, you run back down here to the horses."

"But how—?"

"I don't know exactly," replied Mercy. "But I've got to try."

"I hope you know what you're doing," said Jess, withdrawing his rifle from its leather pouch. He turned and headed up the trail in the direction they had been riding. In a few minutes he was out of sight. Mercy sat down to wait, collect her thoughts, and pray.

When fifteen or so minutes had passed, she rose, made sure the horses were secure, then led Loretta's tan out of the woods, back to the narrow trail.

"Well," she said to herself, "here goes nothing!"

She mounted Loretta's horse and rode straight up to the ridge and confidently down the other side without slowing, and straight toward where she'd judged the cabin to be located. Heart pounding inside her, she knew her only chance was to pretend to be as tough as the three outlaws she was trying to outwit. There sat the mine shaft to her right. Out of the corner of her eye she glanced upward toward the water tank.

I hope you're up there, Jess!

Down a slight slope to her left, around a huge boulder, and there it was—a small plank cabin. Almost the moment it came into view, a man she did not recognize walked onto the porch and stood waiting.

"That's far enough, lady," he said gruffly. "What do you think you're doing here?"

"I'm here with a message for Ross Fletcher," Mercy answered back as she dismounted, trying to make her voice sound tough. "He inside?" she asked, walking straight up toward the cabin.

"I told you to stop where you were," said the man.

"Yeah? Well, I told you my business is with Fletcher," rejoined Mercy, walking straight up the two steps to the porch. "So either tell him I'm here or else stand aside."

The man continued to eye her skeptically. "All right, I'll tell him," he said. "No need to get riled."

He turned and walked back through the door. But Mercy was not about to be left standing outside, and continued on his heels.

When Ross Fletcher glanced up from the table where he sat and saw a woman with a six-gun on her hip and what looked like Loretta's hat on her head following Stoner through the door, he had no idea what it was about.

Before his partner had a chance to speak, Mercy walked straight into the middle of the room and stared straight at the man.

"You Fletcher?" she said.

"Yeah," replied Fletcher, rising slowly, his eyebrows wrinkling in question. "Who're you?"

"A friend of Loretta's," replied Mercy.

"Why didn't she come herself?"

"'Cause she's tied up with the Forbes fellow. She said she had to get word to you quick and couldn't afford to leave him. She offered me ten dollars, so I said I'd deliver the message. I'm from the saloon."

Fletcher listened suspiciously.

"And say I don't believe you?" he said.

"That's just what Loretta said you'd say," laughed Mercy. "That's why she gave me her hat and bandana and told me to ride her horse out here, so you'd know she sent me."

Mercy reached into her pocket and took out Loretta's red bandana and tossed it to Fletcher. He caught it.

"Yeah, well, this is Loretta's. That don't prove nothing."

"She's on the tan, all right, Ross," put in Stoner.

"All right, all right, lady—what's the message?" said Fletcher. "Deliver it and get back to town and tell her next time she better come herself."

>-+‹›-O-‹›-+‹

From where he sat tied up in the corner, Eagleflight had nearly dozed off when he heard a horse approaching outside. He paid no attention, even when Stoner reentered the cabin, and scarcely noticed the form following him inside, assuming it to be Loretta.

At the words *You Fletcher?* Jeremiah's eyes suddenly shot open in disbelief. He glanced across the floor, glad neither of the men was looking his way, for his face went pale and his mouth gaped opened in astonishment.

Mercy! What are you doing here? he cried silently to himself.

Mercy knew better herself than to glance toward him. If their eyes met once, her heart would leap and her eyes would instantly betray her. She allowed herself only to note the fact out of the corner of her eye that someone else sat on the floor at the far end of the room. She dared not glance more closely in that direction.

It *had* to be Jeremiah. She would look when the time was right.

"She said to tell you she couldn't come," said Mercy, "because the Forbes fellow was about to skip town. She said he's got the jewels, and he's going to leave with them and forget his partner. She said you needed to get back to Denver quick, and she'd keep him there as long as she could."

Fletcher took in the information thoughtfully. If it was true, it explained well enough why Loretta would send someone else.

"Well, that's her message," said Mercy, "so I figure I'll be getting back myself. Hey," she said, turning toward where

Stoner still stood by the door, "would you get Loretta's horse some water before I go?"

"Uh, yeah . . . sure, I reckon," Stoner answered. He turned and walked back outside.

Mercy gave the door a shove closed behind him. The next instant, while Fletcher was still distracted, turning the message over in his mind, she drew the gun from her holster. When Fletcher looked up, he was staring down the barrel of a .45.

"Hey, what the—?"

"I've got one more message, Fletcher," said Mercy in a soft voice. "Keep your mouth shut, and go untie that man over there."

"What are you talking—?" he said, still bewildered at the sudden turn of events.

"Untie him, Fletcher!" barked Mercy, motioning in Jeremiah's direction with the gun.

A smoldering thundercloud of anger now coming over his face, Fletcher complied. "You little hussy!" he growled as he loosened Jeremiah's hands. "I don't know what you've done with Loretta, but I'll get you for this!"

Glancing quickly out the window, Mercy saw that Stoner had walked some distance from the cabin and was now holding the reins of Loretta's horse while it drank from a wooden trough.

"That's good for now, Fletcher," she said the moment Jeremiah's hands were free. "Now stand back."

He did so. As he did, Mercy dug her free hand under her belt behind her shirt, withdrawing a small thirty-six-caliber derringer.

"Jeremiah!" she said, tossing it toward him.

The next instant Fletcher found two guns aimed at him.

"I don't know how you did it," exclaimed Jeremiah, "but am I ever glad to see you!"

At last Mercy allowed herself to smile. But only briefly. She could not let down her guard quite yet or she would faint straightaway. They still had to get away from here!

"Where's the third man?" she said.

"I don't know—he went out about an hour ago," replied Jeremiah, struggling to loosen the ropes around his feet with his left hand while he kept Fletcher covered with his right.

"Well, hopefully if he comes back, Jess will spot him."

"Jess!" exclaimed Jeremiah, throwing aside the last of the cords and jumping to his feet.

"He's on the hill above here, covering us. Can you tie something around Fletcher's mouth so he can't yell?" she asked.

The next instant Loretta's red bandana was serving the useful purpose of silencing the mouth of Ross Fletcher. Jeremiah now proceeded to tie him with the same ropes that had so recently held him fast.

"I'll go outside first," said Mercy. She reholstered the gun she had just bought an hour before, then walked outside, down the steps, and toward Stoner.

"Thanks," she said as she approached. She took the reins from him, and he started back toward the house. The door opened, and suddenly Stoner found a derringer pointed straight toward him. He turned back toward Mercy in bewilderment, only to see a second gun now in her hand.

"Inside, Stoner," said Jeremiah, stepping aside and motioning for Stoner to continue.

Two minutes later both outlaws were bound.

"Let's get out of here!" cried Jeremiah, running through the door.

"I have a horse for you down in the woods," said Mercy, following.

"Then I'll run theirs off first," said Jeremiah as Mercy mounted.

A moment later he leapt up behind where she sat in the saddle. Mercy dug her heels into the horse's sides. They had not gone more than ten yards when suddenly another horseman appeared in front of them, blocking their path. In his hands he held a rifle.

"That's far enough!" he said.

"McLeod—where'd you come from?" said Jeremiah.

"I happened to come back right in the middle of your little game," answered the third outlaw. "But you've had your fun, and it's over now. Get down off of that horse."

Suddenly a shot rang out from high on the hill above them. McLeod's horse started as McLeod turned to return the fire. Jeremiah leapt from behind Mercy to the ground and flew forward, grabbing McLeod from behind and dragging him out of his saddle. The rifle fell to the ground.

Mercy jumped down, ran to it, and kicked it aside. As McLeod regained his feet, he spun around and leapt toward Jeremiah, who, weakened from his days in captivity, was light-headed from the sudden activity. The next moment he found himself on the ground with McLeod on top of him.

But the shot from Mercy's gun ended the fight as quickly as it had begun. McLeod turned to see her standing, pistol in the air, hand trembling.

"Get off him!" she said.

Cursing, he complied. Footsteps came running down the

hillside, and the next moment Jess came into view. Jeremiah struggled to his feet, finding Mercy's arms waiting for him.

"Oh, Jeremiah!" she sighed.

"How did you possibly . . . ?"

His voice drifted off in contented confusion. He realized there were too many questions to possibly be answered here and now. He pulled Mercy close.

"I'll just see if I can find something to tie up this varmint," said Jess. "Get in there!" he said to McLeod, who now climbed to his feet, muttering obscenities at no one in particular. "Watch your mouth," said Jess, jabbing him in the back with the barrel of his rifle. "Can't you see there's a lady present?"

With Jeremiah's feet solidly under him, Mercy collapsed in his arms. Now that it was over, every ounce of strength seemed suddenly to drain from her body.

"Jeremiah . . . Jeremiah . . . I didn't think I could do it," she murmured.

"I've never seen such a brave lady," he said, stroking her hair tenderly. "You saved my life, do you know that?"

"I just know that I love you," she sighed contentedly, "and I'm so happy you're safe. I was so worried."

"Not half as much as I was!" laughed Jeremiah. "But I had better go give Jess a hand before he gets us into any more trouble!"

Three minutes later, Jess running on foot and Mercy and Eagleflight on the back of Loretta's horse, the three hurried back down the trail to where the other two horses were waiting for them.

BACK IN DENVER

Meanwhile, back at the Grey Falcon Inn in Denver, Beula Sterns and Loretta Monroe were about to embark upon the most surprising adventure of their lives.

After sitting for nearly an hour in tense silence, suddenly Loretta jumped up from the chair she was sitting in and walked across the room toward the door.

"This is the most ridiculous thing I've ever seen!" she

exclaimed. "Sitting here with a black lady staring at me and not saying a word! You don't have a gun. I'm not tied up. What am I sitting here for? I'm getting out of here!"

Slowly Beula rose, her intimidating presence filling the space between Loretta and the door.

"You got me in yo way, dat's why," she said. "I don' need no rope or no gun, 'cause you ain't gonna go no place, honey. So jus' sit yoself back down."

Foolishly Loretta tried to shove Beula aside. But she might as well have tried to budge a stubborn bull, for indeed Beula's girth was nearly as great as her stature. Her employer and guardian until earlier today may not have treated her with respect, but when he was on the trail, he liked to eat well and Beula saw to it that they both did, which was one of his primary reasons for keeping her. She could have matched her skills with any chef at any of the South's finest restaurants.

Temperamentally Loretta flailed at Beula with no more effect than her initial attempt. Finally Beula could help herself no longer and began laughing aloud.

"I tell you, chil'," she chuckled, "you ain't gonna git outta here nohow."

Now something occurred that neither woman had expected. Realizing the futility of her effort, Loretta shrank away, fell back a few steps, and slumped to the bed. And then, to her own amazement as much as Beula's, the poor girl began to cry.

Beula stood immovable, her years with Brother Joseph hardening her against emotion and making her suspicious of anything resembling pangs of convenient repentance. She stopped laughing and remained, arms crossed, feet still planted firmly on the floor, her thick eyebrows gathering together slightly in wary caution, waiting to see what would come of this latest ploy. One thing she was *not* going to do was leave the door unguarded and let the cunning little thing bolt past her.

In truth, however, Loretta's tears were not contrived. Something in the utter futility of her attack against Beula's large frame broke unexpectedly through the tough exterior she had been trying so hard to maintain. The tears came, and she could not prevent them. As she lay there, in rushed a tumult of hurtful memories and pent-up feelings and frustrations she had kept hidden for years. She was a young girl again, beating upon the chest of her father.

By degrees, the mother's instinct of the tired old heart of Beula Sterns began to revive. The recent years had not been kind to her, but they could not altogether extinguish the innate compassion with which the Creator endowed the heart of woman. Truly these two had been sent, each to work toward the salvation of the other, though neither yet knew it. For when any heart opens toward another of its kind, the door swings wide for selflessness to enter, and then salvation itself may not be far behind.

With tentative steps, Beula approached the bed, apprehensive, yet moved. She stretched out her arm and laid one of her large, hardworking hands gently upon Loretta's back.

Had Loretta paused to consider the implications, she might have flinched and drawn back from the touch, for never in all her twenty years, except an hour earlier when Beula had restrained her, had her fair white skin once touched that of a Negro. Her father had taught her not so much to despise the colored race but to fear it. Loretta, however, did not start at Beula's soft caress, only wept more freely.

Beula now eased herself down onto the edge of the bed at Loretta's side. If the girl was faking it, that was a chance she would have to take. But the soreness in her own soul vibrated with identification. She, too, knew the loneliness that came from the prostrate form on the bed, and her soul went out to the girl who only minutes before had been her enemy.

"Dere, dere," said Beula tenderly, stroking Loretta's back with the love of genuine womanhood, "everything's gonna be all right, chil'."

"Nothing's going to be all right," whimpered Loretta, her face buried in the pillow. "I'm caught and I can't get away, and I'll probably go to jail, all because of Ross. I hate him!"

"Hate's a fearsome word, chil'."

"I do hate him, I tell you!" sobbed Loretta. "It's been a nightmare ever since he took me in. I thought he was trying to help me! How could I have been such a nincompoop?"

She wept for another minute or two. Beula continued to stroke her back and hair, uttering soft and soothing motherisms.

Suddenly Loretta turned over on her back, sniffed a few times, and gazed up into Beula's compassionate face.

"I'm all alone," she moaned. "I've got no one but Ross. What am I going to do?"

Beula stretched her arms around the girl's shoulders and pulled her upward from the bed. The next instant Loretta threw her arms about this stranger who had shown her more love in two minutes than she had known in the last five years.

Beula drew her close, cradling Loretta, who began to weep again. Something very cold had begun to thaw within both hearts, and the ice of reticence and restraint now melted more rapidly in the light of their shared humanity than would have been possible under the warmth of ten suns. For there is no more powerful warming agent in all the universe than love.

Great warm tears now fell from Beula's eyes onto the top of Loretta's head. Neither considered how shocking some might have considered the scene, for they had altogether forgotten about the color of skin, and their weeping was without shame.

They remained on the edge of the bed, clutching one another for several minutes more as if their very lives depended on that embrace.

SURPRISING
FRIENDSHIP

Beula noticed Loretta stiffening. The young girl had wept in her arms like a child who had lost her kitten. But as the sobs subsided, the child grew up again.

Loretta sat back on the bed and wiped at her tears a few times.

"I didn't mean to do that," she said in an embarrassed

tone. "I'm sorry." She gazed down as if speaking to the floor at Beula's feet.

"Ain't nuthin' to be sorry 'bout, chil'. Cryin's good fo da soul. Here, you needs t' gib dat nose a good blow."

She handed Loretta a handkerchief. Loretta blew her nose, then tried to smile.

"What yo name, chil'? If you an' me's gonna be friends, we oughta know who we each is."

At last Loretta allowed her eyes to lift toward the black woman's face. She smiled again, the former quarrelsome antagonism fading from her countenance.

"My name's Loretta . . . Loretta Monroe," she said, already her voice sounding five years younger from the loss of its hard edge.

"Well, I'm Beula Sterns," said Beula, extending her large, rough hand. Loretta returned the gesture and found her tiny, white fingers swallowed entirely in Beula's grasp as the two shook hands. Beula closed her other hand over the back of Loretta's and gave it a squeeze.

"I haven't cried like that since I was a girl," said Loretta.

"Why in heaben's name not? You still be a girl, an' girls is supposed t' cry."

"Ross doesn't like it. He gets real mad if I cry."

"Who's dis Ross you keep talking 'bout? He yo man?"

"My cousin."

"What make him think he got da right t' tell you you can't cry?" asked Beula indignantly, already feeling the spirit of the mother bear rising up over this tender newfound little cub.

"He took me in when my ma died. I didn't have anywhere to go. That was six years ago. He's taken care of me ever since the funeral."

"Why him?"

"He said we was family and had to stick together. But he's not a good man." Loretta's voice began to tremble as she spoke. "Oh, Beula," she said, "I've been involved in all kinds of terrible things since. I can't stand to think of all he made me do." She turned away and began to cry again.

"Don' you worry 'bout showin' dem tears t' me, Loretta, chil'," said Beula. "Dat's what I's here for, t' help you get caught up on da cryin' you been missin' all dese years. So you jus' let dem tears come."

Loretta nodded.

"But why don' you leave dis here Ross," asked Beula, "if he's such a bad feller?"

Loretta sat straight on the bed in silence. She appeared to be searching deep into the recesses of her mind for a response. She had asked herself this same question dozens of times but had never yet found an answer.

Beula knew how to wait. Indeed, she had asked the same question of herself hundreds of times in regard to Brother Joseph and intuitively knew that perhaps there was no answer. As different as these two women appeared on the outside, they had in fact arrived in this hotel room together out of more similar circumstances than either could at present guess.

"I . . . I don't know, really," said Loretta at length. Her voice sounded more thoughtful and mature than it ever had before. "I always wanted to, I suppose," she went on, "especially after he made me start helping in his outlawin'. He didn't at the beginning, you know. At first he was decent enough to me. He and my older brother were real good friends. They did everything together. My folks sort of raised Ross as one of us, seein' as how his folks never came back."

"Neber came back from what?"

"They was goin' West on a wagon train."

"Why dat Ross stay wif you?"

"When it was time for the wagon train to move farther on, Ross was a mite sickly, so they left him with us. They said they'd come back for him or send word when they got settled. But we never heard nothin'."

"Kinda a low-down thing fo parents t' do," huffed Beula.

"Ross used to say it was just a trick to get rid of him. But I think my folks heard somethin' about a real bad blizzard that year in the direction they were going. I don't know. I was pretty little."

"But you still ain' tol' me why you was hooked up wif jus' him."

Loretta blew her nose on the handkerchief, turning over the edges and absently studying the torn edge of the fabric.

"I had nowhere to go, no money, hardly any clothes," she said. "My older brother had gone back to the East 'cause he wanted to study to be a preacher and wanted to go get some more schoolin'. Ross was pretty mad when Walt left. The idea of Walt preaching seemed so ridiculous to Ross that he took off, and we never saw him again. Not till the funeral, I mean. My father died the next year fallin' off a spooked horse."

Loretta's voice began to tremble again. She wiped once more at her nose and tried to steady herself with a breath or two before going on.

"After that my ma just sort of wasted away," she said. "I was only fourteen, and I did my best to help her. But with Pa and Walt and Ross all gone, we couldn't even keep the animals. And we lost touch with Walt. I don't know if he died or just stopped caring about us. Ma kept selling the

stock off until we didn't even have any horses left. Then she took sick and just died one day."

"Lan' sakes, chil'," said Beula, "dat's a sad story. I'm jus' sorry I wasn't dere t' gib you an' yo po ma a han'."

"I don't know how Ross found out," said Loretta, "but he showed up at the funeral and told me I was coming with him."

"An' you went?"

"Like I said, I had no place else to go. Nobody else had offered to take me in, and I didn't have any other kin that I knew of. He offered to take care of me, and so I went. I didn't know he'd been outlawin' since he left us."

"Was he good t' you, chil'?"

"He took care of me. Even though he was an outlaw, I couldn't hate him at first on account of that. By then I was still only fifteen and I didn't know what else to do. At least he kept other men away from me, and I was thankful for that."

"I reckon dat's somethin' all right."

"His partner was sweet on me, and as I got older he would have taken me if he could. But Ross wouldn't let him so much as touch me. I had to do all the cooking and women's work, he called it. I didn't mind too much at first. At least I had a place to be. It would have been all right, I reckon, except then he started making me help with the outlawin' a couple years ago."

"So you didn't leave 'cause you was stuck an' you didn't know *how* t' leave — that about it, chil'?"

"I suppose," Loretta said with a nod. "Where could I have gone?"

"Well, I reckon I understan', 'cause I been stuck like dat, too. But I ain' stuck no mo, an' maybe neither is you."

"What do you mean?"

"Jus' that maybe now you's *got* a place to go," stated Beula with firmness in her voice.

"But I *don't* have anyplace to go," repeated Loretta, tears beginning to fill her eyes. "I can't even get out of this room! And when this is all over, Ross'll find me, and it will all be the same again."

"Maybe now' da time fo you t' start a new life—you eber think o' dat? Wifout Ross an' da others."

"How am I going to start a new life? I don't have a cent to my name."

"I don' neither, chil', leastways no mo than I took when I lef'. Look at me, Loretta, chil'. What you see?"

"I don't know . . . just you," Loretta said with a shrug.

"What you see is all I got, too. I ain' got nuthin' neither. But I'm startin' me a new life—jus' today—thanks t' dat Mercy girl. I was jus' like you yesterday. I bin travelin' fo years wif a sort o' outlaw man, jus' like yo Ross, but his was a different kin' o' stealin'. I didn't like what he was doin'. But I had no place t' go neither, jus' like you said. But den dat Mercy girl, she jus' come along an' tol' me t' come wif her, an' here I is."

"But what does that have to do with—"

"She says she has a place fo me t' go. An' so I'll jus' tell her dat you's wif me an' you's comin', too."

"But I still don't see how . . ."

"We'll ask Sister Mercy. She'll know what to do."

"Sister Mercy?"

"Da young lady what put you in here wif me," laughed Beula. "She promised t' help me, so maybe she'll know how t' help you, too. She's a good an' brave young lady. She almost got caught in da same trap I was in, but she had da

good sense t' up an' leave when she saw what was
happenin'."

"Why do you call her Sister?"

"'Cause she used t' be a 'vangelist."

"What!" exclaimed Loretta, unable to bring the memory
of the lady who had drawn a gun on her an hour earlier and
the word *evangelist* together in the same place in her brain.
"That's the last thing I would have taken her for!"

"Well, dat's her."

"But how is she going to help you?"

"I don' know exactly, but she said I could come wif her."

"Well, I can't go with her. Besides, Ross'd come after me
and kill me if I left. When he gets riled or starts drinking, he
can get so angry."

"I tell you dat you an' me's makin' us a new life startin'
here an' now. We been leanin' on dem two no-goods all dis
time, but we don' gotta be no mo'."

"I'd be afraid."

"If we stay together-like, we don' need to be afraid o'
nobody."

FIRST FALTERING
PRAYERS

Now, after years of being an unwilling part of a religious

sham, a remnant of the dormant faith that resides in the

spirit of every man and woman arose in the heart of the old

black woman. The words that next came from her lips

would no doubt have caused Brother Joseph to laugh aloud

had he heard them even then, as he searched frantically up

and down the river for any trace of her. In reality, however, they were words to set angels singing.

"Maybe folks like you an' me's gotta start learnin' t' trust the Lord more'n we been in da habit o' doin', Loretta," said Beula.

Loretta said nothing, just sniffed a few times and dabbed at her nose.

"Lan' sakes," Beula went on, "I ain't no one t' be preachin' t' nobody after what I been watchin' in silence this many a year. But maybe I'm finally wakin' up t' what I been asleep to fo too blame long."

"What's that—what do you mean?" asked Loretta.

"Dat maybe ol' Joseph's lyin' and fibbin' don' change da fact dat God's still a body folks in a fix like us can go to an' ask t' help us."

"I don't know how to ask him for help."

"I don' know much 'bout it, neither."

"I've never prayed in my life, Beula."

"I reckon I prayed afore, but I don' know dat I eber meant it much since I was a young'un. Maybe it's time we bof learned how, 'cause I figure if eber a couple o' women needed somebody's help, it's us, an' dat time's now."

The room fell silent.

"I suppose you're right," said Loretta after a minute, "but if either of us is going to pray, it'll have to be you, because I don't have any idea what to say."

"I reckon you's right dere," rejoined Beula. "An' I reckon dat's fair 'cause I brought it up in da first place. So I reckon here goes afore my feet gets too cold."

She drew in a deep breath, bowed her head, and closed her eyes.

"Well, Lord," she began, "it's Beula Sterns talkin', though

I reckon you knows who I is already. I ain't been much in da way o' prayin' like I know I should. I reckon I been a heap blinded by Joseph's ways t' what you mighta wanted t' say jus' t' me, an' I'm sorry, Lord. I shouldna let somebody else keep me from what I oughta done mysel'. I don' know what I been thinkin'. But now eber since Sister Mercy came t' da wagon today, suddenly it's like my eyes is openin' an' I'm seein' again. So I thank you fo bringin' her back t' look fer me, an' fo carin' 'bout an' ol' slave woman dat nobody's cared much about all dese years, an' dat didn't show da poor girl much tenderness when she was wif us, God forgib me. But I inten' t' make it up t' her, Lord, if you'll gib me da chance. An' now me an' Loretta, we don' know what's gonna become o' us, but we's askin' fo yo help, Lord, 'cause we're pretty sure you love us even if dere ain't too many other folks dat do, an' we're gonna try t' listen t' you a mite better from now on."

Again there was silence.

"That was a beautiful prayer, Beula," said Loretta sincerely.

"You really think so?" Beula said with childlike pleasure.

"Yes . . . I mean it. It was beautiful."

Loretta took a deep breath. "Well, I suppose it's my turn now, though I can't help being a little afraid."

"Ain't nothing to be feared of, Loretta, chil'," said Beula.

"I suppose you're right. Well . . . I guess I'll try. God," she said, then stopped. "Oh, I forgot!" she added, bowing her head and closing her eyes. "God, I don't know how to pray, but I just want to tell you that I'd like your help, too. I'm not sure how you help people that are in trouble, but if ever someone was, it's me, and I don't know what to do. I'd like to ask you to help me get away from Ross and be able to start a new life, because I don't like livin' the way I've been. I don't know what I'm supposed to do, but if you'll show me, I'll do my best to do it. I don't know if I'll do it very well, because this is all new to me and I never thought about you before. But I'll try to learn if you'll help me. And like Beula prayed about Sister Mercy, I want to thank you for Beula, too, Lord, and that she showed me she cared about me."

She stopped, then glanced over to where Beula still sat with her eyes closed.

"Are you supposed to say *amen* when you're done?" Loretta asked.

Beula looked up at her.

"I reckon," she answered. "Most preachers I eber heard say it, and now dat I think o' it, I recollect my mammy endin' her prayers dat way, too."

"Well then, *amen*," said Loretta.

Both women let out sighs.

"Well, I reckon we done it," said Beula. "Dat prayer o' yours was beautiful, too."

"Thank you," said Loretta. "And I meant what I said . . . you know, about you."

"Thank you, chil', dat's one o' the nicest things anyone's eber said 'bout me in my whole life."

Beula drew in a deep breath and glanced around. "You know what?" she said. "I'm gettin' powerful hungry. You got an appetite, Loretta?"

"Now that you mention it, yes."

"Let's us go down t' da dinin' room an' git us somethin' t' put into these po stomachs o' ours."

"But . . . but I thought you said you didn't have any money."

"I don' have much, dat's fo sure, but I think I might have three or four dollars in my carpetbag. I didn't want t' leave Joseph's wagon wifout *somethin'*, so I helped myself t' a small portion o' his las' night's collection. God forgive me if dat's a sin, but I reckon dere ain't a much better way o' spendin' da Lord's money than feedin' a couple o' poor women what ain't had much t' eat all afternoon."

Beula started to chuckle. "Joseph don' know it, but I've known da combination t' his little safe fo years!"

44

PNEUMONIA

Prayers of a different kind rose as dusk descended
on the Bar S ranch that same Saturday several hundred
miles east. The Father hears and heeds all the entreaties of
his children, however diverse their requests. Even as angels
of protection were being sent to a hotel in Denver, angels of
healing were hastening toward the small bedroom of a ranch
in Kansas.

Almost immediately after Mercy's departure, Rachel had taken a turn for the worse.

What brought it on neither Zeke nor Jody could say, for she seemed for a time to have almost completely recovered. The revival of her spirits had enabled Mercy to leave her sister in Jody's capable care without anxiety for her welfare.

Now Rachel was back in bed, coughing badly and clearly weakening. Doc Haggerty had been summoned immediately and had unhesitatingly announced the unwelcome diagnosis.

Jody followed him out of the sickroom after his examination.

"Is it . . . ?"

"That's right, Mrs. Simmons—it's pneumonia all right."

Jody's face whitened as her hand went unconsciously to her mouth.

"I could hear the rattling in her lungs the minute I walked in," Haggerty added.

"I was afraid of that," sighed Jody. "She's been coughing blood."

"I expected as much. That's one sick young lady, Mrs. Simmons."

"I had hoped maybe there might be some other explanation."

"I'm afraid not. She's going to need a heap of care."

"What should I do?"

"I reckon you're doing most everything you can already. Don't prevent her coughing. It may sound like the very devil, but we gotta get her to cough up all that mess in her lungs."

"Can she eat?"

"She's gotta try. Get some food and liquid down her so that body of hers has the energy to fight off the infection."

"She doesn't keep anything down."

"You'll have to be persistent. Use some sugar water. Alternate that with good strong beef broth. Give her a teaspoon every ten minutes."

Jody sighed again. "I'll do my best, Doc," she said.

"I'll check back with you in the morning."

Zeke walked into the house about twenty minutes after Doc Haggerty's departure. Jody gave him a report on Rachel's condition.

"I reckon it's time we started praying a little harder," said Zeke. "The Lord must have something more he's wanting to do through this than we thought."

He sat down in the large sitting room. Jody joined him.

"Lord," Zeke prayed softly, "we place dear Rachel into your hands. Do with her and in her what you purpose. Heal her in body, soul, spirit, and heart. Accomplish your will, Father, in Rachel's life and in all the lives she touches."

The days following Doc Haggerty's visit were exhausting for Jody. Yet the natural mother within her knew instinctively how to care for this child who had become so unexpectedly her charge, and joy filled her heart to do so.

On the afternoon of the second day, a change seemed to come to Rachel's eyes, a new light of calm. Jody hoped it might indicate the breaking of the fever, yet placing her hand gently upon the girl's forehead produced only an involuntary shudder in the rancher's wife. Rachel's skin was as hot as ever.

Rachel's eyes opened at the touch. "Thank you for taking such good care of me," she said in a barely audible voice, casting a thin smile up from the middle of the pillow.

"You precious dear," replied Jody, struggling to keep away her tears.

"Would you bring me some paper . . . and a pen and ink?" whispered Rachel.

"Yes . . . but . . . you mustn't tire yourself," objected Jody.

"I need to write a letter."

"But I don't — "

"Please, Jody," implored Rachel.

At length Jody consented. How could she refuse the poor thing? She left the room and returned a few minutes later with the necessary supplies, which she set up on a bed tray Zeke had made for her. With several extra pillows, she managed to prop Rachel's limp frame into enough of a sitting position that she could reach everything.

The effort that followed was taxing, and Rachel could only keep at it for a few minutes at a time. As weak as she was, however, she was determined to complete the task.

45

TEARFUL NEWS

The letter that arrived a week later at the Louisville home of Sinclair and Ernestine Randolph had been eagerly watched for, but its content could not have been more unexpected.

Having two of their three children away from home and out of contact for what would soon be two weeks in itself signaled a great change for the banker and his wife. They knew that, for Rachel especially, these weeks could not help but be ones of great adventure. They did their best, therefore, to rejoice in the opportunity for their second daughter to safely spread her wings beyond their own nest, and they gave God thanks for the walls that had come down between them all prior to the girls' departure.

Yet this latter development only made the letter, when it came, all the more heart-wrenching to bear.

With trembling fingers and an eager smile, Mrs. Randolph tore at the edges of the envelope, anxious to hear how the trip had gone and how Rachel was faring at the ranch.

"Dear Mama and Daddy," she read,

> *I have had much time recently to lie here and think about many things. I cannot say it has been pleasant. Not only am I so weak and tired that sometimes I cannot stay awake, but now I also feel so badly about the wrong attitudes I have had toward both of you that the guilt I feel makes this time all the harder to bear.*
>
> *We encountered a dreadful storm on our way back to Jody's ranch — with terrible rain and even a tornado. I'm afraid I was neither as brave nor as strong as Mercy, for even by the time we got to their house I was becoming exhausted and sick, and now — though I wish I did not have to worry you by telling you this — I have been in bed ever since with pneumonia.*
>
> *I am sorry — please do not worry. I know I have already caused you so much trouble that I cannot stand the thought of adding to it. Yet that is why I am writing, so that you will know of my condition.*

Both the doctor and Jody put as brave a face on it as they can and say that I will soon be fine. But I can tell they are worried from the looks in their eyes and the hushed conversations I can hear in the next room when they think I am not listening. I am trying to be brave, too, like I know Mercy would, but I am not succeeding very well.

I am afraid. I am certain I am dying, for I am so very weak and I cough all the time, sometimes blood. This letter has taken me ever so long to finish, but I dare not let Jody help me with it or she will insist that I try to be more optimistic and not tell you such things. But if I am trying to face the truth about myself and what I have been, then I ought to be honest about the seriousness of this illness.

Long before now Ernestine Randolph's eyes were flowing with tears prompted by the full gamut of a mother's emotions.

If I am to die when I am only eighteen . . .

Mrs. Randolph went on—and at the words, a choking sob burst forth from her lips, though she nevertheless continued to read the words from her daughter's weakened hand . . .

I cannot do so without telling you again how sorry I am to have taken your love for granted as I have done. You have loved me as much as ever any father or mother could love a daughter, though I did not have eyes to see it because of thinking you cared more for Mercy and Thomas. I see now how wrong I was, though I fear it is too late. How I wish I

*had not been so foolish and could have seen your love sooner!
Please forgive me.*

*Now I wish I had never come to Kansas. Yet being away
from you makes my heart long for you as it never has before
in my life. Oh, I love you suddenly so very, very much, and
now I fear I may never see you again.*

*But please, do not worry about me. Though I am afraid,
I am at peace down inside because I have said these things to
you.*

Mama, Daddy – I do love you both. Good-bye.

Rachel.

"Oh, Sinclair, what are we going to do?" burst out Mrs.
Randolph.

Mr. Randolph, who had been reading Rachel's words as
he sat at his wife's side, was silent several moments. He, too,
was filled with many thoughts and feelings, which to even
try to express would have instantly turned his collar wet
with tears.

"My first impulse," he said at length, "is to tell you to
pack our bags while I ride down to the train station to buy
two tickets for Kansas. But Rachel is curiously silent about
Mercy. I think under the circumstances it may be prudent
to begin with a telegram to Mercy. If she confirms Rachel's
condition to be as serious as it sounds from the letter, then
we shall indeed be on the next train west."

RETURN

When Mercy, Jeremiah, and Jess galloped back into Denver that fateful Saturday, knowing nothing of Doc Haggerty's visit to the Simmons ranch, the sun was about to set on a long and eventful day.

Mercy dismounted in front of the inn and flew up the stairs to her room, concerned to have left Beula so long alone with her captive. When she ran into the room and found it empty, her first thought was that Loretta had escaped and Beula had gone back to the Tent of Meeting.

Slowly she turned back toward the stairs just as Jeremiah and Jess reached the landing.

"Why the long face?" asked Jeremiah.

"Beula's not there," answered Mercy. "I don't —"

"'Course I ain't, chil'," sounded a voice downstairs in the lobby. "How can I be in da room when I's down here?"

"Beula!" exclaimed Mercy. She bounded down the stairs faster than she had run up them. "I am so relieved to see you, I thought — well, never mind what I thought! But —"

All at once she saw Loretta standing patiently, though a little nervously, behind Beula. A look of confusion spread over Mercy's face.

"Don' worry, Mercy, honey," said Beula. "Loretta's wif us now. Her an' me's good frien's. We was in da dinin' room eatin' some dinner — not so good as I coulda made mysel', but we was too hungry t' complain — when we heard the three o' yous trampin' up dem stairs like a earthquake! Dat's when I came out here t' see what da fuss was, an' saw you standin' up dere."

"I . . . I don't understand any of this," laughed Mercy. "But I'm too relieved either to complain or to ask questions. You can tell me all about it later."

"I am sorry for trying to deceive you," said Loretta, stepping forward. "Hello, Jess," she added with an embarrassed expression, glancing toward him as Jess approached. "I suppose I owe you an apology, too. My name isn't Doretta but Loretta Monroe. I was mixed up with Ross Fletcher. He made me try to trick you into telling me where the jewels were."

Jess nodded. He had realized the truth long before now.

He felt too foolish for being taken in, however, to be angry with her.

"I am glad to see that you are all right, Mr. Eagleflight," Loretta said to Jeremiah. "I am so sorry."

"Well, I *am* all right," replied Jeremiah with a smile, "so don't mention it. By the way, Beula," he said, turning toward Beula and extending his hand, "it is good to see you again. Mercy's told me everything."

"I'm glad you's been takin' care o' her since I las' saw you, sir."

"No *sir* when you're talking to me, Beula—just *Jeremiah.* I for one am extremely hungry!" he added, glancing toward the dining room. "Your Mr. Fletcher, Loretta, did not feed me very well. What's on Boone's menu tonight?"

"A middlin' sort of chicken stew wif biscuits," remarked Beula with undisguised dissatisfaction.

"It sounds delicious!" said Jeremiah. "What do you two say to some supper?"

"It ain't delicious," rejoined Beula, "but it's food, if dat's what you's lookin' for."

"That's all I care about," said Jeremiah, leading the way back toward the dining room. Then he paused. "You all go on ahead," he said. "I'd better go over and tell the sheriff what we've done and where to find Fletcher, Stoner, and McLeod. Mercy, order me a big bowl of chicken stew, lots of biscuits, and a pot of the hottest, blackest coffee they can make!"

He turned and left the Grey Falcon while the others continued into the dining room.

Fifteen minutes later, Jeremiah returned and took a chair next to Mercy. She glanced up at him with a look of question.

"The sheriff's rounding up a posse to head out to the old mine tonight. He wants those three behind bars!"

"What should *we* do?" asked Mercy.

"I say we enjoy ourselves tonight," said Jeremiah, plunging his spoon into the steaming bowl in front of him, "and head back for Kansas in the morning."

There was one at the table who took in Jeremiah's words with something less than enthusiasm. Jeremiah was quick to notice it.

"You're coming with us, aren't you, Jess?"

"Aw, shoot, Jeremiah," Jess replied, "how can I show my face again at the Bar S after running off like I did? Zeke'll tan my hide."

"Don't you know Zeke better than that by now? Why, he'll walk up, shake your hand, look you square in the eye, and say, 'Welcome home, Jess, my boy—great to have you back!'"

"Yeah, I reckon he probably would at that. Zeke ain't exactly like other men."

"By the way, Jeremiah," said Mercy, "Loretta's coming with us."

Jeremiah looked up, spoon poised between bowl and mouth. He glanced first at Mercy, then at Loretta, then back to Mercy.

"It seems she has no place to go, just like Beula. I know Jody will take them both in."

"What about—?" Jeremiah did not complete his sentence.

"Did you tell the sheriff about me?" asked Loretta.

"Yeah, I did—told him we had you with us for now."

"What did he say?"

"Not a word. Didn't seem too concerned about it. He said there's no warrant on you specifically, that you're just listed as a companion to the gang for purposes of identifying them."

"But am I free to . . . just leave town?"

Jeremiah thought for a minute, then rose from the table. "I'll go back over and talk to him before he rides out and see what he says."

Jeremiah left the hotel a second time for the sheriff's office. He returned in less than ten minutes.

He sat down and resumed his meal. "The sheriff says that if you want to leave with us, that's fine with him."

"May I . . . do you suppose I could stay here, with you, tonight?" she asked, turning to Mercy.

"You be stayin' right in our room wif us," Beula answered for her.

"I have a room at the Rocky Mountain," she said, "but I'm afraid . . . that is, if Ross was to come looking for me —"

"He's going to be in jail by morning," said Jeremiah.

"I would still be afraid to stay there."

"We'll go get your things right after supper," said Mercy. "You'll spend the night with us, and we'll catch the train in the morning."

They continued to make plans as they finished their stew.

"You know, Jeremiah," said Mercy, "there is one more errand I have in Denver, that is, if we're not too late."

She explained. Everyone but Jess said they would accompany her.

REVIVAL OF
A DIFFERENT KIND

When Mercy and Jeremiah, along with Beula and

Loretta, approached the small church, the evening service

had just begun. From within they could hear the organ

pumping out the tune to one of Brother Joseph's favorites,

"Bringing in the Sheaves."

Presuming that he had returned to his wagon at some

time during the afternoon, by now Brother Joseph would

know Beula to be missing. It was doubtful, thought Mercy, that he would have divined the entire truth, but no small amount of anxiety, mingled with profound annoyance, must already have set in.

It had been the evangelist's hope to enlist the services of one or two attractive young assistants during this swing through Denver. He had hoped to begin the winter season of his fleecing operation in the more temperate climate of the Southwest. Thus far, however, no hopeful young missionary had ventured forward to answer the call. He had planned to leave town on the following day, after Sunday-morning services. Now Beula's disappearance had thrown doubt upon his plans.

The four entered through the rear door and settled inconspicuously near the back while Brother Joseph's head was turned briefly giving instructions to the church organist. Their entrance was not so inconspicuous, however, that a number of congregational heads did not turn. For this was one of those revival services, sadly more the norm than not, in which most of those in attendance were members of the sponsoring church. The sight of a single stranger entering their midst, therefore, immediately roused the hope that such was a prospective "unbeliever" who might answer the call at the end of the service. For four strangers to walk in together was unheard of. Perhaps, thought one or two, revival would visit Bethel Baptist Church after all!

When Brother Joseph turned again to face the congregation, he spotted Beula immediately. How could anyone miss her in the midst of the sea of white faces? She sat stoically staring straight ahead. The reverend gave no external indication of discomfort or recognition, however, and continued leading the next verse of the song, inwardly fuming at

Beula's presumption in coming here. He did not know the faces of the congregation well enough to realize she had been accompanied into the church by the others beside her, and was too distracted by his anger to recognize any of them.

The service proceeded. Announcements and various Scriptures and prayers and preliminaries followed from the church's pastor, who then announced Brother Joseph with accompanying fanfare. Rev. Mertree strode to the pulpit with even more confidence than usual to counter his continued anxiety over what Beula's game might be. Perhaps she had merely come to watch, he had told himself a dozen times as he sat in the front row awaiting his introduction. Yet his suspicious instinct whispered otherwise. He tried to convince himself that she could not possibly know a thing about his two plants in the audience. Even if she did, she would not *dare* to speak up.

The Reverend Brother Joseph Mertree preached with something less than his usual eloquence to be sure, yet sufficient eloquence to arouse once again the tearful spirit of confession and repentance on the part of two gentlemen who were, like the four in the next to last row, strangers to Bethel Baptist.

When congregational *Hallelujah*s and *Praise the Lord*s and *Amen*s had subsided, Brother Joseph again addressed the flock.

"It is this which you see before you this evening, my friends," he said, "which we who take the gospel into the far reaches of this land are privileged to witness in town after town across the prairie, in the West, in the Midwest, in the South, on the plains and deserts, in the mountains, in valleys. Wherever men and women gather, hungry souls await the gospel. This is why I feel that the Lord has led me here to

Denver, and to Bethel Baptist, to send out the invitation once again to join me in spreading and expanding this harvest of eternal life. The generosity of your tithes and offerings, as I have told you, will accomplish mighty things for God's work, sending forth workers unto the fields, and planting churches in needy communities throughout the West. Yet as much as your generous donations, ladies and gentlemen, we need workers to labor in the vineyards that they might reap with me what we have sown. Again I urge you young people to prayerfully search your hearts to see if one among you, capable of playing the organ and leading singing, might be one whom God is calling even now. Do not delay if the Lord is speaking to your heart. Take courage from these two men who have repented this night before us all. Come, join my evangelistic team that the —"

He paused in midsentence, his eyes lighting up as his face broke into a smile.

"Ah, yes!" he exclaimed. "I see there is a young lady among you whose heart the Holy Ghost has touched."

He stepped down from behind the pulpit, hand outstretched, to greet the young woman now proceeding down the aisle from the rear of the church.

"Bless you . . . bless you, my dear!" he said with enthusiasm, striding toward her.

Suddenly a familiarity in the face rose before him. His step faltered, though many years of acting enabled him to hold the smile upon his lips for a few seconds longer.

Where had he . . . ? But it couldn't . . . What was she —?

At last his face displayed dawning recognition. The glow left his eyes and was replaced by momentary confusion. He remembered Mercy's disappearance well, and now she had returned.

That was it! And now Beula had found her and brought her to the service that she might rejoin them!

The smile again broke across his lips. The two met in the middle of the church and clasped hands.

"Sister Mercy!" he exclaimed. "How wonderful it is to see you again! You don't know how worried dear Beula and I have been about you."

He turned ebulliently first toward the one side of the congregation then the other with an expansive gesture of his arm. "This is one of my former colleagues and assistants," he said in a triumphant tone, "Sister Mercy. She was lost from me some time ago, and I have been praying ever since for her safe return. It would seem the Lord has seen fit to answer my prayers in your very midst! She has come to answer the call once again and rejoin in the evangelistic effort."

A few scattered *Praise the Lord*s and *Hallelujah*s followed.

"Perhaps, Brother Joseph," said Mercy, loudly enough so that the congregation could hear, "I might be permitted a few moments to tell the congregation of my experiences while traveling with you, so that others might be encouraged to respond appropriately."

"I think, Sister Mercy, that —"

"Please, Brother Joseph," said Mercy, loudly enough to be heard by everyone, "it was such a memorable time in my life, and one of such profound revelations, that I genuinely feel these people will benefit from what I have to share with them."

"Yes, brother," put in the pastor of Bethel Baptist. "We would dearly love to hear a firsthand account."

"Ah . . . yes, well, *ahem*," faltered Brother Joseph, clearing his throat, "then I, uh . . . see no reason why I should object," he added with a smile. Having all this time convinced himself that Mercy had simply gotten lost in the town, and with no idea that she had witnessed his duplicity, the good reverend still had no premonition of what was coming. Reluctantly, yet still doing his best to keep up a smiling appearance, he took a seat toward the rear of the church, while Mercy continued up the aisle to the front.

"I had the privilege," Mercy began, "of traveling through Missouri and Kansas with Brother Joseph. I played the organ and led singing and passed out leaflets in the towns through which we passed, inviting all to attend our services. I had grown up in a Christian home, perhaps like many of you here this evening. But nothing in my Christian upbringing prepared me for what I would see and hear during that time."

She paused and let her eyes rest a moment on Brother Joseph, who sat smiling smugly. He had been involved in this charade for so long that even he was occasionally duped by it.

"It was in a little Kansas town by the name of Sweetriver where my most profound revelation came," she went on, still gazing straight toward him. "We had just concluded a series of three meetings, which to all appearances were highly successful. Much money was raised, and many were the tearful conversions witnessed by one and all. Imagine my surprise, therefore, when, while out walking in the town early on the morning prior to our departure, I should overhear Brother Joseph and two of the men whose repentance had been most dramatic—"

Again Mercy paused. The face of her former colleague and employer was ashen, for at last he had begun to realize exactly *why* Mercy had not continued on with them beyond

Sweetriver. His once-confident form was beginning to slip down in his chair. He was suddenly conscious of the discomfort of a few eyes beginning to rest upon him.

"But why should I tell you?" she continued. "Perhaps these two men who have confessed *their* sin among you here this evening . . . no doubt *they* could tell you far better than I of the prior financial arrangements between themselves and the good Brother Mertree."

Every eye in the church now turned toward where the two men sat in the second row. Neither had bargained for anything like this, and both continued to sit immovable for a few seconds.

"What do you gentlemen have to say for yourselves?" asked Mercy.

"Uh . . . *praise the Lord?*" replied one in the tentative tone of question, as if he hoped such a reply might suffice.

"I meant," said Mercy, "would you like to share with the congregation how much Brother Joseph paid you to come here tonight and do what you have done?"

A hushed gasp of astonishment went around the church. All eyes spun around toward where Rev. Mertree had been sitting only moments earlier. But the chair was empty.

Perceiving how badly things had turned against him, the evangelist had slipped down from his chair, which was next to the aisle, and had crawled on all fours to the door, managing in the dim light of the evening service to get out of the place unseen.

Even as the faithful of Bethel Baptist now proceeded to question the two converts more closely, the not-so-reverend Joseph Mertree was running as fast as his legs would carry him back to his traveling Tent of Meeting and Healing to hitch up his two horses as best he could in the darkness and make good his departure from Denver during the middle of Saturday night.

Beula and Mercy could remain behind if they wanted, and good riddance. They had never had it so good as while traveling with him, and one day they would both regret making sport of him.

In the meantime, he had better make haste before the sheriff could be notified.

OUT OF
DENVER

A knock came to Eagleflight's door at the Grey Falcon.

Then a second. A loud knock.

"Eagleflight . . . hey, Eagleflight!" said an importunate

voice on the other side.

Jeremiah rolled over in his bed. It was pitch-black. It was

probably two or three in the morning.

Slowly he rose and went to the door. He opened it a crack. There stood the sheriff.

"Sorry to disturb you, Eagleflight," he said, "but I figured you'd want to know."

"Yeah . . . what?" said Jeremiah, opening the door the rest of the way.

"Fletcher and the others—they was gone when we got there. Not a trace. You must not have tied 'em up too good."

"What is it, Jeremiah?" called out Jess groggily.

"They escaped," replied Jeremiah over his shoulder into the room. "No . . . no, Sheriff," he said, turning back to the sheriff, "can't say as we spent a whole lot of time at it. We were just trying to get out of there as fast as we could."

"Well, you might ought to have done a little better job, 'cause they're gone now. And knowing you got their gal, that Loretta you was telling me about, and knowing the kind of varmints they are, I thought you ought to know. I figured you might want to get out of town."

Jeremiah sighed.

"Hmm . . . yeah—I see what you mean," he said, rubbing the sleep out of his eyes. "But you'll be watching for them?"

"'Course," replied the sheriff. "But me and my deputies can't be everywhere every minute. And you gotta figure they know where you are since they was watching your friend Forbes even before you showed up. It's up to you, of course, but if I was in your shoes, I wouldn't want to stick around."

"Yeah," Jeremiah said with a nod. "All right, Sheriff— thanks."

The sheriff turned and left, and Jeremiah went back inside.

"Get up, Jess," he said.

"What for?"

"We're not waiting for the train," replied Jeremiah, pulling on his breeches. "We're getting out of Denver tonight — right now. I'll go wake Mercy and the other two."

He left the room in his stocking feet while Jess crawled from his bed and did his best to dress in the darkness.

The knock on their door, coming as it did in the middle of such a black night and a deep sleep, startled Mercy even more than it had Jeremiah. She nearly leapt out of bed in fright, grabbed her robe, and crept to the door on tiptoe, heart pounding.

The knock came again.

"Who is it?" she whispered.

"Mercy . . . it's Jeremiah."

She opened the door an inch or two, letting out a deep breath of relief to see his face.

"Mercy, we've got to leave the hotel . . . now. Fletcher and the others escaped. The sheriff just warned me. He's afraid we could be in danger."

"I'll wake the others," she replied, instantly alert. "But, Jeremiah," she added, "what are we going to do?"

"That I'm not quite sure of yet. All I know is that we've got to get out of the Grey Falcon. They know where we've been staying."

Mercy shut the door, lit the lamp, and woke Beula and Loretta, and all three began to dress and gather up their few belongings. In the meantime, after thinking a minute or two, Jeremiah descended the stairs and went to wake Boone.

Jeremiah had no more explained their predicament to the owner of the hotel, than his friend was buttoning his breeches and pulling on his boots.

"If we wait around for the train in the morning," he was saying, "I'm afraid it may be too late."

"I think you're right," replied Boone. "The eastbound doesn't pull out of here till ten-forty, and they'd be watching the station as well as the hotel."

He fell silent, obviously thinking.

"I'll take you all out of Denver by wagon," he said after a minute. "You can catch the train down the line."

"You can't leave the city," protested Jeremiah. "What about the hotel?"

"I've got people who'll take care of things for a day or two. It's the safest way. Besides, if they do track you down, you'll need an extra gun. With you and me and Jess, at least it'll be a fair fight."

"Where do you suggest we go?"

"Wherever I can get you onto the train. Probably Limon, that's the next stop—hundred miles from here."

"We'll never make that by the time the train gets there."

"I'm thinking of Monday's train. But why're we standing here talking? We gotta get you out of town."

Boone rose, grabbed up his coat, and headed for the door. "I'll be out back hitching up the team," he said. "Go get your people ready. Then come down and help me with the horses. But tell the women it's going to be a bumpy ride. I got no other way to move five people than my old freight wagon."

Both men left Boone's room.

An hour later, Jeremiah Eagleflight, Mercy Randolph, Jess Forbes, Beula Sterns, and Loretta Monroe sat huddled in coats and blankets in the back of Hank Boone's wagon, rumbling slowly along the wide eastbound dirt road out of Denver.

A more incongruous assortment of individuals it would

have been difficult to imagine—two card-playing drifters, an erstwhile woman evangelist, a former black slave, a female train robber, and the proprietor of a Denver hotel. Yet here they all were, allies bound together in a single cause—to get Boone's five passengers on a train for Kansas before Loretta's cousin and the rest of the Medicine Bow Gang could find them.

As for the latter two women, they were leaving behind not only the city of Denver but also everything their lives had been up till that moment. Each had a change or two of clothes and a few assorted odds and ends, comprising the whole of their worldly possessions. What was to become of them, neither had an idea. But Loretta trusted Beula, Beula trusted Mercy, Mercy trusted Jeremiah and Jody and Zeke, and *all* of them were learning—in unique ways and according to different timetables—to trust that God would take care of them. To accomplish this end, the Almighty had thrust them together in this manner. They all sat in the early-morning chill, bound together as one, while at the same time they sat silent and alone with their own thoughts and prayers. . . .

The night was still black, though a quarter moon gave Boone's two faithful horses just enough light to see their way. It was approximately three-forty in the morning as they left the last building of Denver behind them.

Cradled against Jeremiah's shoulder and with his arm snugly around her, though she was cold and the ride uncomfortable, Mercy thought she had never been so contented in all her life.

Gradually the women dozed. Two hours later it was still dark. There was no sound other than the rhythmic *clop-clop-clop* of the eight shod hooves over the hard-packed dirt road.

In another hour the gray light of dawn began to spread over the flat plain east of Denver. They had only covered eight or ten miles, but they were well enough out of Denver to feel safe for a while. They would have to increase their pace as the day progressed if they hoped to make Limon by the time Monday's train from Denver arrived. But for now it was enough that they were moving steadily.

A FAMILIAR SIGHT

Late Sunday afternoon, as the sun began its descent

toward the Rockies behind them, Boone and Eagleflight

were discussing where to make camp for the night. They

had seen Sunday's train pass in the distance late in the

morning. The sight had prompted a quickening of the horses'

walk as a result of the increased activity of Boone's reins.

But they had only covered some half of the distance to

Limon and needed to get another fifteen or twenty miles today before stopping.

The sun was just setting about an hour and a half later when Jeremiah, who was then directing the team, spotted something in the distance.

"Whoa," he said, reining in the team.

"What is it?" asked Jess from the back.

"I don't know," replied Jeremiah. "There's something up ahead. Looks like a campfire and a wagon of some kind. Maybe one of us ought to go on up on foot and take a look. What do you think, Boone?"

By now all the weary travelers were looking forward. Beula had risen to her feet to stretch her legs and now gazed in the direction Jeremiah had indicated, hand over her eyes even though the sun was at her back.

Gradually she began to chuckle, then laugh aloud.

"What is it, Beula?" asked Mercy.

"I don' know whether t' be riled or whether t' laugh," she said.

"Do you see something?" asked Jeremiah.

"Dat I do. . . . Dat I do indeed," she said. "An' if you can trust me, Jeremiah Eagleflight, I can tell you dat you can go ahead an' keep right on goin'. 'Cause right up dere ahead's da Lord's provision fo our supper!" She began laughing again.

"I don't know what you're talking about," said Jeremiah with a smile. "But I'm too tired and too hungry to argue, so I'll trust you, like you say. Sit down, everyone. He-yah!" he cried to the horses, flicking the reins.

Again the wagon jerked into motion. But now all the others except Beula were so curious that they kept their

eyes peeled as they gradually approached the strange camp-
site Jeremiah had seen in the distance.

"You know . . . ," said Jeremiah after another few minutes,
"unless my eyes are mistaken . . ."

"It is . . . it's him!" exclaimed Mercy suddenly, knowing
what Jeremiah was thinking.

"It's what?" said Jess. "I still see nothing but a wagon."

"But a very special kin' ob wagon!" laughed Beula.

"It's Brother Joseph!" said Mercy, now fighting between
a rekindling of her anger and the humor of what was bound
to be a very awkward encounter for the good reverend.

Jeremiah continued on, leading the horses straight into
the camp of the fleeing Tent of Meeting and Healing.

He reined in the horses, jumped down, and strode forward
to where Rev. Mertree stood.

"Good evening, kind sir," he said. "I have with me a wagon
of weary pilgrims." He gestured behind him, though most of
his entourage was seated and yet out of sight. "Do you suppose we might impose upon your hospitality for supper?"

"I, uh . . . I don't—" Brother Joseph hesitated, somehow
recognizing the fellow but momentarily taken off his guard.

Beula and Mercy now stood up in the back of the wagon.
Brother Joseph's face turned pale.

"Ain't no need t' ask his permission," said Beula, climbing
down now and walking forward. "I've been da cook for dis
Healing Tent more years than I like t' think. I know where
all da fixin's are. Evenin', Joseph," she said to her former
boss. "You won' min' if I put us together some vittles?"

Under the circumstances, Brother Joseph could hardly
argue, seeing he was so thoroughly outnumbered. And in
truth, he was starving himself, and one of Beula's meals
sounded better than he was likely to admit.

An hour later, the seven itinerants were seated around the campfire enjoying a stew the likes of which none had expected in this wilderness. Two rabbits that Jeremiah and Jess had shot provided the meat, and Beula's deft hands provided the rest.

They would camp around Brother Joseph's fire for the night and set out the rest of the way for Limon an hour before daybreak.

BACK AT
THE RANCH

Mercy and Eagleflight and their companions from
Denver arrived back at the Bar S without further incident,

neither seeing nor hearing anything from the Medicine Bow

Gang. For most of the journey, by train and by stage, Jess

had avoided the looks of both Loretta and Mercy. He'd been

pulled out of many a scrape by Jeremiah, but he wasn't

used to being rescued from his schemes by women.

Subdued by fatigue, all five had been content to sit and watch the Colorado and Kansas plains go by, and the trip had passed in relative silence.

Jody's reception of the two pilgrim women could not have been warmer or more full of genuine love. As Loretta and Beula lay down in their beds the night of their arrival, sharing a hastily tidied and assembled room on the second floor of the ranch house, both experienced a sense of homeyness they hadn't felt in years.

Beula was downstairs bright and early the next morning, bustling about the kitchen even before Jody made her appearance.

"If I'm gonna partake ob yo hospitality, Miz Jody," she said in reply to Jody's protests, "den da least you can do is let me do 'bout da only thing I knows how t' do."

And when the men began to exclaim over the biscuits and ham gravy, Jody could not help laughing. It was already clear enough that Beula's home would be in the kitchen for as long as she was with them. Within a week Jody declared that she couldn't imagine how she had managed all this time without her.

Mercy immediately took Jody's place nursing Rachel back to health. The fever had broken almost the hour her letter had left for Sweetriver with one of the men. Upon receipt of her father's frantic telegram a few days later, Rachel had hastily asked Jody to go into town to wire back a reassuring message to her parents. And now with Mercy back, the recovery grew even more rapid. Mercy wrote a long letter home the day following their return.

Jess was welcomed back among Zeke's hands as if he had done no more than ride into Sweetriver for the afternoon. Almost exactly as Jeremiah had predicted, the rancher's first words to him, accompanied by a great slap on the back, were, "Welcome back, Jess—good to have you home, son!" The next afternoon he was out working alongside Bart Wood, and never enjoyed strenuous, honest labor so much.

Their first evening back, Mercy and Jody rose and began clearing away the supper things. Instantly Beula jumped to her feet, the right of servanthood already beginning to assert itself, and proceeded to chase them out of the kitchen.

"You ladies go spen' time wif yo menfolk," she said, shooing them away as if they were children. "Loretta an' me can do jus' fine in here wif da cleanin' up."

Mercy sought out Jeremiah. He and Jess and Zeke were standing outside, each with a cup of hot coffee in his hands, gazing out over the prairie, where a chilly mist was beginning to form faintly over the moist ground. Jeremiah saw her and eased away from the other two. He and Mercy walked away toward the large oak. It was the first quiet time alone they had enjoyed together since Denver.

"Did I ever thank you for coming to rescue me?" asked Jeremiah with a grin.

"I don't know," replied Mercy with a contented smile. "I think you may have. But having you safe again is all the thanks I need."

"You are some kind of brave young lady, you know."

"I didn't really think about it. When I didn't hear from you, I just went looking. You were in trouble, and it all just sort of happened," laughed Mercy.

"Things like that don't just happen. You made it happen. I gotta say, you made me awfully proud."

Mercy slipped her hand gently through Jeremiah's elbow as they walked, leaning her head against the side of his arm.

"I need to think about returning to Louisville with

Rachel," she said after a minute or two, "as soon, that is, as Doc Haggerty gives his assurance that her lungs are clear."

Jeremiah nodded. "Zeke told me what the doc said. A winter out here would be the worst thing for her lungs. The winds on the prairie can bite right through to your bone."

"But I don't want to leave you again," said Mercy. "The last time I left, you went and got yourself kidnapped!"

Jeremiah let out a delighted laugh.

"I mean it," said Mercy, trying to sound serious. "I wouldn't want anything like that to happen again."

Jeremiah stretched his arm around her and gave her a squeeze. "Don't you worry about me," he said. "I doubt anybody ever got kidnapped more than once in his life."

"You *will* come to Louisville for Christmas?" Mercy asked.

"Ain't a thing that could keep me away!"

They reached the giant oak. Jeremiah placed his hand on the trunk, reminded of the prayer he had once prayed in this very spot.

"Something's on your mind, I can tell," said Mercy.

Jeremiah smiled as he leaned back against the tree.

"I was just thinking of a conversation I had with Zeke when you were in Louisville."

"Tell me about it."

"It was about trees . . . and growth," said Jeremiah thoughtfully.

He paused, snatches of the conversation darting through his brain.

"Did you know," he said after a moment, "that Zeke planted this tree himself—from a tiny seedling?"

"No, I would never have imagined," replied Mercy. "Just look at it now!"

They continued to talk quietly and happily at the foot of the great prayer oak until well past nightfall.

><del>·</del><del>·</del><del>·</del>○<del>·</del><del>·</del><del>·</del><

Only Loretta felt shyly out of place at the ranch. Indeed, how could she not? She had never even known, much less lived among, real Christians before in her life. Being treated with courtesy and respect, especially by men who were gentle and kind to her and didn't swear—that was hard enough to get used to. But to be taken in and actually made like one of the family—that was altogether more than she knew how to handle. The poor girl spent at least some portion of every day for two weeks quietly fighting back tears. But the healing had begun, and the tears served to wash clean many places within her, places that the love of her new friends would in time fill with a reborn sense of worth and personal value.

Loretta followed Beula around like a faithful puppy. Beula's naturally bubbly spirit and inborn sense of service blossomed rapidly from the love she felt in the Simmons home. And thus she possessed an abundant supply of smiles and good cheer to shower on her new young friend.

In time, as Rachel improved, Loretta could be found more and more in the sick room. It began at first as simple ministry, Loretta seeking to give to another in the same way she felt everyone was giving to her.

Mercy noticed the movement of Loretta's heart toward Rachel and gradually withdrew. Very quickly the two girls became as sisters themselves, which could not have pleased Mercy more.

Winter was coming to the prairie of Kansas. The land

browned, the leaves fell, the air grew cold, the winds crisped up, and more rain and snow came.

Mercy and Rachel returned to Louisville, leaving a certain quiet emptiness behind them for a week. For was not Mercy the reason that the Bar S family had grown as it had? And was she not therefore herself, without realizing it, the heart and energy and sinew connecting the many varied relationships represented?

MEMORIES

The sun had not yet peeked over the horizon. But the roosters knew that the light was coming and had already begun their screeching attempts to coax it out more quickly.

Beula Sterns lay in her bed, listening to the sounds of the early morning.

"You crazy ol' birds," she said. "You neber stop lookin'

ahead. No matter what happens, you always lookin' t' da
nex' day."

She stopped and thought to herself.

*Time was when I couldn't wait for da nex' day t' come. Goodness,
but dat were a long time ago! I used t' hear dem ol' yard birds every
mornin', an' already hab da whole day planned out.*

Beula sat up in bed and shook herself awake. As her feet
touched the floor she quickly lifted them up again.

"Lan' sakes! Dat floor's cold! I better go git dem fires
goin'!" she exclaimed under her breath. Yet even the basic
need for warmth could not chase away thoughts of the past
that had intruded into her consciousness with the calls from
the throats of Jody's roosters.

Old Beula could not have analyzed it had she tried. But
cold feet notwithstanding, her whole being was warming
from the inside out. As it did, she was herself, without knowing it, giving warmth to all those around her in far greater
ways than merely by the fires she kept going as winter
slowly gripped the plains.

The warming had begun when Mercy had taken her from
Brother Joseph's wagon. More ice had melted when she
had likewise helped Loretta escape. But the greatest change
of all had come upon her arrival to this home. She had been
more than a little afraid at first. Mercy had assured her that
her friends were different from most people. But how could
she believe it, never having met the likes of Zeke and Jody
Simmons?

But how right Mercy had been!

Was it possible that two strangers could make her feel so
welcome? And now, just a few short weeks later, Beula had
a little room of her own, with her very own bed. Spread
over the top of it lay one of Jody's bright-colored quilts,

which brought back memories of a home far away and times long passed.

Every day it seemed that more and more of the past gently stole into Beula's consciousness. Not the recent unpleasant era of dependency on Brother Joseph, but the old times of childhood and adolescence, with warm, sunny smiles and forgotten melodies and happy thoughts. These had been long buried with the pain of remembering. But now that the present contained happiness again, it no longer hurt to remember joyous days of the past.

She could not keep the newfound warmth of her nature from spilling out. She was happy in Jody's kitchen with people to watch over and cook for! And now that life had purpose, the faith of her fathers also began to return. Unconsciously she began to hum the old spirituals, Scriptures she hadn't thought of in years came to mind, and with them returned deep faith in a good God who looked after his children.

"What a silly ol' woman!" she scolded herself. "Here I sit jus' reminiscin' when I got me folk t' take care ob."

Beula stood, dressed herself quickly, and hurried downstairs to stoke both fires, shuffling along with marvelous silence considering the bulk of her frame—she would wake no one if she could help it. Entering the large sitting room, she saw the evidences scattered about of several projects Jody had been busy with the night before. The rancher's wife had just that afternoon asked Zeke to bring out the boxes of Christmas decorations, and had spent the evening cleaning and sorting through them and making plans for the season.

"My, my!" Beula exclaimed under her breath, gazing about the room. "I almost done forgot about Christmas!"

She stood as one transfixed for several moments. And now the warming of personhood within her had nearly completed its work, for warm tears began to stream down her fleshy brown cheeks.

Thank you, good Lord, fo dese dear folks, she prayed silently. *Hep me t' gib back jus' a little ob what dey done fo me. An' hep me, Lord, t' gib back t' you, too. All dese years I done forgot 'bout you more'n I should hab. I'm sorry, Lord. I don' know what coulda made me get so blame thickheaded. Eben Joseph shouldna been able t' do dat to a body like me. But I won' forget you agin, Lord. Dis is Christmas, da time fo us t' be rememberin' you, an' I promise I will, Lord, better from now on.*

She moved over to the big stone fireplace, knelt down, inspected the state of the coals, added a few dry sticks, blew at them rather than making use of Zeke's hand bellows, and within a minute had succeeded in producing a healthy blaze to which she added several fresh logs. Her brain had not been inactive as she stoked the fire. For now as she stood, eyeing the flames with satisfaction, a great smile spread across her face.

"An' what's Christmas," she said to herself, "wifout a thick, gooey, southern pecan pie!"

A wide smile on her lips, she now made her way to the kitchen to rekindle the embers in its great cast-iron stove.

BEULA'S PLANS

After breakfast that same morning, Beula nabbed Bart
as he stepped outside on his way back to the bunkhouse.

"Bart Wood," she said. "I'm needin' a ride t' town. How
'bout you dribin' me?"

Bart stopped and turned. "Zeke's goin' in tomorrow,"
he replied.

"I know dat," rejoined Beula. "Miz Jody, she says Zeke

can git me whateber I need. But I got me private businez an' I gotta go today."

Bart stood momentarily uncertain.

"I got me *kitchen* businez," Beula added with a sly smile, "an' if you hep me an' keep yo mouth shut, dere jus' might be somethin' extra in it fo you when I's done."

Bart possessed enough of a man's appetite to have a general idea what Beula was hinting at, and he required no further convincing. His lips parted into a grin of his own. The two of them were on their way into Sweetriver within the hour.

Bart pulled up in front of the general store and said he'd wait in the wagon.

"I don' want nobody waitin' for me," replied Beula, climbing down. "I got me some long-forgotten businez t' ten' to, and I want t' take my time. So you jus' go on an' do some man businez ob yo own, an' I'll jus' see you in a couple hours."

Bart complied, taking no offense at the good lady's abrupt words. All the Bar S hands had taken such a liking to their new cook that almost nothing she would have done could upset them. Nor was their affection a result of Beula's cooking alone. Jody's observations to Mercy about the men were accurate enough. Most had no family, and though it took some skill to keep from showing it, they all felt a strange sort of comfort in the bossy mothering that came their way from Beula. Jack Rice, too, was old enough to remember his own upbringing in Mississippi before the war, and Beula reminded him of the mammy who kept the household together when his own father was a hired hand.

The Bar S cook, known by this time to every man,

woman, and child in Sweetriver, made her way into the
general store. She marched straight to the counter.

"Billy," she announced, "I want me some good southern
pecans—a couple poun's oughta do it—an' two jars ob dark
sorghum syrup."

The young lad behind the counter offered no word of
reply. He turned and went in search of the items. A moment
later his father emerged from the back room.

"Ah, Beula—good morning!" he said. "How are you
today?"

"Jus' real fine, Mr. Wingate—an' yoself?"

"Pretty well—cold enough for you?"

"Christmas be on da way," replied Beula, "an' I reckon a
body's gotta put up wif da cold if dere's gonna be a Christmas
in da year."

Billy returned to the counter with the two jars, then set
about in search of a canvas bag, which he began to fill with
the unshelled pecans.

"Shall I put these things on Mrs. Simmons' account?"
asked Mr. Wingate.

"No sirree—no," said Beula. "Dis all be my own businez,
an' not a word ob it t' nobody from either ob you!"

"I understand," replied the shopkeeper as Beula dug out
a few coins from some concealed pocket about her person.
She laid them upon the counter as if they represented a vast
fortune—as indeed they did, for she had brought with her
into town every cent she possessed.

Beula, in truth, had taken very little of Brother Joseph's
money. His little safe had contained easily thirty or forty
dollars at the time she had opened it, and she had availed
herself of little more than a tenth of its contents. She
wanted no more than enough to safeguard her against

emergency, nor would she have taken it all had he offered her the entire sum. That was not the kind of money she wanted. She was no thief.

Till this moment she had spent nothing of it but the seventy-five cents she had contributed to the alleviation of her and Loretta's hunger back in Denver. Now, with the pecans and sorghum taken care of, she quickly took stock of the remaining coins in her hand. Her dwindling fortune was hardly sizeable, but it was sufficient to give her more inward joy than she had ever experienced shopping before in her life. For Mr. Wingate's general store now became the site of a Christmas shopping spree that, if surpassed by others in total expenditure, had certainly never been matched in size of heart. Not a penny did Beula spend upon herself as she pored over every shelf, discovering now this, now that small gift she thought Loretta or Zeke or Dirk or Clancy or one of the other men, and especially Jody, would enjoy. Never more regally did a queen reign over the imagined happiness of her subjects than did Beula Sterns that morning as for more than an hour she made her way among Mr. Wingate's crowded shelves and aisles, until at last she computed that her fortune exactly equalled the value of items waiting upon his counter.

How rich she felt to be able to spend her *own* money on those she loved!

When Bart returned, he found Beula standing outside the store waiting, a large bundle in each arm, a small wooden box at her feet, and smiling from ear to ear.

He reined in the horses and jumped down to help her with her packages. But she was already headed toward the wagon. Bart moved toward the box sitting on the boardwalk.

"I'll fetch dat, Bart," she said. "You jus' git yosel' back up in da wagon."

"What are you so happy about, Beula?" he asked, knowing better than to argue.

"You neber min' what I's so happy about," she rejoined, the smile immediately disappearing from her lips.

"And what's all this shopping for? Zeke always picks up the supplies."

"My, but you's gotten a heap too inquis'tive fo yo own good! Neber you min' what it's about. I done tol' you befo, dis is my own personal businez."

Chuckling to himself at Beula's attempted brusqueness and knowing full well she was still smiling inside no matter how gruff she attempted to sound, Bart flicked the reins, and the wagon lurched into motion.

"What kind of business do *you* have here in town, Beula?" Bart asked after they were out of Sweetriver, half in continued jest, half to make conversation.

"Same kin' o' businez you oughta be tendin' to yosel'. Dis here's da season fo rememberin'."

"Remembering what?"

"Christmas time's da season t' be rememberin' each other, an' specially da little baby what came t' teach us 'bout God's love."

Bart was silent a moment. Now it was his turn to remember what God had done for him earlier that same year. How intricately were the histories of these two once-lonely individuals linked, though neither knew it. For Beula did not know Bart as one of Brother Joseph's hired plants in the Sweetriver revival, nor did Bart know Beula to have been the good evangelist's former cook and maid.

"Yeah . . . yeah, you're right, Beula," said Bart thought-fully. "I got me plenty to be thankful for all right."

"Speakin' fo mysel', Christmas ain' been such a happy time since longer'n I can recall. Now I got me a family t' be wif on Christmas, an' I inten' t' make da most ob it."

"Zeke's been mighty good to me," added Bart, nodding his head.

"Well, I plans t' do somethin' fo dem," said Beula, "an' *dat's* what my businez in town's all 'bout."

They rode on some distance in silence, the only sound to be heard the steady clopping of hooves along the dirt road.

"What do you suppose I could do, Beula," said Bart at length, "to show Zeke and Miz Jody how grateful I am?"

"Well, now dat you ask," mused Beula, "I reckon if you was of a mind to, I could use some hep wif what I's plannin' fo Zeke."

"I'd be obliged if you'd let me," said Bart.

"I's plannin' t' gib everyone a little somethin'. But since Zeke gibs us all a home at his ranch, I figured we oughta let him know how much we 'preciate it."

"You're right there!" said Bart. "Just tell me what to do."

"When I was growin' up on a plantation in da South," said Beula, "I had me a master who was good t' us, jus' like Zeke. When I got older, I took care ob his young'uns in da big house, though I must not hab done too good a job o' it if a body was t' look at how one ob dem turned out. I still be a mite confused at how dat boy coulda come from such a good mama and pappy who was so kind t' folks, black an' white. Every year, Master Mertree he had all da slaves write deir names on a big slab o' wood—dem dat *could* write deir names, an' da others he wrote it for 'em—an' he put dat wood on da wall right in da hallway ob da big house. A body could walk down dat hallway an' remember all da folks who had been dere befo. An' I done thought about how dat might make a nice memory for da Simmonses, on account o' dem havin' no young'uns ob dere own, to hab a slab like dat nailed up on a wall ob da house. Den every Christmas we could make a new one, an' remember da past at da same time as we's lookin' forward to da new year."

"That sounds like a real good idea, Beula!" said Bart enthusiastically. "You just tell me what to do!"

The remainder of the ride home was filled with spirited discussion between the aging white man and black woman, both well beyond what many would consider their prime, yet each filled with the childlike happiness that comes from starting life anew.

FESTIVE
SEASON

Christmas at the home of Sinclair and Ernestine

Randolph was always festive throughout the month of

December, but never more so than as the year 1891 drew to

a close. Both their daughters were home and safe. Rachel

had nearly recovered from her serious bout with pneumo-

nia, yet was forever changed by what the illness had

wrought in her heart. The quiet spirit radiating from her

now was due to far more than innate temperament and was growing more Christlike in nature daily. Thomas kept busy with his schoolwork. And Mercy's husband-to-be, Jeremiah Eagleflight, had arrived two weeks ago to celebrate the season with them all.

Mercy made arrangements with a photographer in the city for herself and Jeremiah to pose for a picture the day the family met him at the train station. She had found a small gold pocket watch to give him for Christmas, in whose lid she wanted to place a miniature of the two of them and whose dimensions she had given the shopkeeper in advance. By Christmas Day the photograph would no more be a surprise, though she would not show it to him before then, but she hoped he would like the watch none the less for that. She asked the photographer to make an extra copy of the picture for herself.

Jeremiah had never known such a holiday!

Mercy's mother had so many traditions to keep alive that the entire house remained abuzz with activity for the entire two weeks after Jeremiah's arrival.

"You are trying to keep Mercy from me," he teased his future mother-in-law after a week, "by keeping her so busy with cooking and decorating and sewing that she forgets I am even here!"

"No fear of that, Jeremiah!" rejoined the banker's wife with a laugh. "Believe me—and a mother knows these things!—she is aware of your presence every second."

Though it was all foreign to a westerner like him, whose family life could not have been more different, Jeremiah loved every minute. He accompanied Mercy on all her various shopping errands, helped with as much of the decorating as the women would allow, and even dressed up in his good suit of clothes one day to spend the morning with Mercy's father at the bank.

If only Jess could see me now! he thought with an inward smile.

Louisville was beautiful at Christmastime. Most of the city's shops were colorfully decorated. Tiny village scenes had been set up in some. Carved wooden toys filled the display windows of more than one store. Green boughs and wreaths of fir and cedar hung about the doors of many homes. And the steeple bells of the churches rang out the tunes of favorite carols.

"Hang up your coats, everyone, and come help me with the greens," Mrs. Randolph called out one afternoon as Mercy, Rachel, and Jeremiah returned from the neighbors' with fresh butter and eggs. The energetic lady was at that moment in the process of dragging a sheet full of fresh cuttings through the kitchen on her way toward the Sunday parlor.

"Here, you two take these," she said. "Rachel, come with me, and we'll fetch the ribbons."

Mercy saw Jeremiah's incredulous expression and laughed.

"It's always like this," she said. "Mother loves Christmas so much that she wears us out with her decorating and baking. But we wouldn't have it any other way."

Jeremiah had not been in the Sunday parlor since the evening of his arrival, when the family had enjoyed coffee and apple pie there together. As he and Mercy now entered the room, he paused and gazed about him with wonder.

"What has happened?" he exclaimed. "I feel like I've stepped into another world!"

"Mother always transforms the parlor into a fairyland for Christmas," replied Mercy. "Do you like it?"

All the furniture had been moved out to the walls to make room in the center for a single large table. The table's surface had been transformed into an entire miniature scene of long ago—a town in Judea and its surroundings.

Slowly, almost reverently, Jeremiah walked toward it. He picked up the small plaster figure of a camel, examined it briefly, then glanced questioningly at Mercy, still not recognizing the scene.

"The wise men traveled to Bethlehem on camels."

"You mean . . . in the Bible story?"

Mercy nodded.

"It's Bethlehem—now I see! It's . . . it's magnificent."

Mercy smiled. "Mother began making these figures when she was a girl," she said. "She added to her collection every Christmas until by now it is so large that it takes a huge table to hold it all."

"There . . . there must be a hundred different people and animals."

"Someone at the paper found out about it, came to look at what Mother had done, and wrote an article about it," Mercy continued. "Now, on Christmas Eve, Mother and Father open our home so that people can come to see it. Mother puts out her Christmas baking."

"I can't wait to see that! How many come?"

"Oh, a great many. It is so wonderful to watch the little children, and how their eyes get so big as their parents tell them the story of baby Jesus."

CHRISTMAS EVE
AT THE BAR S

Mercy and Eagleflight's absence notwithstanding,

Jody determined that this would be the most joyous Christ-

mas the Bar S had ever seen.

There was something so fulfilling for her to have others

for whom she could make it meaningful. She would make it

a wonderful and happy time for Loretta and Beula, as well

as Zeke's winter crew of men. Jeremiah had asked Zeke

especially to watch out for his nephew. Jeremiah didn't want to go traipsing all over the country another time after him!

Jody had her own traditions, just like Mercy's mother. And now, with her family so suddenly expanded, everything became exciting and new. She felt like a mother to the orphaned Loretta, and in some mysteriously wonderful way she felt as if in Beula she had discovered a long-lost sister she hadn't known she had.

When she asked Zeke to bring down her boxes of Christmas things from the storeroom, Jody's anticipation was greater than for any Christmas she could remember in years. She wanted everything to be festive, but most of all she wanted to help the others remember the Savior's birth. They would enjoy one another . . . and they would give God thanks.

For days Jody sorted through the decorations she had collected over the years. These boxes contained so many memories!

They had no children of their own. Yet she and Zeke had so much to be thankful for. They had enjoyed a full life.

For several years, however, Christmas had been a melancholy time as they looked forward, year following year, to the time when they would have children yet felt that hope gradually dimming within them. They had long since adjusted to the fact and had had good and happy years together since.

And now at this time, as they often did during holidays, Jody's reminiscences turned inward. More than once her eyes filled with tears as she placed around the house the reminders of the past—tears of mixed emotions in which a quiet, thankful contentedness prevailed.

And now suddenly they had a houseful!

She would banish any melancholy memories of
Christmases that had never been and replace them with a
joyful memory of *this* year, and future years, when they
would share in making *new* memories together.

Jody sat down with Beula and Loretta one morning after
breakfast to plan out several special meals. The joy of the
season came with serving, and she would bring the other
two into every bit of it possible, for they were eager companions in making the most of this holiday.

Two days before Christmas, Zeke, Jess, Bart Wood, Dirk
Heyes, Clancy Phillips, and Jack Rice headed off on horseback into the southern hills. It was part of Zeke's own
Christmas tradition to go out on a tree shoot, as he called it,
with all his men. They did not return until late in the afternoon, laughing and talking among themselves. All six
marched triumphantly up to the door of the house.

"We herewith present you," announced Zeke when the
ladies came to the door, "with three plump turkeys, ripe for
roasting, and one Christmas tree, ready for decorating."

"It's beautiful!" exclaimed Loretta.

But the look of delight and anticipation that filled Beula's
eyes when Bart, Dirk, and Jack held up to her their three
dead birds by the necks was something to behold. Christmas
trees were one thing, but a fat turkey to dress and stuff and
roast — *that* was altogether something else! The expression
on Beula's face was payment enough for their efforts in
stalking them. She did not even look back into the house but
proceeded, with the three men in tow, to the cleaning shed.
They set down their quarry and left Beula to her business.

Beula took to the birds like an artist to his paint and
brushes. It had been much too long since this particular art-

ist had been able to do her work on such prized specimens of poultry. The men's mouths began to water almost immediately. If Beula could prepare beef as they knew she could, just think what she might be able to do with these!

Christmas Eve arrived, and with it the first of several long-awaited sumptuous feasts.

Supper that evening was to be later than usual. Jody warned the men to wash "extra good," put on clean shirts, and come to the table with hearty appetites. With all three requests they more than willingly complied.

When at length Jody rang the bell and the men came across the yard to the house, they seemed to hesitate on the porch, then entered the house one by one with almost timid steps. Heyes and Phillips had been around long enough to know about Christmas at the Bar S. But this was all new for Jess, Bart, and Jack. They walked inside, hair slicked down, faces scrubbed, the faintest hint of soap lingering in the air about one or two of them. And there stood Loretta in a newly made green dress, hair clean and done up with new curls, smelling of bath oil, beaming, and looking prettier than any of the men had ever seen her. Beside her, Jody looked every bit as stunning in a colorful skirt, white blouse, and black suede vest. She had the added benefit of some gray hair and eyes of experienced wisdom to add stateliness to her natural beauty. Zeke, in tie, dress shirt, and slacks, greeted each of the men with a handshake and a warm welcome as if he hadn't seen them in months.

"What you all be gawkin' at—as if you neber laid eyes on one another afore?" scolded Beula as she came in from the kitchen. "We's got us food t' eat. You can finish yo gawkin' later."

Zeke broke into a laugh and was immediately joined by

the others. Jody led the way into the large front sitting room, where they had set out a buffet.

Slices of buttered bread and thick slabs of cold ham and beef proved easy fare without a table. The men loaded up their plates and then took chairs about the room, several wondering to themselves at the scarcity of the provisions.

"Hey, Clancy," cried Jess as he stabbed a slice of ham, "look over there. I didn't see all that when I walked in."

He pointed to a second table on the other side of the room. There needed be no worry for provision with Jody in charge. She and Beula and Loretta had been in the kitchen baking almost from morning till night for three days. And now the men saw the fruit of their labors—cookies and candies and turnovers of a dozen or more varieties. There were so many goodies, they would last a week!

"And tomorrow, there'll be fresh pies to go with the turkeys!" added Jody. "I guarantee every one of you men will put on five pounds!"

Everyone relaxed as the evening went on, and the conversation and laughter flowed freely. When everyone had eaten their fill, Jody rose and nodded for Beula to follow her. They returned several minutes later, each holding a tray from which they passed around mugs of warm, frothy, fresh eggnog.

As they did so, Zeke took the opportunity to gather their thoughts together upon the reason for their celebration.

"You men know—and you women, too, I'll have to start saying!" he added, glancing first at Loretta, then at Beula. "You all know that I consider every man who works for me, as I know Jody considers everyone who shares our roof . . . we consider you family.

"I'm not going to preach to you," he continued, "'cause

that's not my way. I know you've all recognized how things are different here at the Bar S than at other places where you may have hired on in the past, or at other places you women may have been. You all know why, 'cause I've told you. But I want to remind you of it again, just like I do every so often. The reason things are different here is because I'm not the boss here.

"The God who's our Father's the Boss of this ranch. The rules we abide by and the ways we do things are by the book, *his* book. He's the Boss, and we all work for him. That means we try to do things his way, as best we can."

Zeke paused and picked up his Bible from the table beside him.

"There was a time, a long time ago, when the Father sent his own Son to his ranch, to work beside his people for a spell so that Son could show them and teach them what the rules of the ranch were. The reason we celebrate Christmas is because that's the day the Son came. So this evening I'd like to read to you what God's book says about this particular night, the night before that great event of the Son's coming."

He flipped through the pages and found his place. A hush fell over the room as Zeke began to read.

"'And Joseph also went up from Galilee, out of the city of Nazareth, into Judaea, unto the city of David, which is called Bethlehem . . . to be taxed with Mary his espoused wife. . . .'"

BETHLEHEM

Christmas Eve came to Kentucky clear and cold and bright.

A steady stream of townspeople had come to the

Randolph home throughout the evening. Jeremiah had

assumed that the atmosphere would be one of informal visit-

ing and milling around. Instead, however, after the parlor

was fully decorated with greens and with many candles

placed around the room and lit, and a blazing fire built, Mr. Randolph closed the door.

As guests arrived throughout the evening, Mr. and Mrs. Randolph showed them inside the room, either alone or with their families, closing the door behind them. No one heard what went on inside or what might be the gist of each individual conversation. But as each group emerged, a glow shown on every face.

A good deal of visiting did take place, and he met dozens of new people, but such conversations occurred in the kitchen and dining room. As the evening progressed, Jeremiah grew more and more curious. Then, when all the visitors were gone and most of the lights in the house put out, as Christmas Eve grew late, the five Randolphs, along with Jeremiah Eagleflight, the newest member of their family, silently entered the parlor together.

The sight to meet Jeremiah's eyes—the candlelit scene of Bethlehem, with eerie shadows from the remnants of the fire dancing about over its miniature shapes—struck marvel and awe into his heart. The village and surrounding hillside suddenly seemed so real, as if he were gazing down from among the angelic host that visited them that wonderful night.

No one said a word, for this was the Randolph tradition. Joining hands, the six stretched themselves around one end of the table and stood in prayerful silence, contemplating reverently, each in his own way, the *fact* of Bethlehem—a fact that changed the universe forever. Beside that fact, nothing needed to be said . . . only thanks given.

When they emerged from the room ten minutes later, the candles extinguished and the fire left to burn itself out, a glow shown on Jeremiah's face as well, though he was not aware of it. Mercy saw it but said nothing. She knew the effect the scene had on people and was content to let God continue his work in her beloved Jeremiah's heart without comment.

Jeremiah had laid down in his bed a few minutes later, quietly at peace and content, yet unable to sleep. Both mind and heart were full.

Zeke had shown him the practical side of Christianity. Mercy had shown him the loving side. But now he saw even more clearly than ever before how much more there was to being a Christian than making good choices or trying to be kind or reading the Bible or searching for truth.

Suddenly the very mystical yet down-to-earth *reality* of Jesus Christ himself entered his soul. And Jeremiah knew he would never be the same.

Gazing down upon the make-believe scene of Bethlehem on that most holy of nights suddenly made the birth of Jesus so immediate . . . so very *real!*

Being a Christian, thought Jeremiah, was not about *Jeremiah Eagleflight* at all, or what *he* did, or even what he believed. *It was about Jesus.*

That's what this night was all about. That's why Mrs. Randolph's scene so moved people. *Because Jesus had really, truly been born!*

56

A LOUISVILLE
CHRISTMAS

Jeremiah's early Christmas reverie was sharply

interrupted by laughter outside his door. He heard giggling

and whispering.

Suddenly Thomas burst into the room.

"Nobody sleeps in on Christmas morning!" he anounced,

then proceeded to attempt to drag Jeremiah from bed.

"But wait," protested Jeremiah, "I'm not even dressed

yet—Thomas . . . hey, hold on there. . . . Thomas, hey—cut it out!"

Both Mercy and Rachel stood laughing just outside the doorway, listening with delight to Jeremiah's outcries.

Jeremiah desperately grabbed at the quilt to cover himself.

"You must come downstairs and join us for gifts," Thomas said.

Jeremiah hesitated only another moment and threw his clothes on, most disheveled, but dressed. Then, prompted into playfulness himself by the giddy snickering from the hall, he followed Thomas from the room. All he saw were Mercy's and Rachel's backs as they scurried away. He and Thomas bolted after them.

The two teenagers and the two young adults tumbled and pushed their way like children down the stairs, through the hall, and at last into the parlor.

Yet again Jeremiah was overwhelmed as he entered the room. Was there no end to the surprises in this house?

Sometime during the night, the holy crèche had been moved alongside one wall. An enormous fully decorated Christmas tree now stood in the center of the room in its place.

Mr. and Mrs. Randolph stood beside it, both smiling broadly, for the joy of Christmas is no less for parents than for children. The sideboard was laid out with rolls, butter, jam, and fresh applesauce. Jeremiah's nostrils filled with the aroma of hot coffee from the direction of the fireplace.

He turned toward it, now first noticing the mantel, which the previous evening had been covered with greens. It was now cleared off and set with six small bowls, five of porcelain, with the names of each family member painted decoratively on the sides, and a sixth of pewter, with the name *Jeremiah* lettered on a card and tied around the bowl with red ribbon.

"I . . . I don't—wow . . . ," he faltered. "It's beautiful. . . . I've never seen a Christmas tree so pretty."

"Mother and Father always stay up half the night on Christmas Eve decorating the tree," explained Thomas, "after we've all gone to bed."

"We don't know how they do it," laughed Rachel. "When I was young I used to think it was magic and that the tree just *appeared* every Christmas morning."

Mr. and Mrs. Randolph now joined in Rachel's laughter to hear their children talk so.

"Then we eat," added Mercy, "and afterward get to go see what is in our bowls. Then we bring our own gifts from their hiding places to put under the tree."

"It's a morning for play!" said Mr. Randolph exuberantly. "So let us make haste with breakfast so that we might begin. Coffee, Jeremiah?"

"Yes—thank you," he replied.

Mercy's father poured out a steaming cup of the fresh black brew. Then the two men followed the women to the breakfast sideboard to serve up.

As he ate, Jeremiah could not keep away the sense of overwhelming privilege he felt to have been taken up and made part of such a happy and loving family. His throat seemed caught between the urge to both laugh and cry at the same time. Consequently he did neither, but sat quietly observing everything that went on around him with something like an inner sense of awe.

Half an hour later, amid laughter and merrymaking, the young people took their bowls down from the mantel.

"Come, Jeremiah," exhorted Mercy gaily, grabbing his

hand and pulling him from his chair. "You have to join us.
You're part of the family now, you know!"

Jeremiah reached up and took down the bowl with his
name on it. In it he discovered a bright orange, a dark blue
necktie, and assorted candies.

"Thank you . . . thank you very much," he said, turning
almost shyly toward Mercy's parents. He picked up the
orange in his hand, turned it over a few times, then smelled
its rough-textured peel.

"I've never had an orange before," he said. "They don't
grow in the north and plains."

He tossed it into the air lightly, then caught it, continuing
to turn it over in his hand.

"It's to eat, silly," laughed Mercy, "not play with!"

"Go bring down your gifts, everyone!" cried Mr. Randolph.

Rachel, Thomas, and Mercy disappeared from the room
in a rush, leaving Jeremiah and his future father- and
mother-in-law alone in the room laughing. From all over the
house squeals of delight and laughter and frenzied anticipation could be heard. Thomas was the first to return with an
armload, then he disappeared again at the same moment
that Mercy returned. Rachel appeared next, then Thomas
with several more packages.

At last, five or ten minutes later, they all seated themselves around the tree, whose base now overflowed with
bright boxes and packages of many different sizes and
shapes.

"I can't wait!" exclaimed Mercy. "I wanted to save it for
the very last, but I just can't. Here, Jeremiah," she said,
handing Jeremiah a small box wrapped in red paper and
tied with a white ribbon and bow. "Merry Christmas!"

"Thank you," said Jeremiah, taking it. He held it a moment.

"Open it!" said Mercy impatiently, fairly wriggling out of her chair beside him.

"With everyone watching?" he said, glancing about at the rest of her family. Every eye was upon him.

"Of course. We all watch every gift as it is opened."

"All right, then," he said. He began timidly tearing at one edge of the paper. Hardly able to contain herself, Mercy's fingers twitched as if they could help him where they sat impatiently in her lap. At length Jeremiah succeeded in removing the paper and ribbon.

Carefully he lifted off the top of the small box, then pulled out the watch. He sat several moments just looking at the decorated gold case.

"I . . . I just don't know what to say," he said.

"Open it!" said Mercy.

"What . . . the watch?"

"Yes!"

Jeremiah lifted the lid. Inside he recognized immediately the pose from two weeks earlier in the photographer's shop.

"You had this planned all along," he said with a smile.

"Of course. Christmas is the season when secrets are allowed, don't you know?"

"Thank you. It's . . . it's the most wonderful gift I've ever received."

Jeremiah glanced down. It was clear he was both moved and embarrassed.

"I . . . I appreciate all you've done for me," he said, glancing around at Mercy's family. "And this watch, Mercy—it's beautiful. I never . . . I never expected anything like this. I've never owned anything as nice as this in my life."

He paused and looked down again.

"But . . . well—I'm afraid I didn't get anybody anything. I . . . I just didn't think about gifts. Now that I think about it, I don't know how I could have been so stupid, especially watching you all shopping every day. I'm sorry . . . I didn't . . . I've been so busy saving money for the new house and all . . . and I just plum forgot about gifts."

"Set your mind at ease, son," interrupted Mr. Randolph. "We didn't expect any. You are our guest, and that is exactly how we want it. It is the *giving* that brings us joy."

"But I should have thought to give you all something."

"Oh, but you have," said Mercy's father.

"I . . . I don't understand what you mean."

"You've given us the best gift of all—better than any watch or toy or new dress or tool. You've come to share the season with us, and that is the best thing you have to give. You've let us know you and share our home and lives with you. You've given us *yourself*, Jeremiah, my boy, and there is no more priceless gift any man or woman has to offer than that."

A moment more, and suddenly Jeremiah stood and hurriedly strode from the room. The tears suddenly flooding his eyes were so unexpectedly new that he could not let Mercy or her family see them. He had not cried since he was a boy, and he did not know what to do but run and hide.

Mercy found him twenty minutes later, sitting composed on the side of the bed in his guest room. The door was open, and she walked in. She approached slowly and placed her hand on his shoulder.

"Are you all right?" she asked.

He nodded, taking in a deep breath.

"Would you like to join us again?"

"Are you through with your gifts?" he asked softly.

"Oh, no—we waited for you."

Jeremiah looked up into Mercy's face and forced an embarrassed smile. She knew what he was thinking and just nodded reassuringly.

"My family really loves you," she said.

Jeremiah nodded. That much was clear, and he knew it.

"Come," she said, reaching for his hand, "it's Christmas—no more looking back."

57

CHRISTMAS
PRAYER

By that afternoon Jeremiah had recovered from his self-recriminations and was laughing at the whole thing.

"I don't know how I could have been in such a daze for two weeks!" he said.

"It was no worse than the daze I was in during my first week in Sweetriver," laughed Mercy.

They took their seats around the table for Mrs. Randolph's

triumphant Christmas feast. Mr. Randolph extended both his hands. Jeremiah and Rachel, seated next to him on each side, took them, and on around the table it went until the circle of hands was complete.

"Our loving heavenly Father," he prayed, "we give you thanks for this day from hearts full of the deepest gratitude. All the prayers we can think to utter dissolve into the two words that we can never say enough — *Thank you!*

"Thank you for this season of giving and remembering, and for your great gift most of all. Thank you for this very precious and special day when you sent to earth your Son so that man might know you as he had not known you before, as our Father! Oh, thank you, God our creator, whom we now know to call by that cherished and wonderful name — Father. Thank you, our Father! Fatherhood is a message of Christmas. Your own Fatherhood is such a great and wondrous gift to us. Let us dare to approach you in intimacy, as Jesus told us we should, and call you, as he did, our Abba . . . our very own Daddy."

Mr. Randolph paused briefly, then concluded.

"We join hearts in thanking you for all you have given us and all you are constantly doing for us. Thank you for your provision, for this food, for our home, for our family, for friends, for Rachel's health, for Mercy's presence here with us, for Thomas' inquisitive mind, and for our dear new friend Jeremiah, whom we all love. Now let us rejoice with thanksgiving for the rest of this day. Keep us mindful of the presence of your Spirit among us in all we do and think, and increase our humble gratefulness to you every day of our lives. Thank you, Father. Amen."

*Amen*s followed around the table.

Mercy's mother picked up the bowl of mashed potatoes and began the seemingly endless passage of serving dishes.

"You can't know how much I appreciate how you've opened your home to me," said Jeremiah as he dug into the tempting plates that came his way. "It means more than I can tell you. And if you invite me back —," he added.

"If!" exclaimed Mercy. "Jeremiah, we're going to be married. This is your home now, too."

"You'll never be a guest again, my boy," put in Mr. Randolph. "You're one of the family now!"

"Thank you," said Jeremiah. "All right, I'll say it like this — *when* I am here again for Christmas — "

"That's better!" said Mercy.

"When I am here again," Jeremiah went on, "I'm going to do better in the way of gift giving. I'm already making plans. I'll make up for this year, just you wait and see!"

"No need to make up for anything, Jeremiah," said Mercy's father.

"That may be, but I'm still making plans!" laughed Jeremiah, then he opened his mouth wide for a bite of turkey. "Ernestine," he added to Mercy's mother a few seconds later, "everything is delicious!"

"Thank you, Jeremiah."

"He's right, Mama," added Rachel. "You've outdone yourself again."

More talk followed, about the food and about several of the gifts that had been exchanged earlier in the day.

"You know, Sinclair," said Mrs. Randolph thoughtfully after a temporary lull in the conversation, during which the six mouths, however, remained active in the business of the meal, "I've never heard you say anything like what you prayed just a few minutes ago. I can't get it out of my mind."

"What, exactly?"

"About God's Fatherhood being the gift of Christmas."

"Did I pray that?"

"Yes, you did, Daddy," said Mercy. "I was struck by it at the time, too."

"I've always thought that God's greatest gift to us was Jesus," Ernestine added, "and that *he* was the gift of Christmas."

"Sometimes when I am praying," mused Mr. Randolph, "I find words or expressions coming out of my mouth I hadn't thought of ahead of time or planned to say. I think this may have been one of those, for I had not given the matter a great deal of thought before now."

"*Do* you think God's fatherhood is the gift of Christmas, Daddy," asked Rachel, "or is it Jesus?"

"I would say both. The Father sent Jesus to us, not as a gift to us merely *in himself as the Son*, but also for the purpose of revealing the Father to us."

Jeremiah listened, intrigued. He had never heard such a religious conversation around a meal table in his life. And yet, he supposed, today *was* Christmas. What better subject to discuss than what the day signified?

"Therefore, I would have to add that when God sent Jesus to live among us on that very first Christmas back in Bethlehem so long ago," Mr. Randolph was saying, "that *he was giving us himself as Father.*"

"What would the teachers at your Missionary College say to that, Mercy?" asked Rachel, turning toward her sister.

Mercy thought a moment, then smiled. "That is a good question," she said. "I'm not sure. But Daddy's right, isn't he, for that was one of the reasons Jesus came after all—to tell us about the Father."

"Exactly," rejoined Mr. Randolph, "to inform man of that startling revelation that had been kept hidden until then. *That* is what the fact of Jesus' birth means—that the Son has a Father!"

"I thought Jesus came to bring salvation, Papa," said Thomas.

"He did, my boy. Jesus came to provide the way to salvation, which exists nowhere else but in the Father's loving heart. Even the cross cannot save by itself. What is a cross but two slabs of wood? Only a Son who knew the Father's love could take us, through the cross, *to* that love. Without God's Fatherhood, there is no salvation. It is because he loves us with a Father's love that *he*—the Father—saves us. Such was one of Jesus' purposes for living, to take us by the hand and bring us to the Father's heart of love."

Again it was silent.

"What you've said is such an enormous truth, Sinclair," said Ernestine. "It sheds an entirely new perspective on what happened that night back in Bethlehem. Already I can't wait to put up next year's scene."

"I suppose I have always thought of this day mostly in connection just with the baby Jesus," said Mercy at length. "But God's gift at Christmas is so much larger than I had ever considered."

"That can be said of everything God does and all he gives," added Mr. Randolph. "*Everything* of his is so much larger than we think."

"How do you mean . . . *larger?*" asked Jeremiah.

"I mean," replied Mercy's father, "that we small-minded men are anxious to place boundaries around what God does, or can do, or *might* do, so that we can explain his ways and means to the satisfaction of our finite intellects."

"And you're saying those boundaries aren't good?"

"Oh, I don't know about bad or good. Some of them might be necessary, I suppose, to help us understand what might not be understandable to our earthly minds otherwise. My point is simply that God's work among men has fewer boundaries than we generally think. Boundaries and limitations speak of finiteness, and God is infinite. And especially God's love is not limited by man's interpretations and by the boundaries man would place around the extent of its reach."

That evening, after all the food had been stored away and the kitchen cleaned up—during which time Mercy's father and Jeremiah had had a man-to-man talk about many things, including the young couple's future—Jeremiah and Mercy bundled up and went outside for a walk. No snow had come to Louisville yet this year, but the cold on this Christmas Day informed the city that it was on its way.

Jeremiah held onto Mercy's arm to make sure she wouldn't slip on the frozen ground.

"You know," he said after they had walked some distance in silence, "I have to start thinking about getting back to the ranch."

"I know," Mercy said with a nod, "though I didn't want to think about it *quite* yet."

"Zeke said that he and some of the boys would help me clear that knoll this winter and get a start on our cabin. There'll be plenty of work once the spring thaw comes to the prairie, so I want to get as much done on it this winter as I can."

"Oh, Jeremiah, it's going to be so exciting! Can you believe that we will have a house of our very own?"

"Don't let your hopes get too high—it'll just be a two- or three-room cabin at first."

"I'll be happy as can be in a one-room cabin," said Mercy, "as long as I'm with you."

Jeremiah drew her close, and she felt the rough coldness of his jacket.

"I am glad that you and Father decided we should have the wedding in Kansas," she went on after a minute. "As much as I love my home and family, it just wouldn't seem right to be married here when *that* is where our life together began."

"The prairie will be lovely in June."

"Oh, Jeremiah, do you think we could have the wedding out at the river, where we had our picnic?"

"I don't see why not—though it may be a chore to get everyone out there!"

"Zeke will find a way."

Jeremiah laughed.

"I suppose I don't need to worry," he said. "You're right— Zeke is a resourceful fellow. Knowing him, he'll probably figure out a way to get a church organ all the way out there!"

SPRING COMES
ROUND AGAIN

Spring was again in full flower on the prairie and ranch
land of south-central Kansas.

A year had passed since the traveling evangelist had
brought such change to their lives, though the odors blowing in from the south and west hadn't changed. Zeke
Simmons was still the first man at the Bar S to sense the

shifts in the weather. A sweet breeze had greeted him this morning, and he suspected rain.

But then, he had been here a long time . . . and the men still called him Boss. He was expected to know things better and sooner than anyone.

"How's that colt, Forbes?" he called, riding up to the corral. Jess lay on his back, dust covering his face, hat several yards away, while at the far end of the corral a frisky young buff-colored pony bucked about, trying to toss the uncomfortable saddle off its back, now that it had gotten rid of the rider.

Jess looked up with a wide grin.

"I just about got him!" he said. "One or two more rides, and that critter's gonna be eating sugar and apples out of my hand!"

"Stick with it, then. You got six days to get him ready if you still want to give it to the girl for her present."

"The colt'll be ready," said Jess, jumping back to his feet.

Zeke rode on toward the house. *Six days*, he mused.

The last six months had gone by quickly. It would be good to see Mercy again. He could hardly believe it had been so long!

They'd all be on the train from Kansas City next week, and he was sending a wagon, two large carriages, and half a herd of horses to fetch them. But it would no longer be a two-day journey. The new line through Atchison, Topeka, and Santa Fe—with a stop in Sweetriver—was at last open. No more long rides to Fort Hays—the train came right here now!

It was hard to believe how rapidly change could happen! Sweetriver was changing. The whole country was continuing to grow westward.

As if in response to his thoughts, he heard today's train clattering along its shiny new rails in the distance. A few minutes later its whistle blew as it pulled into the new, freshly painted Sweetriver station.

It would have been simpler, Zeke thought, for them to have just gotten married in Kentucky. The preacher was there. Mercy's family was there.

But no, they had to get hitched right here at the Bar S, even if it meant bringing the whole clan—brother, sister, parents, grandparents, uncles, aunts . . . and the preacher, too!—out to Kansas on the railroad.

Of course, Zeke and Jody could not have been more delighted!

Was this not where the young couple had met and fallen in love? This was where they planned to live. And so *this* was where they were going to pledge their futures to one another.

Zeke was glad he'd found a couple new ranch hands last month. There sure had been a lot of extra work about the place these few weeks—not to mention all the usual spring work, with new calves and repairs all over the Bar S from winter damage.

Zeke glanced up toward the ridge east of the valley where the new house was started. He and Jess and Jeremiah and the rest of his boys had cleared the foundation for it as soon as the snow let up. They'd gotten a floor down and a start on framing up the walls before Jeremiah left for Louisville two weeks ago. There the newly married Eagleflights would live one day.

He and Jess and the rest of the boys would have continued working on it while Jeremiah was in Kentucky if he'd have let them. But Jeremiah insisted on building it himself and wouldn't let so much as a board be set in place before he got back. Zeke had been happy to comply with his wishes. It would make enjoyable summer work. And while Jeremiah didn't have much money, Zeke had offered to buy most of the lumber and let Jeremiah work it off.

It didn't matter, said Jeremiah, if it wasn't done by the wedding. He and Mercy would roll out their bedrolls wherever they could! They'd get the walls finished and the roof overhead soon enough, and then they'd be happy. The house didn't need to be fancy as long as they had each other!

Well, thought Zeke with a smile, they'd have each other all right. And half of Kentucky besides! In another week this place would be full of life, with ten or a dozen guests! The population of the Bar S would double the minute that train arrived in Sweetriver!

Zeke glanced up at the house again. What a quiet joy it gave him to know that Eagleflight wanted to stay on at the Bar S and continue working for him!

He hadn't admitted it to anyone but his wife, but the young man was like the son he'd never had. That he would choose to stay and let Zeke provide a house for them on his own land while he continued to work on the ranch — there couldn't have been a happier ending to the whole unexpected episode for the childless rancher. Maybe he would sell Eagleflight the new house and a chunk of the Bar S someday . . . or even give it to him!

Who could tell what the future might hold? Maybe the Bar S brand would someday be changed to the E and S Connected.

Zeke's wife was experiencing a similar sense of fulfillment. No one would ever replace Mercy in Jody's heart. From that first day the hapless failed evangelist had appeared as a stranger on her doorstep just about a year ago, Jody's mother heart had gone out to the lonely young lady who was so far from home.

So much had happened since then! Now Jody had Loretta, too—who was making clothes and mending breeches and even learning the craft of saddle making, just like Mercy had—and Beula to help with the cooking and housekeeping.

And what had begun as little more than a stopover in Sweetriver as the wagon of a traveling evangelist had passed through had led eventually, through the past winter and spring to weekly Sunday gatherings at the Bar S, during which Jody or Zeke would open the Word of God to those who came to join them.

There was no preaching, only openhearted sharing. Whenever Zeke heard himself referred to as "the preaching rancher," he was quick to say, "I am nothing more than one who was thirsty for life myself, telling the rest of you where I have found water to drink." By the end of April, even Eagleflight upon occasion shared what was on his heart.

The home meetings became talked about more and more throughout Sweetriver. No one could deny that the whole atmosphere of the community was gradually changing as a result of the meetings. Business at the Silver Ox was down. Goodwill and smiles as people met on the sidewalk were in abundant supply.

There had even been continued talk on Zeke and Jody's part of building a church for the community, and the talk had gotten back through the Randolphs to Rev. Walton in Louisville. The reverend would therefore be coming to the wedding in Kansas with two motives on his mind.

Throughout the winter and spring, news of the wedding

caused a different mood to settle not merely over the Bar S but also over all of Sweetriver.

A sense of anticipation seemed to pervade the entire community. Everyone was anxious to have the two young people back. The whole town was abuzz with anticipation as the day drew closer.

59

GRATEFULNESS
FOR A FULL LIFE

Zeke rode up to the house, dismounted, and walked inside.

He and Jody had been counting the days for three

months now, ever since the date had been set. Jody had

been fussing nearly the entire time over her dress and a new

fancy coat for Zeke.

Jody met him with a hug and a kiss.

"What's that for?" said her husband.

"Because I love you," she said. "Maybe planning for a wedding makes me feel romantic."

"Well, you can feel romantic anytime you want!" rejoined Zeke, taking his wife in his arms and planting another kiss on her lips.

He held her for a moment.

"The Lord has given us such a good life, hasn't he, Zeke?" sighed Jody after a minute.

"Who could have thought all this would come to us?"

"Our Father is always full of surprises. You never know when a simple knock on the door is from the hand of someone who is going to change your life."

"Or when a soft-spoken livery-stable laborer is going to become your right-hand man!" added Zeke.

They stood quietly in one another's arms a few moments more.

"Oh, Father, we are so grateful to you for the blessings you've added to our lives!" whispered Jody.

"Amen to that, Lord," added Zeke. "Help us to always walk exactly in your will for us."

Beula had been watching from the kitchen window. She could hardly believe her good fortune to have been welcomed as she had at the Bar S. These were good people, and God had surely been good to her!

"What you be wantin' fo supper, Mr. Zeke?" she asked as she emerged from the kitchen. "You can hab me fix up a roast ob yo beef or chicken wif dumplin's."

"How can a man be so blessed as to be given choices like that?" laughed Zeke. "Everything you make is delicious, Beula."

"Dat may be," she replied with simple humility, "but I'd still like t' fix whateber you's got you a hankerin' fo."

"Well, then," sighed Zeke, "I think I shall order . . . the chicken and dumplings."

Satisfied, Beula turned back to the kitchen. She came out a moment later, clutching a wicked-looking cleaver in her stout hand, and headed outside toward the chicken coop with a purposeful step.

"She's quite a lady," mused Zeke as she went.

"That she is," rejoined Jody. "She practically waits on me hand and foot."

"Good!" said Zeke. "You deserve it!"

"Jody, is this supposed to be —," came a voice. "Oh, I'm sorry," Loretta said the next moment, entering the room with a handful of linen. "I didn't know you were busy."

"It's just me, Loretta," laughed Zeke. "How are you today?"

"Very well, thank you, Zeke."

"You had a question about Mrs. Carter's order?" asked Jody.

"Yes — if you have time."

"Of course," replied Jody, leading Loretta back toward the sewing room, "what is it?"

Zeke watched them go. This certainly was a busy place, he thought to himself. And Jeremiah and Mercy weren't even here yet!

Things were bound to settle down after the wedding. Then he and the boys would get back to ranching. *And* finishing the new house for his adopted son and the new bride!

Maybe later in the summer he would take all the hands down to Texas, mused Zeke, to bring up a small new herd of cattle. That was an experience any self-respecting western man ought to have.

Times were changing so fast — why, some of his boys had never even driven cattle on the open prairie.

ARRIVAL

The mass of humanity at the train station in Sweetriver was unlike anything the new stationmaster had beheld since his transfer to the sleepy little place. The townsfolk had been expecting the travelers all morning, and now it seemed as if every one of the inhabitants had gathered as the train slowly approached, filling the landing to capacity and spreading up and down the tracks.

"Who are these people you've all come to meet?" he kept asking now one, now another as the crowd continued to increase.

The only answer he received was, "Mercy and Eagleflight!" two enigmatic words from which he could derive no satisfactory explanation of the phenomenon. To witness the sight, the man declared, you would think President Harrison himself were aboard!

The train had barely stopped and steam still puffed in great white blasts from underneath the engine when Mercy jumped onto the platform from an open door in one of the carriages and flew into Jody's waiting arms.

"I missed you, dear," whispered Jody in Mercy's ear.

"And I you," replied Mercy, eyes overflowing with tears of love. "Oh, it is good to see you," she added, stepping back with a smile, then taking a moment to gaze into the eyes of her friend. But the moment could only last a second, for behind them came bustle and commotion and activity as all the new arrivals followed Mercy out of the car and disembarked after their long ride. Mercy and Jody released one another and turned toward them.

"Ernestine!" said Jody warmly. "At last I can welcome you to *my* home." The two women embraced.

As Jody took in Mercy's mother, even more than at their first meeting, she was struck with the calm look of serenity in Ernestine's blue eyes. Her shoulder-length brown hair fell in natural curls and had ample strands of gray. Her face was a long one—handsome, striking, and full of hidden life—and the smile that now came to the lips perfectly complemented the peacefulness of the eyes.

"And, Sinclair," Jody added, stepping back and looking

past Mercy's mother to her father, "how wonderful to see you again! Welcome to you, too."

"Thank you, Jody," replied Mercy's father.

By now the rest of the entourage from Kentucky was climbing down onto the platform. Zeke made his way to his wife's side.

"Mother, Daddy," said Mercy, "this is Jody's husband—Zeke Simmons."

Handshakes followed all around.

"We feel like we already know you, Mr. Simmons," said Mercy's father. "Mercy never stops talking about Kansas."

Zeke laughed. "The name's Zeke," he said. "I hope our hospitality will be able to match Mercy's enthusiasm!"

"Jeremiah!" exclaimed Jody as Mercy's husband-to-be appeared in front of her. "It's so good to see you again!"

Eagleflight took Zeke's wife in his arms, hugged her tightly, then planted a light kiss on her cheek.

"Oh, Loretta!" exclaimed Mercy, suddenly seeing her friend standing shyly with Jess behind Jody. The two embraced. Jess and Jeremiah shook hands, and out of the train continued to pour the rest of the Randolph entourage.

Now came Rachel, who ran into Jody's arms even as the tears rose in her eyes. "I feel like I am coming to my second home," whispered Rachel. As the women embraced, Mr. Randolph introduced his son to Zeke.

"Welcome to Kansas, Tom. I've heard that you are quite a young scientist!"

"Jody . . . Zeke," said Mercy as Rachel and Thomas stepped back, "I want you to meet some more of my relatives—"

The rancher and his wife smiled and welcomed each of the newcomers in turn.

". . . and my aunt Alma . . . and my uncle Dink," continued Mercy.

"Welcome to you all!" exclaimed Jody. "I'm still not sure where we're going to manage to put everyone, but at least I can promise you Kansas hospitality!"

"And you remember Rev. Walton. . . ."

Jody nodded while her husband and the minister shook hands for the first time.

"I would like you to meet his wife," added Mercy, completing all the introductions but two.

"Mrs. Walton, I am happy you are here," said Jody, shaking first the lady's, then her husband's, hand. "It is good to see you again, Rev. Walton."

"Mama, Daddy . . . ," said Mercy, now drawing her parents together and leading them to one side of the bustling crowd where Jess and Loretta stood together, "these are two of our very special friends I've been telling you about — Jess Forbes and Loretta Monroe."

All four shook hands warmly. Had Mercy's parents met Loretta in Denver, they would not have recognized her now, so thorough was the change upon her entire countenance. If Jody was about to lose one adopted daughter to marriage, the Lord had given another in her place. Loretta had never been happier.

"Where's Beula?" said Mercy, glancing all about.

"Where do you think?" laughed Jody. "Back home in the kitchen, preparing your welcome-home feast."

By now everyone was off the train. Greetings and introductions extended into the crowd, as many of the townspeople present tried to get to the young man and woman known, to the stationmaster's consternation, simply as Mercy and Eagleflight. Bags were set down on the platform as the train personnel attempted to keep to their schedule. It was fifteen or twenty minutes, however, before the gathering began slowly to make its way out through the building so that they might load everything into Zeke's waiting wagons outside the station.

"My," said Mercy's mother, glancing about as they crossed the street toward them, "this certainly doesn't *look* like the Wild West. From all the commotion, I would think I was in the middle of a New York parade."

"Just wait until our first Indian attack," said Jeremiah at her side.

"There aren't really—," she exclaimed in alarm.

"No, Ernestine," laughed Jeremiah, "this is the 1890s. Everything is positively civilized, even here in Kansas."

"What about snakes?"

"Well, there are plenty of rattlers in these parts," replied Zeke, overhearing the conversation. "But as long as you don't wander out into the prairie alone, you won't see too many."

The train had long since continued its journey westward by the time two carriages, a wagon full of carpetbags and trunks, and at least ten riders on horseback thundered out of Sweetriver, to further shouts and waves of friends and well-wishers from the shops. On the way, Rachel showed her parents where the tornado had nearly overtaken them, able now to laugh at the frightening memory. Twenty-five minutes after leaving town, the assembly crested the ridge and noisily clattered and galloped and rolled down into the valley of the Bar S ranch.

Most of the ranch hands, except Phillips, who was out on the south pasture inspecting a section of broken fence, had wandered in to welcome back Eagleflight and his enormous

new family. Besides the winter crew, three new hands—
Oscar, Bob, and a young broncobuster who had wandered
in from the Oklahoma Territory and went by the name
J. D.—had been added and were already practically members of the family.

"All right, you men!" Zeke called out loudly. "Let's get
these ladies' luggage into the house and the men's gear into
the bunkhouse, and then get these horses unsaddled and
unhitched. We're all nearly ready to starve."

"Fresh rolls an' beef stew, potatoes, hot coffee, an' berry
pie are waitin' in da kitchen!" Beula called out. "Come on
in, all ob you, else it'll git cold!"

At the sound of her voice as she stood on the porch watching everyone climb down out of the carriages to the ground,
Mercy ran forward to embrace the dear black lady.

"Lan' sakes, Mercy, chil'—what's dat for?"

"It's because I love you, Beula," replied Mercy, "and I
missed you. Come," she added, taking Beula's hand and
pulling her forward off the porch, "I want you to meet my
family."

"I don't know about the rest of you," said Jeremiah
meanwhile to the men, "but I know Beula's cooking, and
I don't need to be told twice. Let's get this luggage in so we
can eat!"

PROCESSION
OF HAPPINESS

Four days later, toward two o'clock on the afternoon

of a warm early-June day, what from a distance might have

looked like a funeral march slowly wound its way from the

Bar S ranch toward the nearest pass through the valley of

the Sweet River.

Ten or twelve carriages and wagons led the two miles

across the prairie, followed by a strung-out gathering of

townspeople on foot and horseback, numbering fifty or sixty. A dozen or fifteen Pawnee Indians, mostly children, completed the procession on multicolored white, brown, and black ponies.

It took some time for the procession to reach the river. No one was in a hurry. This was a celebration that would last the rest of the day.

At last the assembly was gathered at the river's side, some standing, some sitting on the green grass that grew lush up and down the banks of the Sweet. This was the only place it was fitting for them to be married, both young people had declared. At last the moment they had long anticipated had arrived.

Rev. Harold Walton, guest from the bride's home in Louisville, Kentucky, stood, Bible in hand, at the edge of the bank, with the river behind him, waiting for the final strains of the music from an old portable pump organ to fade away before he began to address the crowd with a few words fitly chosen for the occasion.

In front of him stood the bride on her father's arm. What a lovely picture she made!

The dress she wore was white but simple, though by no means plain. The fabric of which she and her mother had made it was full of a lacy stuff they had found in Louisville. The collar came high up the neck, and a round yoke with an extra row of lace extended around the shoulder. Its long full skirt hung easily from Mercy's waist, with three rows of the same lace sewn around the bottom of the skirt. The sleeves were long and narrow. A pretty sash of pale green ribbon was tied about Mercy's slender midsection, extending around to the back, where it was tied in a bow whose ends hung down halfway to the ground.

Mercy's light brown hair was adorned and tied loosely with narrower strands of the same green ribbon, playing colorfully amid the natural, wide, bouncy curls she had inherited from her mother.

In her hands Mercy carried a prettily fashioned bouquet Jody had made with strands of wheat and blue cornflowers tied together with more of the green ribbon. Her sparkling green eyes completed the accents to her dress. The only remnant of her old life still clinging to Mercy on this special day was the sturdy pair of black boots she had worn into Sweetriver under her black missionary dress so long ago.

Today, however, she wore them under a flowing dress of the purest white, a fitting symbol of the change in her countenance, heart, and spirit.

The groom stood waiting to one side. As fond as the minister was of Mr. and Mrs. Randolph, he could not help but admit that Mercy and Eagleflight made an even more striking couple.

Next to the bride, in handmade dresses of brightly colored fabric, stood Rachel Randolph and Loretta Monroe. Beside the groom, attired like him in brown, stood Jess Forbes and Zeke Simmons.

In two rows of chairs borrowed from the Silver Ox, sat family and some of the town's most elderly women. Behind them, throughout the standing crowd of observers, beamed the smiles of friends and well-wishers. Most were in attendance because they could personally attest to things being different since Mercy and Eagleflight had turned up in Sweetriver the year before. They wanted to express their friendship, their thanks, and their best wishes. The town had seen nothing like this since before anyone could remember!

Bart Wood, slimmed down, clean shaven, and with the

calluses and muscles of hard work evident on his hands and arms, stood sedate, calm, and thankful, enjoying this wedding far more than he had Brother Joseph Mertree's revival service where he had first laid eyes on the lovely young lady now dressed in white.

Doc Haggerty still didn't know quite what to make of Jess Forbes' seemingly miraculous recovery in his office the previous summer. But he'd stopped trying to figure it out. Plenty more things equally surprising had been seen in Sweetriver on account of these two, and by now he had almost come to expect it.

Similar thoughts flitted through the minds of the rest of the observers.

"Dearly beloved," began Rev. Walton, "we are gathered together this day . . ."

62

MERCY AND EAGLEFLIGHT

The minister concluded his brief homily on marriage and now proceeded with the vows.

"Do you, Jeremiah Eagleflight, take this woman to be your wedded wife . . ."

As Jeremiah listened to the words, he reflected on his two recent visits to Kentucky. How thankful he was for the strong ties that bound all the relationships of Mercy's family together.

He smiled inwardly, remembering what Mercy had said to him as they were walking together just after supper, courtesy of Brother Joseph's larder, on the way back from Denver.

"I do love you, Jeremiah Eagleflight," she had said. "But never have I been involved in so many scary things as I have since meeting you and Jess. Loving you is turning out to be a dangerous occupation!"

"Any regrets?" he had asked.

"No," Mercy had answered. "But I would just like to live long enough to marry you!"

Well, they had lived long enough, Jeremiah thought. Now this day had come without so much as another peep out of Ross Fletcher and the others, though Jeremiah would like to know if they were behind bars yet.

He hoped that he and Mercy could put such dangers behind them for good.

"... to have and to hold from this day forward, for better, for worse, for richer, for poorer, in sickness and in health ..."

It hadn't taken long last December for Jeremiah to realize what kind of family he'd stumbled into! Mercy's father and mother were cut from a different cloth. Like Zeke and Jody, they were a man and a woman possessed with a clarity of purpose as people of God. It still puzzled him at times that Mercy and Rachel had not always recognized the richness of their parents. If anything, he thought, being around their parents every day, they should have been able to recognize the spiritual maturity all the *more* readily. He supposed they'd had to discover if the truths and principles by which their parents lived were real for them, too.

But puzzling as it was, he was glad that that time had come in Mercy's growth. For had not the divine hand used it to lead him to her and ultimately to the Father of them both? He saw, too, when the reality broke personally into Mercy's heart, why she had grown so rapidly to possess a spiritual stature of her own.

". . . to love and to cherish, till death do you part, according to God's holy ordinance?"

As the minister fell silent, Jeremiah's eyes met the deep green eyes of the woman he loved.

The gaze of those emerald pools extended deeper than any icy mountain lake, deeper even than her heart itself, down to the very core of her being where spirit, soul, and flesh united as one.

This was not the same young woman who had stood up over a year ago to preach in front of a community where she did not know a soul. In truth, in the twelve months that had passed, if one individual could be said to have become the soul of Sweetriver, it was the beautiful woman into whose face he was now gazing.

She had not only captured the heart of the town . . . she had taken his as well!

Jeremiah allowed his mouth to form the merest hint of a smile meant only for her. Then quietly he answered Rev. Walton's question. "I do."

Mercy's eyes glistened. Jeremiah knew tears were not far off. As the minister turned, beaming toward his wife-to-be,

Jeremiah glanced away momentarily. His eyes took in Mercy's mother where she stood a few feet away.

The resemblance between the two women was striking. It was not, however, a resemblance of facial characteristics but of spirit and character and inner fiber.

"Do you, Mercy Randolph, take this man to be your wedded husband . . ."

That was her daughter's name, thought Ernestine Randolph, as she heard Rev. Walton intone the words.

Her daughter was getting married!

She took in the scene spread out before them. Her mind drifted back to just moments before as she had ridden toward the river in the buggy with Jody Simmons, Mercy, Rachel, and Loretta.

As they had approached, she had realized why Jeremiah and Mercy had insisted on having the wedding way out here. It was indeed a lovely spot! The blue-green of the river, the brown of the prairie, the green of the grass, and the white and blue of the clouds and sky all seemed to join together in colorful display to welcome them.

She had glanced over at Mercy sitting next to her.

She had recognized the glow in her daughter's face. She had felt it herself what seemed not so many years ago. It was the glow that comes of knowing you are loved. Ernestine had known that Mercy glowed not only with love but also with the knowledge that she was in God's will.

Mercy had that look now, and Ernestine was glad. Her eldest daughter had not always had it. She had gone away to the Missionary College without that same assurance. But now Ernestine knew that Mercy was at peace and yet was as thrilled as a woman could be.

As they had approached the river, Ernestine had turned her focus toward the other woman in the seat with them.

What a jewel Jody was!

Mercy had been fortunate to find her. She was grateful to God for such a woman to help her daughter over a difficult time, offering help that even she herself had been unable to give.

Ernestine's mind came back to the present and to the vows in progress.

She looked out over the crowd of townspeople who had gathered for the wedding. Could Mercy possibly know what a joy it was for her mother to see how many people cared for her and Jeremiah? Since the day of her arrival, there had been a steady stream of visitors at the Bar S, most of them coming to see Mercy. Even three Pawnee families had come, whose children, they had said, had made gifts for Mercy.

Ernestine's heart swelled. *Thank you, Lord, for watching over my daughter!* she sighed. Poor Mercy had gone West so desperately in search of a meaningful faith she could call her own. Just look at all God had done in answer to all their prayers!

She was so glad they had come. It was right, after all, to have this wedding in Kansas.

> ". . . to have and to hold from this day forward, for better, for worse, for richer, for poorer, in sickness and in health . . ."

Mercy gazed upon the man who would be her husband. As she listened to Rev. Walton, she thought back to their arrival here. As the buggy had driven up, music had already been playing.

She had glanced over to the flatbed wagon where dear Beula was playing the organ.

Mercy smiled to herself. What a change this was for both of them from their days together in Brother Joseph's Tent of Meeting and Healing, and his poor old melodeon! As much time as they had been side by side, they hadn't known each other at all back then. Now they were friends for life!

She looked over at Jeremiah. He looked so tall and handsome!

The light brown suit he wore she had seen before. He had worn it the day he'd arrived on the train in Louisville just before last Christmas.

But he looked different now, and she knew it was more than the ruffled shirt and fancy tie he hadn't had in Kentucky.

Now he was preparing to be her husband!

Rev. Walton's words brought her quickly back to the present.

". . . to love, to cherish, and to obey till death do you part, according to God's holy ordinance?"

"I do," breathed Mercy softly.

"Who gives this woman to be married to this man?" asked the minister.

"Her mother and I," replied Sinclair Randolph, taking Mercy's hand, giving it to Jeremiah, and then taking his own place with the men next to Zeke Simmons.

The lady called Mercy and the man known as Eagleflight now stepped forward.

Rev. Walton now led them through the remainder of their vows to one another. So softly were the words spoken that only those six who stood with them, and the man of God before them, could hear their mutual promises of love. By the time he was through, of the nine who stood before the silent throng, only Jess Forbes' eyes remained dry.

Jess now stepped forward with Jeremiah's ring.

Jeremiah placed the ring on Mercy's waiting finger. Rev. Walton prayed softly.

Then, in a voice loud enough for all to hear, he declared: "Forasmuch as Mercy Randolph and Jeremiah Eagleflight have consented together in holy wedlock, and have witnessed the same before God and this assembly, and hereto have given and pledged their troth, and as the groom has given his bride the ring declaring the same, I pronounce that they are husband and wife, in the name of the Father, and of the Son, and of the Holy Ghost. Amen."

Behind them, the crowd broke into spontaneous applause and cheers.

"You may kiss the bride!" he added with a great smile to Jeremiah.

Instead, Jeremiah took Mercy in his arms, wrapping his arms tightly around her. She melted into his embrace, and for the moment there was no one else in the world save the two of them.

"I love you, Mercy," he whispered into her ear.

"Oh, and I love you, Jeremiah!" she returned.

Yet another moment or two they stood.

Then he released her. Mercy took half a step back. Jeremiah leaned forward, hand on her shoulder, and gently brushed his lips against hers.

Behind them, another round of applause burst out, though neither heard it.

"Ladies and gentlemen," said Rev. Walton, nearly shouting to be heard, "may I now take the extreme pleasure of presenting to you . . . Mr. and Mrs. Jeremiah Eagleflight!"

63

ON WINGS
OF EAGLES

*Immediately upon **Rev. Walton**'s announcement, the* bride and groom were smothered by the hugs and kisses and handshakes of their best men and bridesmaids, and within moments, the front two rows of chairs also emptied with a rush of relatives and friends.

The standing crowd gradually began surging forward as

well, threatening to force the wedding party into the river behind them!

To the frantic accompaniment of Beula's stout but dexterous fingers, trying to be heard amid the pandemonium, Zeke jumped onto the music wagon to call out an invitation to come to the house.

Few heard him. No one was in a hurry to leave the happy scene. Beula's cake would keep.

Half an hour later, standing in a row and greeting and shaking hands with well-wishers, Jeremiah suddenly realized that both his partner on his left and his wife on his right had deserted him. They had slipped away easily without being seen in the throng. But the press of people was too constant for him to take time to look around for them.

Meanwhile, some fifty yards away, the bride and best man walked along the riverbank. Mercy didn't know why Jess was taking her away like this, but his voice had sounded urgent.

They reached a clump of trees. He told her to wait, then continued on himself. He returned a moment later, holding reins that led a brown-and-white-spotted pony.

"Oh, Jess, it's beautiful!" exclaimed Mercy.

"He's yours, Mercy," he said. "It's my wedding present for you."

"Jess . . . I—I don't know what to say!"

"I wanted to give you something special, as my way of thanking you for . . . well, you know, for everything—for making me feel like I'm still a part of Jeremiah's life."

"You are, Jess."

"You know what I mean. These last six months with Zeke and Jody's been the best I can ever remember. I ain't known anybody like them all my life. My own folks, you know—"

"I know, Jess. Jeremiah told me."

"I'm more grateful than you can know for all you've done, not just for Jeremiah, but for me, too."

"Thank you, Jess. This pony will be a treasure!"

"I found him and broke him and trained him myself, just for you, Mercy."

"Jess . . . you are a dear!"

"I hope you don't mind—I already gave him a name . . . you can change it if you want."

"What is it, Jess?"

"Well, you see, for his size he's awful fast, and he has the sharpest eyes I ever saw in a horse. I've been calling him *Eaglewing.*"

Mercy stepped forward and kissed him on the cheek.

He blushed, then handed her the reins.

Mercy caught his eyes and held them a moment. "Thank you again, Jess. It's the most beautiful name I could imagine. I wouldn't dream of changing it. I'm so happy you're here with us today!"

"And I'm happy Jeremiah married you. The two of you's made for each other just about more perfect than any man and woman I ever saw."

Mercy smiled. "Shall we get back to the celebration? They'll probably be missing us by now."

"Not missing me . . . but they're sure in tarnation going to wonder what happened to you!"

As they turned, Mercy saw the glint of moisture in Jess' eyes. She looked away and said nothing.

His time was approaching, she thought. The gentle stirrings in his heart were well begun.

"Where have you two been?" exclaimed Jeremiah as they approached two minutes later.

"Your best man kidnapped me," replied Mercy.

"And left me all alone after being married only half an hour!"

"I'll never leave your side again, I promise!" laughed Mercy. She slipped her arm around him as her husband unconsciously cast a quick glance upward. She saw the look and followed his gaze.

High in the sky, floating effortlessly on the gentlest of June breezes, a lone prairie eagle squinted his eyes, taking in all the land on both sides of the river, with the keenest vision of creation.

The giant outspreading span of his wings hardly moved while his small head turned this way and that, now spotting the movement of tiny creatures far below him.

He arched about in a wide circle, curious at the proceedings, then soared around again, realized there was nothing here for him, and finally continued on with his solitary flight.

His calling, like that of all eagles, was to let nature's wind bear him upon its breath to his eternal destiny. Toward that end, though he knew it not, the magnificent winged creature now disappeared from sight.

The eyes of two who *did* know such to be their purpose watched quietly until the great bird became a speck against the deep blue of the heavens . . . and then was gone.